VIOLET'S STORM

A Stormy Encounters Series Novel
(Book 1)

Tanya Benoit

Violet's Storm

First Printing, October 2014

Second Printing, January 2015

Third Printing, February 2018

This is a work of fiction. Names, characters, and incidents either are the product of the author's imagination or are used fictitiously, and any resemblance to actual persons, living or dead, business establishments, events, or locales is entirely coincidental.

Printed by CreateSpace, An Amazon.com Company

Available on Kindle and other devices

ISBN 798-0-9947668-0-9

CONTENTS

DEDICATION

For Markee and Molly
You ladies keep me inspired

ONE

1858 IRELAND

B rady fought back his anger and thundered toward his cottage deep in the forest. He couldn't get his charger to move fast enough, couldn't get far enough away from *him,* and he could think of no better place in the world to seek refuge from his father.

The cottage was a half days' ride from the main stronghold, through thick forests, over grassy knolls, and beyond a gentle stream. It was a tranquil retreat that was built for his mother when he had been just a lad. Like Brady, his mother took no interest in her husband's business affairs, she never quite understood it all. They were Kelly and Son's Shipbuilders, therefore, they built ships. She never acquired the desire to learn any more than that.

Instead, Caitlyn Kelly would seek out her calm sanctuary, residing there for days and weeks on end. As a boy, Brady had loved this place. He'd had an divine adoration of the natural beauty of his surroundings, the calming sounds of the stream dribbling in the fall when the water was low. And he was always in awe in springtime, when the high water seemed more rapid and its constant rushing lulled him to sleep at night in his mother's arms.

Yes, his cottage, the memories of happier, simpler times, was his safe haven from his father and the unattainable expectations attached to his father's love. No one seemed to understand that Brady just wasn't interested in building ships, leading a crew of carpenters, or bookkeeping for the family business.

But as Brady dismounted his steed, his thoughts weren't of happy times, and this place failed to have a calming effect on him for the first time in his life. His anger raged out of his body in the form of a low deep roar as he dropped to his knees in front of the lone stone step. He ran his fingers through his thick, shoulder-length black hair, and pulled tight on the locks as if he were deranged, insane.

"Ma, I tried! I swear by Jesus and Mary, I tried to do as you and Da told me. I tried to be a good student. Building ships holds no interest for me, why can't he just leave it to Liam?" he cried. "Liam, augh! He's the good brother, he's the one who wants it all anyway. Why can't they all leave me be?" His cries fell upon the wind, for there was no one there to hear them. Not anymore.

His anger transformed into something much worse. Grief. It struck him as hard as a battering ram, right through the heart. It had been months since is mother fell sick with Pneumonia and battled for her life for nearly a fortnight. Brady had sat by her sick bed, stifled within the confines of the keep, refusing to leave her side. He'd held her hand, folding her frail fingers in his. He prayed with her at times when she was well enough, and he prayed alone when she slept. *Ye have to get well, Ma.*

He'd watched, as her beautiful, fair face distorted, growing hollower every day, and her coal-black hair which once mirrored Brady's, seemed to grey overnight. Instead of the spark in her blue eyes returning, she surrendered to the fever and died peacefully with her eldest son by her side, crumbling like a little boy from the loss.

For the first time since she'd passed, he was back there, in their special place, mourning a mother who would never hear his cries again, who would never soothe his hurts, and who would never again play mediator between a tenacious husband and a free-willed son.

He entered the cottage, wiping his tears with the back of his hand, trying to erase all sign of emotion. He went to her chair in the bright corner by the large window, and wrapped her patchwork quilt around his shoulders. He shivered as he felt his loneliness wash over him. He scanned the room with brooding eyes. The cottage seemed different somehow.

His mother's needle-work still sat on a small wicker table next to her chair. On top of the wood stove in the far corner of the kitchen, was a large pan that she'd used to make fresh bread. This place appeared untouched, the same as he'd left it – but altered. The emptiness felt almost like a living, breathing entity that Brady was desperate to be rid of.

His anger seized his rational thought as he threw the blanket off, picked up her sewing, and strode to the woodstove, using it as kindling to put a fire in. Once he'd lit the fire his vehemence spiked, and he leveled everything in his path as he tried to rid himself of the rage, and rid the cottage of *her*.

Her cookware, her clothes, her books and blankets – all and everything that reminded him of how things used to be – he demolished or burned. He took a long breath as the adrenalin began to wane.

With little air left in his lungs, he caught sight of a beast in the long oval mirror which hung on the wall between the two bedrooms. It was a reflection of a thing he could no longer recognise. There was a coldness penetrating his sapphire eyes, one he hadn't ever seen before. His long, dark lashes were wet from tears – fury, pure fury. He inhaled a steadying breath, held onto the door frame and willed his wrath to dissipate.

With a fire in the stove, and warmth starting to touch his arms and legs, and his numbness subsiding, he sat at the small, round table in the middle of the room.

He sprawled his long legs underneath, and put his head in his hands, repentant of what he'd just done. The cottage was nothing more than an empty room now. All that remained was taciturn furniture. Devoid of all life.

From the corner of his eye, he spotted a shiny item on the floor next to the doorway. He eyed it for a few minutes, unable to discern what it was.

Instead of dismissing it, he wearily rose from his chair and retrieved it. Brady picked it up and observed it curiously, rubbing the silver between his thumb and forefinger. The Claddagh was a perfect match to the wedding ring his father had given her when they'd wed. Now, the pair was forever broken, for she'd been buried with the ring.

As he rose, he spied a piece of parchment poking out from the door facing. He pulled it out with little effort and sombrely began to read.

My dearest Brady,

I know this is a hard time for you, and I wish I were still with you. There was a time when I remember you and your Da enjoying one another's company, but now darling, it breaks my heart to see you at such odds. Your father has only your best interests in mind and wants you to have all of the good things life has to offer. Brady scoffed at her statement but continued.

Be patient with him, Brady, he loves you dearly. I know your heart is set on making your own way, but all

I ask of you is this. Give him a chance, learn from him, whatever he has to teach. It is hard to make a good living as a farmer these days, and I would never want you to struggle. There is no shame in living off the wealth your father has earned and provided for you. Please, if nothing else, give him your forgiveness.

Keep my necklace close to your heart, take from it, my strength and wisdom, and always know that your mother loved you like no other. I am at peace with my passing, and I hope you can make peace with God as well for calling me back to His kingdom.

All my love,

Mother

Brady leaned into the closed door, bracing himself on his thick forearm. He cursed under his breath. It was like she was there, reasoning with him to *be good,* as so many times before. She must have written the letter on the odd time when he'd slept in a cot next to her sick bed, and had a messenger deliver it. In his hysterical rage, he'd almost missed it, on a day that he'd needed her guidance the most.

Brady plummeted to the floor and with knees pulled close to his body, he shook his head. He thought of all the things that were said earlier that day in his father's study. Words he could never take back.

He had accused his brother, Liam of being a lazy, pompous arse, who had no thoughts and dreams of his own. He had all but spit on his father's hopes that Brady would someday be heir to the family fortune. And with the fortune, came the responsibility of keeping Kelly and Son's successful and productive. This was not the path Brady would see himself travelling down without a fight.

"Why can't ye just hand it all over to Liam, Da?" Brady shouted, unable to concede. Sean Kelly rubbed his face in annoyance. This was an argument that he had had with his son before. Many times.

"'Cause my boy, I have only two sons. In the event of my passin', 'tis tradition in our family that the wealth be split, and the eldest and *presumably* wisest son, will become head of the clan. Head of the household. 'Tis yer duty to take care of the rest of yer kin," he explained. "Why are you loathe to do what is best for yer family?"

Liam, despite Brady's harsh words interjected softly, "Da, you know I would never disappoint you. I can carry on your legacy and make you proud if you'll let me."

Some would think this was a sibling rivalry but Brady was supportive of Liam and knew that his little brother would, in fact, make his father proud – being a better fit for the business side of things.

Although Liam was seven years younger than Brady, at twenty and one, he was well-tutored and an eager learner. He was fascinated by the architecture and planning that went into crafting a sea-worthy vessel. Because of his extensive education in England, he understood the mathematics and engineering which made constructing something so large, so imposing, yet functional, possible. He lived for it. In this and all other facets of life, Liam and Brady were complete opposites.

Where Brady was hot-tempered, tough and strong, Liam was quiet and soft spoken. He even dressed the part of a businessman, wearing a freshly laundered linen shirt under a dark burgundy top coat, brown knee breeches, and carefully knitted knee socks. Brady observed that his shoes even made a clicking noise as he sauntered across the study to stand next to his big brother. One might even doubt they were in fact related.

Their physical features were as if Brady's mother alone created him, and Sean alone had created Liam. His light hair and hazel eyes were in direct contrast to Brady's black locks and steel blue irises. He laid his hand on Brady's shoulder, in a show of support for his brother's cause.

"Liam! Stay out of this! You're only a lad yet, you know nothing of what is important in life. You're not the eldest, 'tis enough from your tongue!" Sean barked. His face was fierce, and his blood was boiling. He yelled at Liam, but never took his dark eyes off Brady.

"Is that all you think about? Tradition? What about my dreams? What about what's important to me?" Brady thundered back. "I don't want this fuckin' life, can't ye understand that? Let it go, old man." Brady turned to storm from the study but was caught dead in his tracks by his father's next words.

"Yer Ma would slap the filth out of yer mouth if she could hear ye speak like that to me. God rest 'er." Sean whispered the last part, but Brady had heard him and was quickly across the room and in his father's face with a tight grip on his collar.

"Aye, Da, God rest 'er. 'Cause there was no rest for the woman livin' here with you," he hissed. Anger boiled up inside Brady with the mere mention of her name. "Don't pretend to know who she was, or what she'd tolerate. Ye've been no kinda husband to her for years – off on your business meetin's, gone weeks at a time. Who do ye think took care of 'er in your stead? 'Twas me, ye bastard." Brady released his father with a harsh shove backward, resulting in Sean falling to the floor, hitting his head on the edge of the bulky oak desk, leaving him on his back and at the mercy of a livid brute.

Brady pressed a sturdy knee into his father's chest, and reared back his fist, but was stopped short when he sensed Liam quietly approaching, gawping at him wide-eyed and disapprovingly.

Their gazes met, and Liam shook his head. Brady looked down into his father's eyes, and for the first time in his life, he saw fear there. The awareness that his Da feared him, both exhilarated and shook him to the core. How could this man who'd had a slight hand in raising him, who was his physical equal, come to fear him? It was a disturbing revelation.

Brady rose from his combative stance, pulling his father up with him. Sean gathered himself, fixing his trousers, and raked his shaking fingers through his peppered hair. Sean looked to Liam, creases of shame painting his face. The disappointment in Liam's gaze seemed to mirror his father's, but Brady could find no shame in what he'd just done. He'd never over-taken the man who'd sired him with such rage before – and so effortlessly. Things would be forever changed between all of them.

Struggling to find his composure, Brady balled his fists at his sides, and turned to leave the study. Just before he reached the massive wooden door, he faced his father once more.

"Never speak of her again," he seethed and added, "Ye didn't know 'er. Ye don't deserve to even say 'er name." Brady opened the door and left the main keep, grumbling under his breath until he was out of earshot.

He rode his stallion from the stables as if he'd stolen it. The horse, as if it could sense the intensity of Brady's emotions, never missed a beat, even when Brady dug his heels into the great beast's haunches. When the cottage came into view, Thunder slowed, blowing steamy puffs from his nostrils.

The small brick structure looked tiny in comparison to the forest in which it was built. But it was inviting. There was only one large window in the front, flanking the front door. Just on the other side of that door lay endless fond memories and reminders of happier times.

But when his shaky hand turned the iron knob, it wasn't a feeling of warmth and comfort that entombed him. Grief struck like a viper and robbed him of his rational thought once again. Like back in his father's study, his pain manifested itself in a torturous and violent way.

Brady always knew he had a mean streak. His entire existence consisted of tempering the beast within. Perhaps his mother knew it as well and was why she'd kept him so close. By taking him with her to her sanctuary in the forest, he could never find cause to fight with Liam or his father.

But now, Caitlyn was gone, and there was nothing and no one that could keep him from turning into the monster lurking beneath his impenetrable surface.

His thoughts carried him back to when he was just sixteen – a boy trying to become a man. Back in those days, it was understood that he was heir to the company, and he hadn't contested it. With Liam away at school, it had been easy to fall under his father's spell, and so he had done his duty, learning as much as he could about the family business.

One evening after the day was done, however, he'd wandered into the tavern where Sean and his friends would always end up on Friday's to conclude the work-week in a celebratory fashion. This day, Brady was eager to drink them under the table and prove he was a man.

Brian Donnelly, one of his father's men, whose job was to oversee the carpenters at Kelly and Son's, took Brady's challenge with an arrogant grin.

Donnelly gulped down his ale, then whiskey, then ale, and whiskey again, until his speech was slurred and his eyes could no longer focus. Brady thought this amusing and was having a hell of a time going drink for drink with the seasoned Irishman. It appeared that Brady had won – until he tried to stand.

"Me thinksss, 'tis….tiiime to taaake a p..iss. Dun' go nooo where b'ys," Brady slurred.

As he tried to steady himself by putting his hand on his father's shoulder, his foot tangled in the leg of the table, and he came crashing down on top of Sean.

"Oh alright, my boy. 'Tis time we get ye home," his father chuckled as he lifted his drunken son from his lap.

All of the men at the table threw their heads back and laughed. All, except for Brady.

"What's the matter lad? Ye can't stay afloat with us mighty ships trying to sink ye," Donnelly scoffed. "Sean, ye better get the wee lad back to his mother. He might need to be rocked b'fore bed."

Brian Donnelly was no slight man. He was a tower compared to Sean, and he stood above most of his men. He was an imposing sight, and everyone around these parts of Ireland knew better than to take him on. But not Brady, and not that night.

Brady seemed to sober instantly, as his pride had been torn to pieces. His nostrils flared and he straightened himself instantly. The alcohol seemed to dissipate from his system, as rage took over.

He was around the table, around all seven of them in an instant, straddling Donnelly in his chair, throwing punch after punch into the man's face until his fists were a bloody mess. Donnelly tried to push him away but ended up toppling over backward in the chair, taking Brady with him.

Donnelly, dazed from the assault was too slow and couldn't possibly anticipate Brady's next attack, as the lad quickly made to his feet and began hurling his boot into the man's exposed middle.

Every time his boot made contact with the man now lying in fetal position in a failing attempt to shield himself, the noise around him, the cheering him on, became louder and louder until it was all Brady could hear. He couldn't hear his father yelling at him and he didn't see the barkeep coming toward him with a long wooden paddle. Brady was in a frenzy, and all he could see was blood. Until he saw nothing at all.

The barkeep whacked him across the back of the head with the heavy wood and Brady fell. Everything around him went black, and he couldn't comprehend sight, smell nor sound.

When he awoke, he was shackled to a cold brick wall in a dark cell. When he tried to open his eyes, the pain in his head was unlike anything he had ever felt. But he knew this place. Brady had been brought home to his father's keep and placed in the prison beneath the stronghold.

"Now, lad, what do ye have to say fer yerself?" The sound of his father's voice startled him, as he tried to focus on the dark figure sitting on a bench on the other side of the bars. Brady jingled the shackles around his hands and found that they were fixed to his feet as well.

"'Tis a tad extreme, don't ye think?" Brady grinned and a chuckle fell from his lips.

Sean stood and closed the distance between them, separated by nothing but iron, confining iron.

"Nay! 'Tis no laughing matter! 'Tis what they do to a vicious animal, is it not? Cage it? If you act as such, ye'll be treated as such." Sean gave Brady a defeated glare, disappointment filling his eyes. "Now that I know yer not dead, I'll leave ye to yer thoughts, lad. Ye almost killed a man tonight. Ye ought to think about it for a while longer."

"Ye mean to just leave me here?" Brady questioned in disbelief, for he never thought his Da would actually leave him below the keep, as cold and damp as it was.

Sean drew in a long, exhausted breath, shook his head at Brady and left the dungeon. Brady knew he was lucky to have been brought home, for the alternative could have resulted in him being locked in a prison far away until his father paid the Donnelly clan for the damages. Brady was fortunate that Brian Donnelly was employed by Kelly and Son's, and agreed to let Sean teach him a lesson in his own way, although Brady couldn't find any gratitude in it.

Sean left his first born in that cold cell for almost a fortnight, living on water and oatcakes. Brady had never known hunger like this existed and devoured the pitiful rations like a savage.

He'd heard through the chatter of the guards, that his mother had been refusing to speak to Sean because he'd forbidden contact with her boy. No doubt, after the very first night, she'd thought the punishment had gone on long enough. But Sean had stood his ground and permitted no one except the servants responsible for feeding Brady to visit or speak to him.

Brady had come dangerously close back then to losing everything, and he knew it. But instead of reforming him, the punishment soured Brady toward his father, and things were never the same again between them.

Brady could only sit and wait to be released, as his hatred for his father took over all logical thought. He knew, in the dark recesses of that cell, that he would never be like *him*. He wanted nothing of his father's, and vowed to make his own way from that day forward.

Brady shook his head back to the present. He stood, his hand tightly clutching his mother's last wishes and examined the destruction he'd left in his wake. He carefully smoothed the parchment out into a flat surface, then folded it until it was small enough to fit into the pocket of his trousers. He hung her chain and pendant around his neck and kissed it as if he were kissing her for the last time. He vowed silently to never remove it from his body, as almost immediately, he felt her presence, and knew she would be forever with him. In his heart.

It was then, Brady had made his decision. He would respect his mother's plea, and return to the stronghold. He would do as she'd asked, despite the past. He would become a shipbuilder and learn how to someday take over Kelly and Son's. In his vow to make her proud, he might even decide to forgive his father for all those hungry, lonely nights below the keep.

He covered the remaining furniture with sheets and cleaned up the mess he had made in his violent, anguished tirade. No doubt, if he hadn't noticed her note, the few remaining boxes of her special things neatly hidden beneath the bed, would surely have been destroyed as well. A small sigh of relief escaped him.

In closing up the cottage for good, his hand lingered on the doorknob as he glanced back at the place which held the most precious of memories. Sadness swallowed him whole as he swiped away a rogue tear that had fled his steely, blue eyes.

He closed the door and whispered, "God keep you, mother."

It was well after midnight when Brady set out for home. He would arrive just before dawn if he rode through the night. Yet, he kept his horse at a leisurely pace, for he dreaded what he would have to do come morning.

He planned to ask his father for forgiveness; essentially giving in. He would become heir to the family fortune and do what was required of him.

His dreams of becoming a farmer, a hunter, a provider for his future family, and of living a simple life in the country would all go up in smoke. He loathed the mere thought of it, yet he vowed to accept it.

TWO

There was nowhere in the world Violet would rather be than in that moment, laying lazily on the grassy edge of the languidly flowing stream. This was her stream, on her family's land, a place where generations of Ryan's before her had cherished and fought to protect. She dipped her hand into the cool water and swirled it around in fascination of her reflection, of how she didn't quite look like herself, but a convoluted image of emerald green eyes, and fiery red hair. She drew in a deep breath of contentment, and let out a long, slow sigh as she rolled to her back, gazing at the few clouds looming overhead.

The spring-time was her favorite time of year, so full of life, creation, and beauty. It was like all the world could melt away. But in that moment, with only her truest companion – a four-year-old mare – chewing on long blades of grass beside her, nothing else mattered. Not even her mother's call off in the distance could snap her back to reality. She was lost so deep within herself that the earth could have shattered beneath her and she wouldn't have flinched.

"Really, Violet! I've been lookin' fer ye everywhere," her mother scolded. Violet could tell her mother wasn't really angry, as she wasn't that sort of woman.

Beth's mouth curved into a small smile and her face sparkled when she came upon her young daughter daydreaming by the stream. She sighed and lay down on the grass, taking her daughter's hand in hers and gazed up at the blue sky.

"Ye know, I used to daydream when I was yer age. Oh, I would sit in my window fer hours watchin' the sky and thinkin' about what it would be like to marry a fine lad and run a home of my own. I even thought about the *obedient* daughters I would someday have," her mother smiled furtively. "Is that what occupies yer mind, Violet? Is that what keeps ye away from yer lessons, when ye know yer supposed to meet with yer tutor at noon? Hmm?"

Violet squeezed her mother's hand and raised it to her mouth, planting a tiny kiss on the back of the soft skin. "Oh Mama, wouldn't it be wonderful to meet a handsome lad? Someone kind and gentle, and patient? Someone like Da. I dream of him all the time, although I don't know him yet." Violet leaned up on her elbows and boldly raised her chin. "I'll know him when I meet him," she asserted. Then she pinned Beth with wide, penetrating eyes. "Do ye t'ink I'm gettin' too old for such dreams?" Violet asked, letting out a hard sigh this time, despair engulfing her. In her mind, a girl in her twenty-second year should be married or at least betrothed. But it seemed her Da wouldn't hear tell of it, no matter who came to call, and from which clan the lad had been born. High-born or low-born – none would be good enough for his only daughter, Vy; although he'd never actually said as much.

"Oh nay, child," her mother whispered, sweetly. "One should never stop dreamin'. 'Tis dreams and hopes that makes life worth livin'. Never stop dreamin', Vy. Your Da will come to his senses soon enough. He's just protectin' what he feels is his greatest achievement. You, my dear." Her mother stood and held out her hands to assist Violet up off the grass. She brushed the foliage from both their skirts and then smiling, she tucked away a few of the rogue strands of Violet's unruly auburn locks.

"You, my sweet child, must return to the main house and be quick about it. Gregory has been patiently waitin' for ye. 'Tis most important ye know, for a girl yer age to know how to read and write. Someday, ye'll not only run a keep of yer own, but ye might even run the finances as well, leavin' your husband to his huntin' and settlin' differences amongst the clan. Yer future husband will appreciate the time you'll free up for him, and might even show his graciousness to you in kind." She laughed a spirited laugh, and added, "Ye know yer father will settle for nothin' less!"

"Oh Mama, why does he even try to pick them for me? He's so fussy. I'm surprised he's not made a betrothal with stuffy-nosed Gregory," Violet whined as they strode toward Daisy, her four-legged eavesdropper. She gave Daisy a loving caress on the neck and clutched the reins. Placing her foot in the stirrup, she effortlessly heaved herself upward.

Once mounted, her emerald green skirts parted across the beast's back and she motioned for her mother to leap up behind her instead of walking back to the manor. Beth arched a brow at her more than trustworthy and capable daughter, but declined with a slight wave.

"Nay, dear. Ye get to yer lessons and be kind to Gregory. And try no' to worry. Yer father would never make such a contract with a man so unworthy of his bonny, wee lass. I t'ink I'll stay and dream a while." She shot her daughter an impish grin and added, "I still dream too ye know, but now mine are about the grandbabies I may someday have, and of chasing them around the great garden on days just like this one."

"If he ever lets me grow up, Mama. If he ever sees fit to let me go," Violet huffed and rolled her eyes. And just like that, she was snapped back to reality, riding Daisy as fast as she could, back to the beautiful home that had sheltered her since she'd been born.

She slowed her mount as she crossed the great garden, inhaling the soft fragrance of the rose bushes flanking the path leading to the back of the main keep, toward the stables.

She dismounted and handed the reins over to Peter, a boy the same age as Violet. They had grown up together, playing, riding, and exchanging stories since they were only in their fifth year. But things had changed so much between them since Violet's body turned from child-like into a woman's. Peter blushed now every time he saw her and seemed too shy to even make polite conversation. Violet could never understand why her friend was so lost to her and she missed his companionship immensely.

"Peter, ye will make sure she is well fed this evening won't ye? I intend to ride her far and hard in the mornin'," Violet smiled, and then adoringly smoothed her hand down Daisy's mane.

Peter's pink cheeks caught Violet's attention, leaving her to wonder yet again, why her presence frequently caused the same crimson hue to engulf his boyish face. *Does he find me attractive*? she wondered, naughtily. An attraction between Violet and Peter would hold no consequence, for her Da would never permit her to court someone so beneath her station. But it was fun to imagine. Violet believed Peter would grow to be quite dashing, with his soft brown hair and green eyes. If he were ever rid of those unruly freckles, that is.

"Aye, Violet. She'll be ready," Peter coughed uncomfortably. He moved quickly, dragging Daisy along to the back of the stable where he could feed and take extra care of the animal.

When Violet arrived through the kitchen entrance in the back of the majestic stone manor, she was greeted by a mouth-watering aroma, hinting a mixture of ginger and cinnamon. To her delight, she spied the still-warm sweetcakes resting on the large countertop in the middle of the archaic room. Just as she reached out an eager hand to snatch one, a voice rang in her ears, halting her in midfilch.

"Git now!!! Yer Da's been lookin' for ye. Gregory's been waitin' in the study for near on an hour!" Nora chastised. "An' git yer hands off me cakes, lass. You'll have one with yer supper."

Nora was very much loved by Violet, as she had been her nanny when she'd been nothing more than a wee babe. When Violet no longer needed a governess, Nora had requested to be moved to the kitchen so she could still have a place within the family and remain close to her charge. "Whatever will become of a lass so hell-bent on breakin' all the rules?" Nora muttered as she straightened out her apron, shaking her head. Violet quickly released the treat, swung around to kiss Nora's cheek in one swift motion, and then ran down the hall to the study.

Violet entered the study to find Gregory and her father discussing the upcoming plans to merge Ryan's Shipwrights with Kelly and Son's Shipbuilders. The Kelly's were from Galway, not far from County Clare, where the Ryan clan had set their roots. The merge with another company promised to be profitable and would surely keep the peace in both counties. Since both families held vast power and influence, it only made sense to fuse such an alliance.

"Aye, as ye can see, Gregory, if we merge with Kelly and Son's, we could use each other's contacts, unify both crews, and build bigger, stronger vessels, all the while, cuttin' cost," Robert pointed boastfully, comparing the proposal with the final agreement, which had not yet been signed.

"And not to mention, Robert, if both clans were merged in business, you can imagine the peace it would bring to all your lands. Smaller clans would keep harmony in fear of suffering the wrath of two, formidable, united clans. I think it will be a glorious day when this merger comes to pass." Gregory patted Robert on the back. A sign of a job well done. Just then, both men noticed Violet's presence in the entryway. Her father's imposing gaze bore into her own.

She feared her tardiness would cause Robert to be angry and scold her, and so she braced herself accordingly. But like so many times before, her father's face softened, his smile widened, and it seemed her indiscretion had been forgotten. The twinkle in his eye – the unmistakable adoration for his only child, caused her heart to swell.

Gregory extended his palm and as always, placed a kiss on the back of her gloved hand.

Gregory was a tall, slim, and studious English gentleman. Violet knew he wouldn't be caught dead in anything but his best clothing, nor without his brown hair combed back into a greasy, shining pelt. Noting how the sun gleamed against his skin through the nearby window, Violet doubted if she had ever seen his pale face when it had not been clean shaven. She'd once heard him say that facial hair was for apes and savages. Unfortunately for him, he'd been so far removed from London society, he had no idea that men sporting a full beard were at the height of fashion these days.

Nevertheless, Gregory exuded an air of superiority and was seemingly unmoved by the fact that he was of no noble blood. Seeing through his brittle façade, Violet merely tolerated him to appease her father's wishes for her to have a proper education – without having her sent to England to achieve it. Being tutored by Gregory, England had come to her.

"Welcome, Violet. I've been talking to your father about his upcoming merge with the Kelly's of Galway. These are exciting times, for it will bring both families wealth and peace," Gregory smiled, while Violet politely pulled her hand from his grip and forced a tight grin.

"Aye, 'twill be a joyous occasion. Perhaps Da can retire and leave all of the family finances and decision makin' to his favourite daughter." Violet came to Robert's side and placed a sweet kiss on her father's cheek.

"Nay, child. I'll never be able to do such a thing 'til I know ye will be a good and obedient daughter, and we find ye a kind and *patient* husband. 'Tis not a good example ye set, bein' late fer everything ye know." Her father gave her a look of slight impatience and her chin a little nudge with the pad of his calloused thumb. "I'll need to know ye can handle things when I am no longer able to." '*Lies!*' "'Tis why Gregory is here twice a week – on time I might add. Now, be a good lass and listen well."

"Aye, Da," Violet blew out exasperatedly. The chance that she would ever take over the family empire was slim. Her father merely humoured her notions of becoming a savvy business woman, and oft-times knowing that fact infuriated her.

In any event, it was well-known that her tutoring served a greater purpose – a ruse to keep her busy and out of mischief. Shielding her father from incessant worry and premature gray hairs.

But she knew she could do it – run a household as well as manage the company. She'd been eavesdropping on Robert's business meetings since she could remember, and felt more than competent to do both. It seemed however, the tutoring only helped to push her closer to Gregory, especially as of late.

She couldn't pretend she didn't notice the hunger in his beady, black eyes whenever her father wasn't about. But *he* was not the man who occupied her dreams. That man was still a faceless enigma.

Violet settled behind the large wooden desk across from Gregory who was visibly trying his hardest to stay focussed. She'd caught him – more than once – undressing her with that carnal glower of his, but instead of unnerving her, the imp inside forced her to use it against him whenever she could.

She could nearly smell his discomfort, as he pulled at his ascot and shifted in his waistcoat. *Good! Wriggle, ye beady-eyed buzzard!*

Violet cleared her throat and smiled sweetly. "Did ye grade my last assignment? Will ye grant me a perfect grade? Da will be so pleased," Violet beamed as if she could read his thoughts. She'd had a sinking suspicion that Gregory's feelings went beyond student/teacher, and she enjoyed watching him in these awkward moments. She never could have imagined how deeply he lusted for her.

"Yes, Violet. Your father will be pleased, indeed." He pulled at his collar again and flew to open the window on the other side of the room, putting as much distance between them as he possibly could. "Your inscription is quite remarkable, but you still need work on your calculations. I can come by an extra hour a week, if you think it would help."

"Oh Gregory!" Violet laughed. "Ye no need to do that. I think with a little repetition I'll get better on my own. And Da has been lettin' me practice with balancin' the books. Perhaps someday he will let me marry too, and then I could help take care of my husband's home and business," she frowned, her heart full of hope – at least until she realised what she had just blurted out. *'Why in the name of Mother Mary, did I just say that?'*

she thought wretchedly. The last thing she needed was Gregory proposing on an assumption that she wanted him to.

Violet strived to be a free spirit, a lady with unpretentious and practical needs. She prayed she hadn't enticed a proposal from the complicated and ostentatious man sweating before her. A man like him would never permit her to have her own mind.

In any marriage, she understood that she would simply be expected to run her home, demand respect and decorum from her help, never taking complete control of the household finances. Not to mention obey her husband at all costs.

The truth of it was discouraging. But the quicker she could be free from these pointless lessons with Gregory, the sooner her father might find her a match and be done with this entire masquerade. Then, the weariness of her impetuous, spirited nature would fall upon that poor fellow's shoulders. It was completely exhausting – waiting for freedom, yet waiting to be shackled once more.

Gregory knew Violet had been longing for love and romance, and used his time to get close to her *and* her father, with the hope that Robert would find that he was indeed a suitable match for his precious jewel.

"I think that will be enough for today, Violet," Gregory choked out after only an hour into his lesson, apparently unable to gather himself. He packed his things into his leather satchel and without meeting her gaze, he quickly strode out of the room. His impure thoughts wreaked havoc on his nervous system today, causing his loins to ache. Just being near her, her sweet innocence permeating the air around them, sparked his senses like wild fire.

He scrambled through the halls of the keep, but before he could make his exit, he heard light, speedy footsteps approaching. He turned to find Violet, running like a child after him, waving something golden in her hands.

"Stop! Wait, Gregory. Wait! You left behind your pocket watch." To his delight, when Violet smiled, her entire face lit up and in turn could brighten any room. He was pleased that his ploy to get her to come running after him had worked, having neglected the watch on purpose.

He yearned to hear her melodious call as she shouted his name and he was gratefully rewarded when the sweet sound resonated the hall, piercing his ear drums. Now, he could return to his tiny room at the boarding house, and revel in delight each time the memory woke him.

He would dream of this woman as he often did, and hopefully ponder some other methods of making her father see that he was a man worthy of making a marriage contract with. He was certain she could come to love him over time. And he was no fool, he knew she was running out of time.

'It would be a shame for a fair and beautiful lady to be unmarried past twenty-five. She would be regarded as a spinster', Gregory thought with a glimmer of hope bubbling in his gut.

Although Violet didn't know it, Gregory and her father had had lengthy conversations about her situation. In the past few years, Gregory had learned that Robert was allowing her to marry for love. She was to choose for herself. *How can I get her to choose me?*

Robert had let her continue to believe the decision was solely his, minimising the risk of fanciful infatuations. If and when she finally met a man and fell in love all on her own accord, he'd know she was ready. And he'd be ready to let her go.

She seemed oblivious to the fact that she was loved by all and desired by many. She'd been too free-spirited and uninterested, to even make time for matters of the heart.

Likewise, Robert Ryan had no idea that his precious Vy pined for love. The kind of love between a man and a woman. An everlasting, burning kind of love was all she could think about, but had given up all hope that it would ever happen.

"If I could only make her fall in love with me..." Gregory sighed and headed back to his lonely little existence.

THREE

Brady dismounted his great silver beast just as the sun peeked out from behind the grassy knoll which created the stunning backdrop for Kelly's keep. He shaded his eyes with his hand to look about the grounds. It appeared everyone was still abed, for the only movement came from the side of the house – the kitchen door to be exact. He watched as Mary, the cook, waddled from the entrance, carrying two large pails to the well.

She would be the only person awake at this hour, as she was to prepare the morning meal. Brady rushed to her side, to aid in her backbreaking chore. She had been the cook for the family since Brady could remember and it seemed she looked more haggard and tired than the last time he'd seen her. The simple task of bringing water from the well was proving to be too much for her to bear this morning. He wondered if his father had noticed her decline as well, and if he had, why she had not been given less demanding duties within the keep.

Brady took the pails from her straining hands with a smile, more than happy to assist.

"God love ye, Lord Brady. 'Tis gettin' to be hard work for this ol' bird," she grinned and wiped the sweat from her brow with her immaculate apron.

Brady regarded her kindly as she held the old iron door open for him and he set the pails of water on the floor in the corner of the kitchen as she directed.

"Now, what would ye be havin' to break yer fast, lad? Ye must be famished, or did ye eat when you were at the cottage?" she asked as she busily went about filling the large, iron cauldron atop the gigantic stove. Brady looked at her like she had just grown two heads. He never understood *how* Mary knew things, never questioned her knowledge of just about everything that went on in the keep. She just knew who was doing what, and where everyone was, at all times. Brady's silence and puzzled look prompted her to explain.

"Aye, the whole village could 'ave heard what went on here yesterday morn'. 'Tis a lucky thing it is, that yer

Da didn't have a band of soldiers sent after ye," she tsked, and shook her head. "He was awfully angry. An' shame on ye! Ye could 'ave hurt 'em a lot worse, you bein' such a big brute."

"How did ye know I would be at the cottage?" He searched her wrinkled eyes for some sympathy to his plight, but found none.

Mary had always tried to remain detached from the family's personal problems, but sometimes Brady just wished she had some kind of opinion either way. But she didn't. She usually remained disengaged and unaffected, until now, that is.

"Lord Brady, everyone knows that when ye need yer alone time, 'tis where you'll find it." Something in her eyes surprised him. Was it empathy? "An' we all know 'tis where ye can be close to your mother and seek 'er guidance." Mary made the sign of the crucifix across her still heaving chest.

In that moment, Brady felt ill at the mention of his mother.

"Nay, I was there, but she can't guide me now or ever again," Brady sighed. "I don't feel much like eatin' just now. When Thunder has been fed and rested, I'll retire to my chambers. 'Tis been a long night."

"As ye wish. I'll have one of the girls bring ye up some fresh oatcakes and leave them outside yer door," she grinned. "Might help to let one of 'em in, ye know."

"Thank ye, Mary. That won't be necessary." Brady ambled out of the kitchen, lost in thought once again. He headed back outside to where his horse still lingered, and took the beast around to the stable. Instead of waking the stable-hand, he quietly made work of attaching the oat bag to Thunder's bridle, and stripped him of the thick blanket covering his large, muscular back. When the horse had had his fill, Brady closed the gate, and returned to the house. His head hung low with exhaustion, feeling defeated and damned.

He quietly moved through the main keep, and up the wide staircase along the far wall. Usually, he took these steps two at a time, but he was not in a hurry to be alone in his chambers, nor was he anxious to sleep, even though the fatigue was overwhelming. He wished he didn't have to face the conversation which awaited when he rose.

Lethargically, he strolled down the long hallway on the third floor of the keep. He passed Liam's chambers, stopping for a moment to listen at the door, curious to hear if his brother yet stirred from his peaceful slumber. *Nothing.*

Just before he reached his own room, at the very end of the hall, the large, wooden and wrought-iron door that hung in front of him, taunted.

'Is father awake yet?' he wondered. The massive grovelling he would have to endure would be much easier to do in private.

He placed his hand on the latch and paused for a moment. He shut his eyes tightly and resisted the urge to fling the door open, go inside and beg for forgiveness. He drew in a breath, and exhaled loudly, turned to his left and clutched the latch to his own chambers.

Once inside, the chill gnawed at him unsympathetically. Even though it was spring of the year and the thaw had begun, the air still possessed a frosty bite. He cursed under his breath as he moved to the hearth to make a fire within. The stone was cold and devoid of waning embers, pointing to the fact that the fire had not been put in.

He looked to the large bed and noticed that the covers had not been turned down for him either, as they had been every single night of his life.

The window coverings were still open, letting the dawn sun filter in, making this room much too cheerful to suit his foul mood. No one had been sent to ready his chamber. More likely than not, the members of the house staff were instructed not to.

Brady lit a candle alongside the bed, then went to the windows and covered them with the large shutters flanking the window frame. He rubbed his frosty hands together and blew warm air into the tightly-wound fists.

Once the fire was licking the bricks, he poured himself a tall tankard of whiskey, and gulped it down in one swift swig. He poured a second drink and fell into the chair next to the hearth. Sleep would come one way or another.

Brady awoke slumped in the chair where fatigue had claimed him, seemingly, only a few hours before. He wearily stood and stretched until the muscles in his arms and back strained, and then rubbed the back of his achy neck. He turned to the window and opened the shutters once more to gauge the time of day.

The sun had begun to set once again, and he estimated that it was either just before the evening meal or just after. In any event, he had to have an audience with his father. He could put it off no longer.

He moved quickly to a basin and splashed in enough water to scrub the sleep from his face. He scoured hard and vigorously, as if he could wash away his inner chaos. With one last glance in the glass, he steeled himself. *I've no other choice.*

When he reached the main hall, it was all but empty, apart from a table of men sitting at the very back. He knew them all, but one face stood out above the rest. He locked gazes with Jack Manning, his best friend since childhood. His friend stood, and greeted Brady with a wide grin.

"Well now, if it isn't the prodigal son?" Jack bellowed above the other voices in the hall. "Have ye returned to finish the ol' man off?" Everyone sitting at the table had turned to look in Brady's direction, and he felt eleven sets of eyes trained on him, waiting for his reaction.

Instead of giving them what they wanted, instead of losing his temper, he thought better of it, and held his breath a moment until the shame and disgrace subsided. He clenched his fists at his sides, and was thankful that Jack wasn't within reaching distance.

Jack and Brady had grown up together since they were barely off their mothers' teat. Although, they were from different stations in the clan – Brady being the chieftain's son, and Jack, the son of a soldier – they had been kindred spirits, and nothing could keep them apart. They got into as much mischief as they could, and no matter whose parents were doling out the punishments, both were punished equally.

Jack had always been a loyal companion, even though he liked to rile Brady up. No matter the situation, Jack could always get a rise out of him, could always push that one button too many. Over the years, it had become a favorite past time of his.

Brady sauntered through the hall, discarding his apprehension at the door. His friends would see only the tough, hard brute of a man in which they knew.

He straddled the bench and sat next to his old friend. Jack patted him on the back in a gesture that meant '*no hard feelin's*'.

"I'm guessin' I missed supper," Brady ascertained, noting the countless empty trenchers scattered about the hall. Serving wenches were busy at work all around them to clear the mess, but were easily distracted by this one table of sexually charged men, coaxing them over to sit on their knees. One girl squealed as a large hand skittered up her skirts. She seemed to like it but blushed, feigning coyness and then rushed away when she noticed Brady's presence.

"Aye, ye missed it. 'Twas a great feast, I must say. Yer father held out no expense celebratin' the news of the merge. You *do* remember the merge, don't ye?" Jack sarcastically asked, and then, "The Kelly's and the Ryan's are creating a great shipbuilders dream. An empire. I t'ought you'd be more enthusiastic. Can't believe ye missed the party altogether," he snorted.

Jack had never understood why Brady only wanted the simpler things in life, why Brady refused to reach out and claim the world that had been handed to him. It was an argument they'd had since they'd been in small pants. Jack would have loved to be employed within the company, but he was merely a soldier's son. His lot in life was to defend the stronghold and be ever ready for combat. Jack was destined to follow tradition, and follow a long line of fathers and grandfathers before him in battle armour. It was unfathomable why Brady couldn't respect the traditions amongst his own kin, especially when it led to unimaginable wealth and security.

Jack wasn't as tall and intimidating as Brady, but what he lacked in sheer size, he made up for in combative skill. No one had bested him in battle yet, and it was likely no one ever would.

His short-cropped blonde hair, sky-blue eyes and faint freckles made him a favourite with the lassies. However, given his station and the rumors surrounding his past, only serving wenches, house maids and maidens of low birth would give him their time – in public, that is. Jack Manning had been known to cause a scandal or two amongst the highborn as well.

"Aye, and I'll be a part of the *great merge*. 'Tis my *duty*," Brady blew out a tired sigh.

Jack slid the remaining contents of his trencher across the table, neither of them acknowledging Brady's admission. The young Kelly wouldn't have to be dragged into the family business kicking and screaming, after all.

"Eat." With a nod and a wave, Jack instructed his men to leave, some of them grunting in annoyance, while others hoisted their chosen wench over sturdy shoulders. After any celebration, it was most common for the men in Jack's unit to have an appetite for rutting like animals. This night would be no different.

Grateful for their inclinations, the hall was finally empty. Brady could seek Jack's guidance regarding the meeting with his father.

"Duty? Git yer supper into ye, then tell me, after all this time, all these years of tryin' to be free of company responsibility, why the change of heart?" Jack asked.

Brady dove into Jack's leftovers like a ravenous beast. It had been the day before last since he'd eaten a bite, and these cold rations tasted like nothing he had ever tasted. Jack watched, absorbed in his friends conflicting emotions. Brady had always worn his feelings like a ragged old shirt – ugly and threadbare, just hoping no one would take notice. Tonight, Brady looked a little older than he had just days before, like his coal-black hair had peppered overnight, and he'd grown creases between his brows.

Brady licked the last taste of roasted pig from his fingertips, stretched his legs beneath the table and began.

"She knew she was going to die, Jack," Brady blandly stated, as his steely blue eyes pinned Jack to the spot.

"Who, Brady? Yer Ma?" Jack asked. Brady nodded.

"Aye, she knew. She let me believe she'd get better. I never had a chance to say good-bye." Brady rose from the bench, and walked aimlessly back and forth the length of the table.

"She was very sick those last days, 'tis likely she knew the end was near. An' ye did say good-bye. Ye never left 'er side," Jack replied. "Now, stop that pacin' to and fro and tell me what this has to do with finally joinin' yer Da and Liam."

Brady sat back down, only now, on the same bench within inches of Jack. He turned slightly, pulled the

Claddagh pendant from its hiding place beneath his shirt and slid the note to the side.

Jack eyed the silver pensively and unfolded the crumply parchment. Brady was fortunate for teaching his old friend how to read when they were young, for he didn't have the strength to read his mother's words aloud.

When Jack had finished, he carefully refolded the letter, and handed it back to Brady.

"Oh, I see. "'Tis yer intention now to live miserably just to make her happy?" Jack asked carefully, and then added, "The dead don't feel happiness, sadness, disappointment, or any other sentiment, Brady. Doin' this for her will solve nothin'. An' throwin' yer life away on an unworkable farm ain't the answer either, brother."

"Jesus! Then tell me what to do, Jack!" Brady roared, fingers instinctively diving into his already disheveled locks. "I can't live how I want. I shouldn't live as *they* want. You tell me then, what is right and what is wrong?" Brady was at his limit and he wondered if it was even possible for Jack to have all the answers.

"I can't tell ye what's right an' wrong. Maybe there's no such thing." Jack reached for his friend and put both hands on his shoulders, steadying him. "There's a middle ground. Find that and everyone will find the contentment they seek."

Brady thought about Jack's words for a moment. Like the kick in the arse he'd been needing, it hit him fast and hard. Finally, he knew what he would say to his father. He quickly swat Jack on the back, and leapt from the bench.

"Ye always seem to make the best sense. Where were ye yesterday when I had the ol' man on the floor with my fist in 'is face?" Brady teased, and then quickly left the hall, hoping that his father and Liam would still be enjoying their after-meal yarn in the study.

Before Brady even reached the large open door, he could hear the voices within. He heard laughter, and thought to himself, *'when was the last time I laughed?'* He shook off the notion and gently poked his head inside. He reminded his inner beast that this night, he would have to conduct himself accordingly. There was no other choice but to make amends, and that meant there were compromises to be made as well. He cleared his throat announcing his arrival.

Liam's expression went from gay to sombre in an instant and his gaze fell immediately to his father. Sean's expression didn't change. A smug grin remained firmly in place, as not to make an upset, and despite how he must have felt, trying his damnedest not to show fear. But Brady sensed his father's lingering trepidation. Instead of letting it fuel him, he regarded his father with a kind smile. Invitingly, Sean nodded at the head bobbing in the doorway.

"Evenin', Liam," Brady said, moving toward them as his gaze shifted back to Sean's peculiar expression, "Da."

"Brady, I hope you're not returnin' to finish me off!" Sean laughed. It was a nervous chuckle more than a laugh, but it shook some of the ice off their reunion. Brady was almost immediately embarrassed and felt a twinge of remorse for his harshness the day before; even though his father would never hold a grudge. He knew his father to be a patient man, most times.

"Nay, Da. I've come 'cause I had to. I know that now. You're aimin' to merge with these Ryan's in Clare and I mean to be there with ye every step of the way." Brady tried a half-smile, but it didn't come easily.

"Aye, ye have come home, then? Ye've come to yer senses as well? Is that what I'm hearin', lad?" Sean asked as he searched Brady's face for any sign of apprehension.

Brady settled into a soft chair, as far away from Sean as possible – across the room, back on to both father and sibling, facing the roaring fire in the hearth. He pulled at his shirt collar to cool the heat coursing through his body. Self-loathing mixed with regret added to the inner inferno, quite nearly burning him alive. Brady never apologised for anything. Knowing that he had to now, was all-consuming.

He breathed in deeply and started. *Pride be damned.*

"Da, I've never wanted the same things as you. I've never wanted the life ye wanted me to live. But I know 'tis a ridiculous notion to think I could go off to the cottage and live off the land. 'Tis no kinda livin' for the future lord of Kelly's Keep. Yer right, I need to come back here and accept the instruction we started. I realize now, this is my responsibility, my destiny even, and I'm ready to accept it," Brady choked out every syllable and added, "What happened here yesterday will never happen again. I am sorry, Father."

Sean was at his side in an instant, placing a hand on his shoulder.

"I know that was hard for ye to say, and I accept your apology." Sean gently squeezed Brady's shoulder with reassurance.

"Could ye sit, Da? There are terms to my agreement."

Sean chuckled, relieved that his boy had returned. He sat facing Brady in the other chair by the hearth – not father to son, but man to man. Liam remained in his father's chair behind the desk but listened intently.

"Of course, there are terms, aye." Sean's eyes gleamed in delight. Though a small victory, and knowing how discontent it would make Brady over time, he had won. "Every business meetin' is subject to terms and compromise. Let's hear it then."

"I want to keep within tradition for the clan and do what is necessary. So, I will reclaim my place within Kelly and Son's that I forfeited so many years ago. I will attend all business meetin's 'til ye feel I am competent and have learned the business well. O' course, in the event of your death, the company, I intend to split down the middle, givin' half to Liam." Sean nodded. He fully understood Brady's need to eliminate sibling rivalry. "Also, I will be movin' back to the country, to the cottage, to live as I wish until I am forced to become head of the clan permanently." It pained Brady to talk about his father's death, for as often as they disagreed, deep down he admired his father and loved him very much.

"How will ye know when you are to meet with potential clients? Nay, ye need to be here, Brady. I can agree for ye to share the company with Liam, but cannot agree to ye bein' an absent partner," Sean said quietly, in fear of angering his intimidating son. Brady sighed.

"Ye'll send a messenger to the cottage. 'Tis only a half days' ride. I am sure this will cause you or the company no strife. It has to be this way, Da. Please understand," he pleaded. "At least during the summer months. Come winter, I'll have to be back here or face starvation, especially if the crop is small. I can do both, you'll see. Let me prove it to ye."

His father regarded him carefully, and silently nodded in agreement.

Brady felt a small amount of relief that the meeting had gone without conflict and his father was willing to let him live the best of both worlds. He stood and turned to Liam, who seemed awe-struck by Brady's generosity of giving up half the company to him in the future. With a wink and a nod, a brotherhood had been solidified.

"Now, Liam, if you can agree to this, pour us a drink in celebration," Sean proclaimed.

Liam rubbed his palms together. "Well, then! What'll it be?"

The Kelly men lounged in the study for what seemed like hours, discussing the happenings within the company, the changes that had been made in refining the art of shipbuilding, new construction methods using steel for the hull, as well as wood, and being on the forefront of this new style to cut costs and labour.

Finally, Brady stood, swallowed the last of his drink and bid the others a good night. He was exhausted and eager to rest. Eager to lay in bed and make plans for when he returned to the forest where he was tethered by nothing and no one. When he'd left the cottage the day before, he'd said farewell to his mother and her dreams to turn it into a real working farm again. But now there was new hope. He would never again have to feel torn between two worlds.

"When is this merge takin' place? Tell me where to be and when, and I'll be there," Brady assured his father.

"We will discuss the particulars in the mornin', but the first meetin' with Robert Ryan takes place here in eight days' time," Sean said as he walked his son to the door. "Get a good night's rest. You'll be needin' yer strength tomorrow. There's much to do before he arrives."

"Aye. Sleep well, Father," Brady replied turning to Liam, who appeared positively drunk, yet still settled behind the desk, nursing a large glass of amber liquid. "Come on little brother, ye can help me to my chamber." Liam shakily stood and let Brady's arm come around him for support.

As if they were still in adolescence, they made their way up the stairs, laughing, and staggering all the way.

After Brady tucked his little brother into bed, he blew out the lamp and stoked up the fire. He wondered if there would be a fire burning for him in his chambers this night.

When he entered his room, it was warm and inviting; such a contrast to how he'd found it mere hours before. What a simple thing it was to have his room readied, a small and insignificant pleasure, but it proved that he was cared for – his father loved him – despite everything Brady had done to prevent it.

This night, his bed covers had been turned down, the coverings on the windows drawn shut, and a lamp still burned on his bed side table. He laughed under his breath. *Someone seen fit to ready the future Kelly lord for bed.* It was difficult to suppress a chuckle at how quickly things change.

He stripped his clothes off, let them fall to the floor, and crawled into his enormous bed. He lay on his back, his hands linked together behind his head, looking toward the ceiling into nothingness and let his thoughts take him away.

He dreamed that night of green fields, the vast forest beyond his cottage and a faceless young maiden round with child, playing hide and seek with a red-haired little boy. It was the most intoxicating and happy dream he'd ever had, and awoke the next morning with vivid memories of the fantasy bettering his mood.

Endless possibilities ignited a spark of hope for the future.

FOUR

Violet's mother settled on the bed behind her, combing the wavy mess back from her face.

"I don't know how ye were able to get your father to agree to let you go with him to Galway lass, but I admire yer determination," Beth laughed.

"Aye! 'Tis an excitin' occasion!" Violet exclaimed. "If ye can keep a secret, I'll tell ye what I told him to change 'is mind."

"Of course, child, what is it?" Her mother came around and perched alongside, wondering what the mischievous lass had gone and done now.

"I told him that I need to see more and experience more if I am ever going to someday be successful as a business woman. And I told 'im that Gregory suggested it to help me gain knowledge in how the company really operates," she said, quietly, so that no passers-by could overhear.

"Aye, so what is the secret?" her mother wearily asked.

"Gregory didn't suggest it, Ma," she put her head down, a little ashamed of her deception. "I only told Da that so he would go along with it. The real reason I want to go so badly, is because I'm twenty and two and have no prospects. No hope in meetin' anyone suitable to marry. I never will if I don't get out from under this keep," Violet explained, dolefully. "I know there's more to life than this. There has to be."

Her mother could see the tears welling up in her daughter's emerald eyes and no doubt felt the weight of the girl's breaking heart.

Beth understood Violet's need to see the world, to fall in love, to find someone who sent shivers down her spine; to make her knees weak. She fondly remembered how lucky she and Robert had been in finding love, despite their arranged marriage.

She'd known so many folks who weren't as fortunate, and swore she would never take that chance with Violet's happiness. There would never be a contract for marriage made for her daughter, unless Violet, herself found someone whom she loved enough to marry.

"I see, lass. Now, what if yer Da finds out Gregory did not recommend you go to Galway with him? Did ye think about that?" her mother scolded.

"Aye, I did. 'Twill be too late. I'll be in Galway, attendin' meetin's and parties, and ye never know who I may meet," she smiled a courageous smile with hope that her mother would understand and not judge her too harshly. And keep her secret.

"Well then, you've two days before you begin the journey. We have to start gettin' ye packed." Beth gave her daughter a kiss on top of her head. "If ye're going to meet the lad of yer dreams, we best pack all yer best gowns."

Both Ryan women began packing Violet's trunks so full they thought they wouldn't be able to close them. Violet carefully folded her favourite red gown, made of elegant silk, brought back from England when her father visited there on one of his business trips. She had never worn it here at home, even though she dearly loved it.

Her father had said that most ladies in England were wearing styles like this one. With a high neck, a low cut-out back, and long sleeves with sequins in every seam, it had been all the craze amongst lassies her age. He'd tried to convince her that it wouldn't be inappropriate for a girl her age to wear such a daring garment, but Violet never found such an occasion worth wearing it to.

Until now, she'd kept the dress carefully hung and confined in her wardrobe. It pained her some to fold it and stuff it into a trunk, but she imagined herself wearing it in Galway, where no one knew her, and she could perhaps step out of herself for a while.

Her mother kept the staff busy, preparing Violet for her first journey away from home, directing chores, and baking extra sweets for her to take; making sure Violet would want for nothing along the way. Her father's patience seemed to be wearing thin, as he didn't see the need for Violet to take *'everything she owned'* to go and meet with the Kelly's. But to her delight, he hadn't complained too much. "After all," he'd said, "girls will be girls."

The dawn's sun arose from behind the last trace of fog and Violet's heart leapt in excitement. She chose her simple, comfortable yellow dress and matching cloak, made of thick, soft fabric to ensure her cosiness and warmth in the family carriage. The color was bright enough that it didn't make her look pallid against her fair, pale complexion, but caused her dark wavy red locks to appear almost cherry. She liked this dress. She felt *womanly* in it, like she was finally a lady.

"Ma! What's takin' them so long? 'Tis not a tricky thing to ready a carriage and load a few trunks on the back, is it?" Violet exclaimed. Her patience was wearing thin as well as everyone else's. For two days straight, this trip was all she could think about and she surprised even herself, when she found that she was also curious about the actual business side of this whole ordeal.

"Be patient, Vy. Yer Da will send for ye as soon as he's ready. I have to tell ye, dear, I'm not havin' a good feelin' about ye leavin'. I will miss ye greatly," her mother said as she enveloped Violet into her warm embrace. "What happens if ye find yerself in love and decide to never to return to me?"

Violet eyed her mother, and let out a small laugh. "Oh, Ma! I'll only be gone a fortnight. Ye won't even have time to miss me. And no matter what happens, I'll return. Promise," Violet replied, as she reciprocated her mother's love.

Just then, her father bellowed at the foot of the stairs. "Lord tunderin', lass! If ye don't want to stay here with yer ma, I think ye better get yer arse down o'er these stairs."

Violet's eyes lit up with enthusiastic delight, and despite her mother falling apart, she didn't try to hide it. She let go of Beth, and spun out of the room, and down the stairs, where her father awaited.

"Aye, Da. I'm ready!" she shouted, her feet barely touching the floor.

Her father mounted his horse once he had Violet safely placed in her carriage. The journey wouldn't be a long one – only a few days, and everyone had made sure she would be comfortable. Inside the carriage, there were books for her to read and needle work to keep her hands busy on her two-day voyage. She peeked out of the covered window and watched in admiration as her father dipped low from his saddle to kiss her mother gently on the lips. She sat back in her seat and sighed. *If I could only find a love like that.*

Her mind was adrift with visions of being kissed, so much that she never watched out the window to see her mother standing there, waving her good-byes. Violet never seen the kisses she'd blown in the direction of her daughter's carriage, and never heard the '*I love you*' carried away by the wind.

If only she had known this was her last moment with her mother for a very long time, she would have taken in every single second and drowned in it.

FIVE

Brady watched as six men, all atop beastly stallions appeared in the distance. He had to look twice when he noticed the carriage in tow as well. His mood quickly soured.

"The Ryan's make it a practice of bringin' their women and children to business meetin's?" he dryly asked his father who was just observing and wondering the same thing.

"I guess we'll soon find out, lad." His father disregarded Brady's foul mood and went to Liam's side, to kindly greet his guests.

The first man brought his horse to a halt, quickly jumped down, and introduced himself as Morgan. The man was an imposing figure, apparently cast from a Norse god mould, but his eyes shone with underlying kindness and genteel. Sean shook his massive hand, introduced himself and turned to both his sons with a smile.

"This is Liam. He's my youngest boy, but make no mistake, he's got more of a mind for figures and business than any one of my senior men," Sean said with a half chuckle and then, "Don't be fooled by his youthful appearance."

"'Tis a pleasure, Liam. I'll be overseein' the construction crew once we've merged." Morgan pointed to his companions behind him who had yet to dismount from their horses. "This here is Patrick, Martin, Seamus, James and of course, Robert Ryan."

Sean smiled at each of them, as they nodded their *hello*. All except Robert, who was moving toward the back of the pack, toward the carriage.

Ignoring Robert's disinterest in introductions, Sean continued. "And over here," he pointed, "my eldest, Brady. He is still learnin', but I've a keen notion that he will someday be workin' right alongside ye, as foreman of the Kelly's fine labour crew."

"Aye. I've heard some fine stories about you, lad," Morgan jeered. "Is it true you almost killed a man with your bare hands before you were even done wettin' the bed?"

Brady fought back his fury and ignored Morgan's taunting. Sean seemed to sense his son's annoyance and intervened.

"Brady has since grown into a wilful, yet sensible man. I'd trust no other to keepin' everyone in line," Sean interjected, coming to his son's defence. It irked Brady to no end that his father would stand there and make excuses for his past indiscretions, and as if that wasn't bad enough, he could feel Morgan's gaze boring into him, waiting for a reaction. *He won't bloody-well be gettin' one today*. This meeting was far too important to let his ire and rage take hold.

Brady watched in brooding silence as Robert extended his hand into the carriage and was met with a tiny gloved one.

When she emerged from the carriage, escorted by her father, Brady stared in awe at the most beautiful woman he had ever seen. She was an enchanted vision for sure and he nearly rubbed his eyes in disbelief.

She wore a simple, pink summer dress with a long white ribbon wrapping about a slender waist, matching her white gloved hands. Her fiery-red hair was half pulled from her face, and fell past her waist in the back, almost to her perfect arse.

Brady swallowed the groan in his throat at the sight, and thought of that sweet, round behind.

Having a woman writhe beneath him didn't instil excitement as it once had. One chambermaid or even whore was no different from the other. They all screamed too much or cried too much. And *if* he'd treated them in a gentleman's manner, they'd expected him to fall in love and propose marriage. It was madness! Love and marriage were things Brady wanted no part of.

But for the first time in so very long, a woman – this slim, red-headed, delightful creature walking toward him, had something stirring inside. He could almost feel his heart beating against the linen shirt he wore.

Breaking Brady's reverie, Robert finally extended his hand in greeting the Kelly's and shook hands with each one of them, keeping his left hand on the small of the girl's back. Brady recognised it as a sign of protection. *Or ownership?*

"'Tis a pleasure to meet you all," Robert exclaimed. "I am anxious to get these meetin's underway so we can all start makin' a great deal more money. May I present my daughter, Violet? She will be sittin' in on our dealin's, as she will someday be heir to my half of the company. I mean, our company," he beamed.

"Hello," she said, with a sweet grin, her pink lips curling ever-so-slightly. "'Tis lovely to meet ye all." Brady had never heard a sound so song-like from any other woman he'd ever met. Instantly, he was spellbound by the sound of it; that one word, *hello*. His manhood twitched beneath his breeches. He had to hear her speak some more.

"Did ye enjoy yer journey, Lady Violet?" By the curious expressions gaping at him, Brady's question surprised both his father and Liam. He really couldn't blame them, for it was so unlike him to be the one extending a welcome for conversation.

Violet's attention suddenly snapped toward the source of the baritone Irish brogue. *Intimidating brute. Handsome brute, though.*

"Aye, I did, thank you," she replied as she looked up into the most chilling pair of blue eyes she had ever seen. She shivered inwardly and her stomach became queasy, like little butterflies were dancing all around in there. She noticed that even though he was introduced as Brady Kelly, son of Sean Kelly, she could see no resemblance connecting them.

Brady's wild raven hair, blue eyes and enormous build, did indeed set him aside from the other two. Violet also noticed that while Liam and Sean were much more suitably dressed for business, Brady wore long, brown trousers and a plain white linen shirt, opened low to expose a small patch of black curly hair on his well-defined chest. While the other two were clean shaven, his square jaw was partially concealed by black stubble.

She liked this Kelly the best. He was mysterious, attractive, and she was amazed by the way his gaze pierced right through to her soul. A deep, crimson heat engulfed her cheeks before Sean broke the spell.

"What do ye think of our shipyard here?" he asked Robert.

"'Tis an impressive display of what ye can do," Robert replied as he scanned the different stations where one vessel was just being started, another looking half finished, with the boom stacks not yet erected, and then to another that was clearly ready for launch.

"She will be called *Caitlyn's Fancy* when we have 'er blessed. We've put it off and rescheduled her maiden voyage, so that you and yer associates can be here to witness what it is we do here," Sean pointed to the grand sight. "She is to be a luxury vessel. Suitable for long voyages."

"She's a beauty!" Robert exclaimed. She truly was as grand a ship as anyone had ever laid eyes upon. "And she's made with the same steel that comes from the mill that just opened here in Galway?"

"Aye, 'tis why the cost is lower for us, we don't have to import any materials," Sean replied.

"Why is it that yer wanting to merge with us then?" Robert asked. "What have ye to gain?" Sean had clearly been ready for this line of questioning, but right now, Violet suspected he was ready to say just about anything to make this deal happen.

"I'll answer that if you don't mind, Father," Liam cut in and then said, "Ryan's Shipwrights possess wealthier contacts. I understand you have dealings in Boston and have made good on all your contracts since you've been in operation," he explained. "And it doesn't hurt that you've had a consistent work force, employing generations of shipwrights who reside within your own villages."

Robert replied directly to Liam, "Aye, lad. Right you are. Ye've done yer homework." He was clearly impressed at the youth's knowledge of business affairs, and nodded his approval.

"So ye see, Robert, bringin' these two ports together as one, with my facilities and materials, and your crew and contracts, we can only do bigger and better things." Sean patted the man on the back. "I hope one of your associates over there is a lawyer. I'd like to get started on this contract first thing in the mornin'. Until then, we'll get ye settled into our guest rooms back at the keep. To-night, we celebrate!"

"Aye!" Robert exclaimed. "What kinda businessman would I be if I came here without two of my best counsellors?" he laughed.

"Violet, me lassie. You could have Liam show ye 'round after the feast this evenin'. How's that sound?" Sean flashed a toothy smile, and winked at Liam.

Violet felt all eyes on her at once, as she turned bright red. She stifled her embarrassment, and stuck out her chin as a show of independence. She wanted to tell them all to go to hell. That she could wander around, all on her own. But then, that wouldn't be becoming of a lady, now would it? She understood she would be expected to have a chaperone everywhere she went; she just didn't want it to be Liam. She hoped someone would suggest Brady, she prayed even more that he would offer. He didn't.

Brady felt a peculiar irritation in his gut when his father recommended Liam as Violet's ambassador to Kelly's Keep.

'*What the hell's wrong with me? Am I not good enough to escort the lass about the castle*?' he thought with rising resentment.

He pictured Violet strolling in the garden with her arm linked through Liam's, laughing politely when he'd make a joke – Liam's jokes were never funny. He thought about how she would look beneath the moonlight, and he yearned to pull the moon down from the sky and watch its reflection dance in her green irises.

Then it hit him like an anchor in the chest. Something he'd never felt before. A gut-wrenching emotion which could only be defined as pure and absolute jealousy. And he was seething in it.

When they'd all departed the shipyard, Sean and Robert led the pack, followed by Liam who was making polite conversation with the Ryan clan lawyers, Patrick and Martin. Morgan stayed in step with his fellow planners and builders, Seamus and James, while Brady took up the rear, trailing Violet's carriage.

All the way back to the keep, the image of Violet with Liam, left him sour and hot tempered.

' *'Tis my own fault. I should've offered to take her around. Not that anyone would 'ave let that happen,'* he chuckled under his breath. For all his twenty-eight years of being a tyrant had come back and bitten him right in the arse.

When the party reached the Kelly estate, the scent of wild iris wafted on the breeze.

Green, rolling hills dotted with purple and white wild flowers were a stunning sight, and spread behind the castle as far as the eye could see.

They were greeted at the tall, stone gatehouse at the front of the yard by four stable stewards, each helping the men from their mounts, and then escorting the horses around back to lodge them for the night.

Once again, Robert escorted Violet from her cozy wagon and the entire party went inside.

Violet was amazed by the grandeur of the great castle. Two imposing towers stood on either side, serving as sentry for the massive wooden doorway between them. No doubt, in times of war and strife, archers would be strategically placed and exterminate anything that dared to threaten the Kelly clan.

As she was ushered inside, her eyes flew to a staircase which winded its way along the far wall. As far as she could see, there were three stories with looming balconies on each level. She also took mental note that although this was an impressive looking home, it lacked some of the things that made her home so comfortable and inviting.

There weren't any wild flowers to be seen in vases scattered throughout the long hallway, and when led into the study, she hadn't seen one hand-made tapestry hanging from the walls along the way. These were things in *her* home, in which her mother took pride in. It was a woman's touch that was deficient here. She wanted to ask for the lady of the house but decided it was better not to pry.

In the study, Violet took a seat in a soft plush chair that had been placed there for the guests. She knew this because there were seven other seats placed around the room which looked as out of place as this one.

She felt a little out of place as well, as the men went to the hearth and lit cigars, poured amber liquid into short tumblers and clicked them together. As if he sensed her unease, Brady brought her a glass filled with the potent liquor.

"Lady Violet," he said as he handed it to her. "As you're to become an heiress to your father's fortune someday, ye should be rightly so, engaged in our celebration," Brady smiled a most wicked smile, causing her breath to catch in her throat.

"Th…thank ye, Brady," she replied, flushing with new sensations, and politely took the glass from his hand. "I think I'll go up to my room, and get ready for the evenin' meal instead."

"Nay, lass. Ye look ready to me," Brady replied as he looked her up and down, starting at her shoes, then up, until his stare was transfixed on her emerald green eyes. The heat in her expression would be impossible to hide, with her cheeks blazing with the intense strength of a wild fire. She wondered how long it would take for the floor to open up and swallow her whole. She prayed it would be soon.

With the implication of his words, she lowered her gaze and stifled a cheeky retort. The tension between them was something unworldly and she didn't think she could endure much more of it.

He cleared his throat.

Their eyes locked for the briefest of moments.

Violet raised her glass, and then so completely unlike her, downed the pungent liquid quickly, nearly causing her to choke the fiery whiskey back up.

"I'll have Mary tend to your every need while yer a guest here. She's the cook, but for such a special ward, I'll have father assign her new duties," he said, holding out his hand. She placed her hand in his, and immediately felt a surge of energy between them.

'Oh, dear Lord, why does he have to be so handsome?' she thought. *'And that voice!'* she swooned.

Brady called for Mary, ignoring the others still congratulating themselves and indulging in the drink. It was astonishing that even Robert had been too preoccupied to see to his daughter's needs.

Mary appeared and escorted Violet up to her room. Once ushered into a small, elegant chamber, with a fire

glowing in the hearth, Violet blew out a breath of reprieve to be far from Brady Kelly.

In taking appraisal of her new accommodations, she
noted the ladies' fashion in which the room had been
decorated. The thick, floral curtains over the windows
had been tied back to let the sun filter in with the warm
breeze which followed. The space was perfectly inviting
in contrast to the lower floor of the manor.

"I 'ope ye like it, lass. 'Tis been quite some time
since a lady's been within these walls, aside from the
help. So, when I spied the wagon comin' up the road, I
hurried to ready it for ye." Mary gave a quick curtsy and
moved to leave.

Violet gently caught her by the arm. "'Tis lovely!
The loveliest room in the entire keep, I would think."
Then Violet bit her lower lip wondering if she should ask
what was really on her mind.

"Is there something wrong, lass?" Mary asked, likely
sensing Violet's lingering inquisition.

"Where is Lady Kelly?" Violet bashfully asked.

"The angels took 'er some months ago. 'Tis why
ye'll see no pretty things scattered about. Lord Kelly 'ad

all and everything that reminded 'im of her put into storage in the tower. I s'pect he will be over it soon and put the castle back to how she'd left it though," Mary explained, almost coldheartedly.

Violet felt a cramp of sorrow deep in her stomach for the Kelly boys. How awful it must have been for the two young men to lose their mother at such a time in their lives. Lady Kelly would never see them married or hold her grandchildren.

"Oh, I see," replied Violet, sombrely. "'Tis a sad thing, for sure."

"Now lass, never ye mind gloomy thoughts. We've a celebration to ready ye for. What have ye in mind to wear?" Mary asked as she went to Violet's trunks and began unpacking her clothes and hanging her gowns. When she shook out the red one, she sighed, smiled and turned to Violet.

"This one," Mary beamed. "Liam will think ye an utter sight of perfection in it." Mary gave Violet a warm expression, but Violet didn't reciprocate.

"Liam?" Violet asked, dumbfounded.

"Aye, he's about your age isn't 'e? An' I seen the way he was gapin' at ye in the study. I'd say he's smitten with ye already," Mary explained, an odd expression beaming from her.

"Aye, I think he is my age." Violet tried her best not to give away what she was already feeling – helplessly drawn to Brady. "But I'm not here to find a husband, Mary. I'm here on business, as are the men," she lied defiantly.

"My apologies, m'lady. I just thought that you and Liam, being the same age an' havin' the same ambitions, ye could make a good match 'tis all. I meant nothin' by it," Mary said apologetically, and then moved to leave the room once again.

Immediately regretting the admonishing manner in which she spoke, Violet gently caught the maid's hand. "Ye don't have to leave. And please, speak freely to me. I'm in need of a friend while I stay under this roof. There are far too many men here," Violet chuckled, easing the tension that had fallen between the two women.

Mary seemed to soften and then smiled once again.

"Aye, there are too many men here now, but just wait 'til tonight. There'll be a sea of wenches, all swooning o'er the little lords," Mary laughed and continued her busying about.

"What of Brady? Is he not married? I would think a gentleman his age would have a wife and babes to come home to," Violet asked, curiosity for the eldest Kelly brother making her bolder than she ever thought possible.

Mary, apparently surprised by the question, stopped in her tracks and no doubt struggled to answer carefully, yet loyally. She sat on the bed, and patted the place beside her for Violet to sit.

"Lord Brady's no gentleman, lass. A tormented soul, that one. Ever since 'e was a boy, he's been obstinate and mean tempered. I don't know what'll ever become of 'im. 'Twill take a patient and understandin' woman to tame that beast. But if it can be done, she'll be awfully lucky. Once ye get Brady Kelly's heart, you've got all of 'im."

Violet understood now, why Liam had been appointed as her escort. Even though Brady was the eldest, he couldn't be trusted to be on his best behaviour. So, Liam, the genteel, no-nonsense business executive had been obliged to take his place. Such a pity, for Brady possessed qualities that intrigued and fascinated her...if she could only put her finger on them. *What is it about him?*

"But you be a smart lass, an' stay clear of 'im," Mary added, and then quickly covered her mouth, obviously regretting that she'd let that last part slip.

But Violet didn't want to stay away from Brady. In fact, the more she was warned against him, the more drawn to him she became. *Charming. Dangerous. Alluring.* So, unlike the boring dolts she'd been avoiding back in Clare.

With butterflies dancing in her belly, Violet donned the risqué gown and Mary fixed her red tangles into elegant curls that tumbled down the open back. She was ready.

Soon, the supper bell rang causing an upsurge of apprehension regarding their choice of that wicked red dress. The result was a sudden urge to empty the contents of her stomach all over the cold stone floor. Only with encouragement from Mary, did Violet finally descend the staircase with a shaky hand grasping the banister all the way down.

To her relief, when she reached the bottom, her father was waiting with his arm held out for her to take. Violet sighed. *I can always count on you, Da.*

"Ye look lovely, Vy. I told ye that dress would be fetchin'. Especially on ye," he quietly praised. "I think ye'll enjoy yer stay here. Sean says there will be a feast like this every night 'til we depart. Ye'll 'ave the opportunity to meet a great deal of new people," Robert said as they made their way to the dining hall. "I know 'tis very important for you to get out of Clare for a while. Perhaps ye may even meet someone special," he added with a wink and a pat on her shaking hand.

Violet didn't know what to say. He knew the real reason why she'd pushed to come along on this trip, and he'd not argued, nor contested it. She looked at him wide-eyed, and as if he could read her mind, he gently kissed her cheek and said, "I knew of yer deception when I spoke to Gregory and he begged me not to let ye come." Robert winked, and Violet blushed. She'd been caught.

"Thank ye so much, Da. I love ye," she whispered.

When the pair entered the impressive hall, she pushed out her chin, and walked straight-backed and proud. Sean and his sons were already seated on the dais, each one flanking their father. Robert led Violet to the setting where they were assigned, and seated her next to Liam. When her father was settled into his seat next to Brady, Sean stood up and made his introductions.

"If I may have yer attention," Sean said, clearing his throat as the entire hall, filled with men and women, came to a complete hush. "I would like to present Lord Robert Ryan and his daughter Lady Violet." Robert stood at his introduction, and nodded.

Violet smiled down at all the curious faces. She feared her shaking knees would cause her to fall on her arse, and hoped a kind nod would serve as satisfactory acknowledgment.

"Tomorrow we embark on new territory for Kelly and Son's. As ye all know, we are merging with Ryan's Shipwrights. This means a long-time contract and security for everyone. I am very pleased to announce that tomorrow mornin', all are welcome to come down to the shipyard as Father O'Malley blesses the *Caitlyn's Fancy*. We'll launch 'er for the first time and then sign the papers necessary to make this merge official.

"Tonight, we feast, dance, and get acquainted." Sean raised his glass, and turned to his guest's one at a time, as a sign of welcome.

Violet sat through five courses, eating very little of anything, laughing at the jokes the common folks would stand up and tell, and making polite conversation with Liam.

When the music started, Violet was relieved that she wouldn't have to hear him going on and on about figures, labour costs, the price of steel, and about the changes he would make to the company when he took over. *Oh, Jesus and Mary, if I have to listen to one more of his jokes!*

Thankfully, the glorious sound of the fiddle had quieted him, as he couldn't speak over it. Violet tapped her toe under the table while the entire hall fell into a frenzy of dance and laughter. She couldn't say whether it was the wine or the fiddle, but a sense of calm finally settled her.

Suddenly she felt glacial-blue eyes pierce her flesh like hot daggers, prompting her to look in Brady's direction. He was perched in his chair, hands clasped together in front of his mouth, leaning in on his elbows. Her belly flipped at the mere sight of him and she suddenly felt self-conscious and naked. She bit her bottom lip until she thought she tasted the salty tang of copper.

Instead of looking away, like any gentleman would, Brady's gaze remained fixed, stripping her bare. Yet, she couldn't look away.

When the band started to play a soft slow melody, she watched nervously, as Brady whispered something in her father's ear, rose from his place and swaggered toward her. Her gaze flickered to Robert. When their eyes met, there was no indication whether or not he was pleased or displeased with what Brady had said. He merely watched tight-lipped as Brady held out his hand to his only daughter.

Only after she'd accepted, Violet felt Robert's disapproving glower. She ignored the warning glint as Brady led her off the dais to the middle of the floor where the other folks were dancing.

Her heart beat furiously as Brady held her tightly against his firm chest. She breathed in, inhaling the faint traces of soap, spice and whiskey. *All male.*

As they began to move to the music, everything and everyone fell away, and it was just the two of them. She looked up into his eyes as he stared into hers, moving sensually to the soft melody.

In that moment, she felt closer to him than she'd ever felt with anyone. Without exchanging one word, he exposed her secrets. For her entire life she'd been someone's daughter or niece, but she had never felt as she did right now; like a woman. She held on to him tightly and he to her, for she feared if she let go, she would never feel this man beneath her touch again.

Brady revelled in her gentle embrace, the heat of her palm scorching his, and he knew in that moment he had to have her. A pain in his groin had him aching with desire, and he knew she felt the severe hardness of him against her. Violet gaped at him with innocence and wonder.

He fought within himself to break free from her body, but he couldn't bring himself to do it. They held on to each other until the song ended and Liam appeared. The magic between them had been broken.

"I'll take a dance with the fair lass now, brother. If, that is, you'll have me, Violet," Liam sneered at Brady as if to say, '*You know I'm better than you. You're not good enough for her*'. Brady let her go, their eyes still connected, feeling as if he'd had the wind knocked out of him. Her expression, lustful only moments ago, suddenly changed, and she politely smiled at Liam and accepted.

Brady could read this female like an open book. She hadn't wanted to break their embrace but necessity of courteousness had most likely been bred into her.

And for the first time in his life, there was sibling rivalry between the two Kelly boys. Brady knew where he stood.

He would never be good enough for Violet Ryan.

SIX

Brady hadn't been able to sleep for more than a few minutes at a time, for whenever slumber had the compassion to claim him, his dreams would take his plagued subconscious to places he wasn't yet ready to go.

He'd dreamed Violet was laid out before him. With hair of flame fanning all around her, she'd been ready and eager for him to take her on a journey into ecstasy. He could almost feel her creamy skin beneath his touch as he ignited fires within her, in places unexplored by any other man.

This morning the memories of his dream left him wanting and aching. He couldn't help but free his erect manhood from beneath the covers, and stroke the hard length of himself in search of release.

Brady pumped, eyes closed tight, picturing his goddess in the exquisite red dress.

Envisioning her soft supple lips, he was certain he would surely die if never given the opportunity to taste them. His pumping fist moved faster and faster until he spilled his hot seed onto his tight abdomen. He sighed with a shaky breath.

Even with his need subsided for the moment, he still couldn't let go of the image of her in his mind. He felt like a man bewitched – tortured and plagued by this woman.

Swinging his legs over the side of the bed, he moved to the wash basin, and poured icy cold water over a cloth to wash and get ready for the morning meeting. *'I have to face 'er again today',* he thought miserably. She would strip him to the core with her astonishing green eyes without realising she was doing it.

'Why now?' he thought. Just as he'd agreed to live a life he didn't want – the life his father had mapped out for him – she'd complicated things. Now, he pictured himself living with her, happily at the cottage far away from everything. Waking up each morning to hear his name on her lips as she woke.

For a split moment, and for the first time in so very long, hope sliced through him. *Perhaps I'm not so dejected and wretched, after all.* But as fast as the thought entered his mind, it fled and was replaced by irritation, suspicion and regret.

He wondered what had happened after he'd left the hall last night; after Liam had stolen his one precious moment with the beautiful Violet Ryan. *'Tis my own fault. I shouldn't 'ave let Liam have 'er.*

Brady had stormed out of the hall like a savage boar, unable to watch his prey being manhandled by another contender. Had Liam danced with her like he had? Had she held him close? Had she gazed up into his eyes like she'd looked at Brady? The mounting questions were driving him senseless.

"Damn her, and damn Liam," Brady swore aloud, wishing a higher power would hear his curse and condemn them all to hell.

When Violet awoke, it took her a moment to remember where she was. She stretched and yawned quietly as she recalled the day before. A wide smile swept across her face, as she thought back to last night's celebration. The feast, the many colourful people she'd met, the music and dancing. She couldn't remember the last time she'd had such a great time in her own village. And even though these weren't her people, they had received her with grace and respect.

She leapt from her bed, just as Mary entered the room to wake her.

"Mornin', lass. Slept well, did ye?" the aged woman asked as she went to the windows to tie back the curtains and open the shutters.

"Aye, Mary. I did, thank ye!" Violet exclaimed.

"Wonderful. But we must be gettin' ye dressed. Yer Da's already waitin' for ye in the study with Lord Kelly and Liam. I figure Brady will be along when he's good an' ready," Mary replied, dryly.

And just then, as if it had been just a dream, Violet remembered Brady and their seductive waltz in the hall. It almost seemed unreal, for she had never felt so amorous and sassy in all her life. And just to think, all from one silly dance. But it was the way he swayed his hips close to hers, the way he held on to her like she were his lifeline. It was the toe-curling way he'd studied her, reading her body. Every facet of this Kelly brute left her longing for more.

At first sight of him back at the shipyard, she had almost been afraid. He'd appeared so dominating and cold. With the mounting anticipation of seeing him again, she knew her fears were justified. Only now, she didn't fear the man. A surge of panic caused her to tremble for fear that she would never again, feel the way she had in his arms.

When Violet entered the study, all three Kelly men were perched around the wooden desk. Patrick and Martin were solidly standing cross-armed behind Sean, and her father was standing over Liam's shoulder looking over him at the papers laid out before them. The two lawyers gave them all the go-ahead, legally speaking, and the contracts were ready to be signed.

"Alright then, that seems to be the last one," Robert said as he made his mark on the bottom-most dotted line.

"Aye, 'tis indeed," smiled Sean, as he extended his hand and both men shook to finalize the deal.

Violet burst in, vexed and outraged that they hadn't waited for her to witness the commemorative occasion. She held her tongue when her gaze fell upon Brady. She hadn't expected him to be there, but out of fear of looking like a spoiled brat about to have a tantrum, she bit the inside of her cheek to quell her displeasure. Her father sensed her discontentment and went to her side.

"No worries, Vy. We've just signed all the paper work to make it legal-like, 'tis all. When we go to the shipyard, we'll do it again so ye can see." Violet sighed. Her father really didn't take her seriously enough to allow her to one day take over in his place; she knew that now. He'd handled her like she was only there *'for show'* too.

"Aye, Da. 'Tis alright," she lowered her eyes, as she felt everyone watching, gauging her reaction. But it wasn't all right. She was angry and struggling to hide her flood of emotion. She looked up, and Brady was watching her intently, eyes flashing with sympathy and compassion. This was a new side of Brady she hadn't yet seen.

Her father left her side, dismissing her displeasure, but Brady replaced him immediately.

"Would ye like to take a walk in the garden with me?" he asked, subtly brushing his fingertips along her bare arm. Heat flooded her. "We've an hour 'til we have to be at the shipyard. Let's enjoy the mornin' outside and leave this lot to congratulatin' themselves."

Violet beamed in reply and forgot about her hurt feelings. She took his arm as he led them out of the back of the keep to the glorious garden.

The twosome strolled about the lush yard making mild conversation at first – the weather, how his clan were recovering from the famine, everyday topics for discussion. But by the time they'd left for the shipyard, Violet had learned how his mother had died, why he'd been branded a ruthless and merciless fiend, and why he had finally given in to this father's pressure tactics and joined with Liam to become an active part of Kelly and Son's.

"'Tis time ye get to the shipyard. The others are 'bout ready to leave as well," Mary declared, reminding Violet of her presence. The maid waggled her eyebrows at Brady disapprovingly and shooed him away, sending him ahead of herself and Violet. "Ye like him?" she asked, intrusively.

"Aye, an' I know I'm not s'posed to," Violet stubbornly admitted. "But I don't care! I think he's charmin'." Mary hadn't pushed the subject and it was a good thing, for Violet had been more than prepared to tell the old bat to mind her own business. Instead, they quietly hurried toward the gatehouse, skirts swooshing against the stone path.

Gallantly mounted on their great steeds, Violet eyed her father and the others with lingering annoyance. Until that is, Brady emerged from the back of the estate holding the reins tethering the most beautiful mare she had ever seen. Even Daisy couldn't compare to this breeder's dream.

"Ye can ride, can ye?" he asked, a slight grin pulling at the corner of his perfectly sculpted lips.

Everyone watched, mouths gaping in disbelief. Surely, Sean's mean-tempered son, the man who cared for no one but himself, couldn't have been suddenly struck with chivalry. But this was a new side of Brady. Yielding and gentle. And with compassion marking his features, he offered his mother's mare to this girl.

"If ye can ride, it'll give ye a break from yer stuffy carriage," Brady chuckled.

Violet smiled warmly and replied, "Aye, I can. She's beautiful, Brady. Thank ye."

"Well, if the boys at the shipyard are to take ye seriously, then ye ought to look the part, like the rest of us then, eh?" Brady replied, his gaze landing directly on her father, as to insinuate Robert's lack of recognizing Violet's proficiency and seeing her as an equal.

Violet smoothed the mare's long blonde mane, grabbed hold of the reins, and flung herself onto the back of the marvellous creature.

"Come along, Vy," Robert called, his cheeks reddening like a child who'd just been chastised.

"Aye, Da," Violet replied, ogling her handsome saviour. Brady made senses within her come alive. She had almost forgotten her father's earlier blunder, or at least now it didn't sting as much.

When they arrived at the shipyard, they dismounted and tied the horse's reins to the post.

There were hundreds of the towns' people and villagers gathered about. Some had set up mobile taverns where anyone who wanted to indulge in the drink while witnessing this historical event in Galway, could effectively do it.

Women dressed in multihued and lively colors were spread about the crowd, and children ran free between the legs of many of them.

Brady pointed to some of the *working-class* girls loitering around the make-shift taverns wearing tattered versions of Violet's red gown. She immediately made mental note that no matter how much she loved it, she hoped she hadn't resembled these women of misfortune. *I'll never wear it again!*

They arrived at the dock where the *Caitlyn's Fancy* was ready for Father O'Malley's benediction. Violet had been to many ship blessings in her life and each one was as exciting as the last. But this time, her focus wasn't on Father O'Malley hurling the holy water to and fro across the bow of the massive vessel. *Brady.* All she could think about was him.

"And now ladies and gentlemen, I present to you, *Caitlyn's Fancy* in all her enormity and exquisite splendour!" beamed Sean. "Could I ask Robert Ryan to approach the dais to sign our merger agreement and break the port across her bow?"

All close parties involved knew the agreement had already been signed, but they wanted to put on a show for the villagers who'd been standing by, watching these two clans come together.

"And tonight," Sean proclaimed, "We shall forget the sophisticated and civilized celebrations. We welcome you all to join us at Peter's Pub instead!"

Being in such close proximity to Violet for an entire morning seemed to instill a sense of calm. As foreign as that was, Brady certainly welcomed it. Strolling through the garden, a gentle breeze catching rogue strands of her glossy hair and carrying them across her plump wanting lips was nearly torture. This – her very existence – was punishment for all the wrongs he'd committed. But he'd not trade the penalty for all the pardons the king could offer.

With her dainty hand resting on his forearm, they'd discussed her interests for the company moving forward. And within her ideas he found her to be exceptionally intelligent and level minded, regardless of how she was treated by her father. There was no doubt she knew the ins and outs of her father's empire, and Brady sensed that her father had been merely entertaining Violet's notion of someday taking over what was rightfully hers. *Christ's mercy on that man!*

Brady had come to like her very much, and at the odd time when Mary wasn't watching their every move, he'd wanted to pin her to the stone wall of the castle and taste her. Feel her breasts heaving against his chest while he stole her breath away.

Brady tried his best to be a gentleman, but his male need grew harder, and his trousers became unbearably tight. Every minute he'd spent with her it became clear she'd been sent from the fiery pits of hell to cause him excruciating, yet delicious anguish.

Augh! Why does the lass vex me so?

Just when he thought he could take no more of her sweet scent and the warmth of her arm linked with his,

Mary interrupted, unwittingly saving Lady Violet from being ravished right there in the garden.

After accepting her gift – the chance to ride the late Lady Kelly's mare to the shipyard – she'd been instructed to ride alongside her father and Liam. Wedged between two men who'd only stifle a spirit, crush a soul beneath their incessant talk of figures and such, Brady knew she deserved much better than that, but was powerless to stop it.

He'd caught her looking back at him with a bored expression; not once, but twice. Was it a plea to intervene and rescue her from the insipid company of dull and uninspiring men?

Common sense had a strange way of embedding itself into the mind when most unwelcome. Despite his ire and jealousy, Brady had no claim to her. It would be most frowned upon and unprofessional were he to wedge himself between Violet and the others – even if that's exactly what her eyes said she'd wanted.

He urged his steed ahead of the party with a grumble of annoyance caught in his throat, a tight lump that refused to vacate his windpipe.

Once they'd arrived at the shipyard, all eyes may have been on the Caitlyn's Fancy, but Brady's attentions were focused on Violet Ryan, who'd left her sentinels to come and stand alongside him once more. He should have felt some small victory, but her nervous energy nearly knocked him off balance.

"Whiskey?" he asked, reaching behind him to retrieve two tankards from a pitifully filthy little boy. The child beamed when Brady left him more than necessary payment and a playful muss of his blonde hair.

Violet smiled and accepted, "Thank ye, kind sir."

The boy blushed at her misuse of title, but grinned widely with missing front teeth. "Just Thomas, M'lady."

"Well, Thomas, I do hope ye take a break from yer hawkin' to enjoy the festivities a bit," Brady asserted.

The boy's gaze tore painfully away from Brady's with words he couldn't say. No doubt the lad had a family whose survival depended upon how well the sales went today. All men, even little ones were burdened with responsibility, and Brady was no different.

Instead of being the ever-dutiful children, standing beside their respective fathers as the Caitlyn's Fancy was blessed, Brady and Violet spent the day going from vendor to vendor in search of a perfect souvenir to bring back to her mother in Clare

Only did their attention return to why they were gathered there, when Sean's voice cut through the din, inviting everyone within ear shot to Peter's Pub.

"Will ye be comin' along to the pub, Violet?" Brady asked, handing her a bag of assorted sweets.

Removing a glove and tucking it under her arm, she took the treat and tossed one into her mouth. "I should think so. 'Tis a celebration for both companies, is it not?"

"Aye, it is. But I doubt very much yer da will let ye go to a place like that. Brimmin' with whores and drunks, that place. Can't imagine why Father suggested it."

Violet looked around, and then pinned him with those green pools of hers. "Perhaps, 'tis so everyone, of every station can enjoy the party."

"Yer too smart, ye know that?" Brady chuckled. "I s'pose yer right."

He found himself easy and carefree…finally able to laugh.

When the Jesus had that happened?

SEVEN

Just as Brady had predicted, Violet was forced to watch from her window as the men mounted their steeds and rode fast toward the village. She sniffled, and with the back of her hand, brushed the tears away from her face.

'How will I ever learn anything if Da can't even allow me to attend the same functions as everyone else?' she thought miserably.

"Augh! Who am I trying to fool? This is purely about Brady!" she said aloud, the solitude devouring her words like a starving abyss.

Violet had never been anxious to get married, always holding on to the promise that when she met the right man, she would know it right away. All other suitors until then were a waste of time. She hadn't been courted like most girls her age, afraid that she would miss out on meeting *the one,* were she out gallivanting with mindless boys. Now that that man had come along, all because of a fateful business trip with her father, she found herself addicted to Brady's presence – her heart and mind in a tortuous loop of wanting. Craving.

Pacing back and forth in the darkness, she waited for some sign of life from the levels below to indicate the men's return. She periodically peered through the window, scanning the grounds for riders who may be approaching with their lanterns cutting through the mist. But to her dismay, no such light appeared.

She let out a defeated sigh, dressed in her night shift, and crawled into the huge four-poster bed, sinking into the down-filled mattress with exhaustion.

Even though sleep clawed its way through her body, her mind was racing. She kept imagining Brady at a tavern somewhere with her father and the other men, all taking advantage of the loose women for hire. She pictured Brady perched in a chair across from her own father, with a wench draped across his lap, his hands caressing places she only dreamed he would someday touch her.

No matter how hard, or how many times she tried to rid her mind of these images, she couldn't seem to shake them. She was in love with him, she knew it. *Is this what love feels like?* It didn't matter that she had only known him for a few days. She wanted nothing more than to be *his* forever. Somehow the family business meant nothing now. Everything had changed so fast. And no matter how ridiculous it seemed, she welcomed it.

Brady stood with his back against the bar, eyeing his father with distaste and aversion. His mother had only been gone a few months, yet Sean's affections with the wenches were effortlessly rewarded tonight. Brady tried to shake off his anger, but the longer he watched, the hotter his blood simmered.

'I can't expect him to be celibate, but this is ridiculous' he boiled.

His gaze wandered to Robert and Liam sitting at a table in deep discussion, over what, he had no idea. And, truth be told, he wasn't interested enough to go over and include himself.

The men Robert had brought with him on this trip were obviously not needed anymore, for they hadn't been seen in hours. Brady surmised that more likely than not, they too, had found comfort in a woman tonight.

Then, his thoughts splintered over *her,* waiting back in her chambers, feeling the crush of knowing she would never be an equal in her father's eyes. Regret for even being there at the pub caused a churning in Brady's gut.

Just in time to add to his budding pestilence, a familiar face swaggered through the gaggle of cheerful, inebriated patrons. Mischief glinted in the playful blue eyes approaching. All the ladies who weren't already occupied, fawned in Jack Manning's direction.

"Ah! My old friend," Jack hollered to Brady. "I didn't think I'd find ye here. What? Did ye decide to dodge yer never-endin' foul mood and come see how people really live?"

Brady snarled at his friend, but Jack took no offense – just as he never did.

"This is a business *thing*," said Brady, nodding in his father's direction. "I had to be here, but I think all the business is done," he chuckled, despite his mood.

"Ye should go an' tell the *little lord* that. Look how he's still up Robert Ryan's arse!" Jack laughed, referring to Liam. "Now let's you an' I get thoroughly drunk and find some warm woman to put up with us for the night."

"Aye, I can agree to the drink, but there's no woman here that interests me," Brady blew out.

Jack gave Brady a contemptuous glare, squinting with an insufferable smirk that made Brady want to drive his fist into his old friend's jaw. "The wee lass from Clare got yer balls in a knot! Seen 'er at the ball last eve…she's a bonny one," Jack winked. "Let's celebrate then, for 'tis the first time I've seen a female do this to ye! An' for Jesus sakes Brady, don't screw it up!" Jack laughed, causing a small smile to form on Brady's lips.

Brady watched his father release his female companion, get up and walk toward the back door. When the girl didn't follow, he assumed Sean was heading out for a piss. Brady turned back toward the bar and downed the shots of whiskey Jack had placed in front of him. They practically ignored everyone in attendance, mulling over some good times and cursing the bad times. They laughed like they used to, almost like they were carefree youngsters again – like life hadn't hardened either of them.

Brady told Jack all about the fire-haired imp who was engrained in his mind, and making his *cock swell*. Jack laughed at his use of words.

"There are some things even a friend doesn't need to know, Brady. You like 'er. Ye want to take her to bed. 'Tis not much more to it than that." Jack threw back his head in a loud, boisterous laugh.

Brady, a little embarrassed, slammed his glass on the bar, shot daggers at Jack's lack of civility and made his way to the back.

"Be right back, friend. Order us up another!" Brady slurred.

A short time later, Brady staggered out the back door, to rid his bladder of the many tankards of ale and many shots of whiskey he had consumed. He made use of the stone wall to guide him to a desired dark corner where he could freely urinate in peace, without anyone catching him with himself in hand, pissing into the wind.

Brady swayed back and forth, emptying his aching bladder. When he was finished, he turned and staggered toward the door.

A dreadful moan from the depths of the alley made his skin crawl, stopping him in his tracks. From an alcove between the tavern and the inn next door, the howl cut through the night air.

He couldn't quite discern what would generate such a grievous sound, and considered dismissing it as an injured stray dog. When his own chilling name pierced his ears in the form of a garbled cough, he instantly sobered and ran toward the stationary object, finding a collapsed small heap.

"Braaddyyy," Sean groaned.

"Aye! Who's there?" Brady searched the darkness for a face to form, and then when he heard the cry again, a chill ran down his spine as he drew closer. "Da! Lord Jesus! Oh Da, what's happened to ye?" Brady frantically asked, immediately cradling his father in his arms, searching for what caused his father to be covered in his own hot crimson blood.

Then, the shimmer of a blade caught his eye, poking out from Sean's stomach. When Brady rocked him, in an attempt to keep him conscious, the wound in his side oozed and the gash on the other side of his chest gushed. Three deep slashes left had his father in an almost lifeless heap in his arms.

"Hang on! You can't leave me too. Who did this to ye, Da? Tell me," Brady cried.

"Robert Ryan...ye...," Sean coughed and sputtered up red spittle, which dripped down his chin, "ye have to...warn..." And then he said nothing. Sean explosively expelled the last of the blood from his throat, spattering violently across Brady's face. The light in his eyes extinguished. The exhale of his remaining breath faded into the air like a soft burble.

No! This can't be happenin'!

Brady shook him hard and aggressively in a futile attempt to bring him back to life. He didn't quite understand what had happened, and was dumbfounded by his father's last words.

Sitting on his heels, he carefully rolled Sean onto his back. Looking to the heavens for strength, Brady clutched the knife handle, painstakingly tearing it from his father's body, as fresh tears dripped from his chin.

He brought the grisly knife up to the glow of a nearby lantern, examining it. That was when he'd noticed the cloth tied to the butt. When he saw that it was a rag made of another clan's tartan, fury took hold and Brady shook with a need for vengeance.

The only other time he had seen a tartan of that pattern, was when Robert Ryan himself wore it as a sash across his chest that first night at the feast.

The realization of it brought back Sean's last words, spoken just moments before.

"Robert Ryan, ye have to warn…" Brady whispered, then it hit him all at once. He leapt to his feet, a new desperation overshadowing reasonable thought, "Liam! Liam!" he shouted.

He ran back into the tavern, where all that remained were a few of the discarded wenches, the bar keep, and Jack. The fire in Brady's fierce, scorching eyes prompted his friend to meet him before he reached the bar.

"What the hell happened to you?" Jack asked, looking Brady over. "Where did all this blood come from? Oh Brady, what have ye done?"

Brady, offended by the implication roared at his friend. "I've done nothin'! 'Tis Da. He lies dead in the alley! From the knife wielded by Robert Ryan himself! Where is the bastard? Where is he? He'll die tonight." Brady held up the piece of Ryan tartan cloth as proof left behind.

He frantically scanned the room and found that except for the few pathetic regulars now huddling close to him with questioning stares, they were alone. Robert Ryan, it seemed, had fled the scene.

"Now, Brady, calm yerself. Robert is gone. Left a while ago. Guess ye didn't notice. Where's yer Da?" Jack quietly asked, trying to appease a furious Brady. But he didn't need to be soothed or pacified! He'd have his revenge. With Jack's solemn gaze boring into him, he knew that would have to wait. Sean Kelly needed to be brought home, one last time.

"Come with me," Brady replied weakly, hanging his head. He dreaded having to drape his father over the back of his horse and carry him back to Kelly's Keep. The clan would be devastated at the loss of their Chieftain.

Jack's gaze fell upon the pitiful sight. "Let's get 'im home, Brady. We can worry 'bout the Ryan's when we get 'im back where he belongs," Jack whispered.

Just then, Brady remembered, "We have to hurry. I think Da wanted me to warn Liam. I have to make sure he's not met the same fate."

As they hurled Sean's dead-weight up and across Thunder's muscled back, Brady's sorrow mingled with panic. Worry for his little brother surged through him, causing his body to shake uncontrollably. While he had to hurry, he was also careful and held the reins with one hand, while the other braced his father.

The trek home was so very quiet and unnerving. Brady wondered if Robert Ryan may still be lurking with his band of hired hands to finish off the whole lot of them.

With time to reflect, Brady couldn't understand why Robert would turn to murder. They had just that day merged companies, a deal which would prove prosperous for all involved. They had found a kin-ship of sorts, and Liam had taken a liking to the Ryan lord, while Brady had been more than taken with the daughter of the murderous bastard.

They'll all pay. By God, they'll pay.

Jack and Brady didn't speak until they reached the courtyard. The tension was so thick it hung low and almost crushed Brady into his horse.

He dismounted carefully. "Go and get Liam, Jack. Bring 'im to me but don't wake the house," Brady instructed. Jack did as he was told and returned a short time later with a pissed off Liam at his side.

"What could you possibly have done to warrant waking me in the middle of the night?" Liam whined, as he pulled his over-coat tight across his body as to keep out the chill.

"Help me, Liam. Help me take 'im down from my mount," Brady said in a slow drawl, no emotion, no explanation.

Liam's eyes went wide and filled with tears when he finally noticed the lifeless carcass set across the beast's back.

He rushed to aid Brady and Jack with removing what was left of Sean Kelly and carry him inside. Sobs wracked Liam's body, and a couple of times he'd almost dropped his father by accident. Fearing the wrath of his older brother, Brady suspected Liam held on for dear life. Unfortunately, he hadn't been able to hang on to his own sorrow and despair.

But for Brady, the numbness had begun to settle in like merciless frostbite, and he daren't offer any words of condolence.

When they reached the master chamber, they gently laid Sean out on his bed.

"Jack, go wake Mary. I'll need her help," Brady instructed icily. Jack nodded and disappeared again.

Finally, Liam took control of his heartache enough to ask, "Brady, can you please explain what happened here?"

Brady pulled the blood-stained knife from the back of his belt and held it out with stained hands to his little brother. Liam eyed it nervously, and looked to Brady for answers.

"Ye see this tartan, Liam? Ye know who wears these colours, don't ye?" Brady's voice began to shake. "Aye! Robert Ryan, that's who!" he roared.

"Why would Robert kill Da? Come on, how could you suspect Lord Ryan of such a heinous crime?" Liam started to sob again.

"Da's words as he struggled to draw his last breath, were of Robert Ryan, and to warn ye of 'im," Brady explained, although he was still as confused as Liam appeared to be.

Silence swept over the Kelly boys and for the first time in a long time, they were connected by a deeper cord than blood. Their sorrow was unbearable.

Just then, Mary burst into the room, paying no heed to her instructions to keep quiet.

"Will someone please tell me, what in the Jesus is goin…" She stopped dead when she seen the pitiful state of her Chieftain, lying grey and lifeless on the bed.

She screamed a high-pitched squeal, her hands then quickly covering her mouth in attempt to stifle the outburst.

"Lord, oh Lord! What 'ave they done to ye?" Her accusing glare flew to Brady, tears streaming down her face. But when her gaze fell upon Liam, it was with compassion and empathy for the little lord.

Mary's finger pointing didn't go unnoticed, but Brady ignored it, with more important things to discuss.

"I'll not explain, Mary," Brady started bitterly, "Make him presentable, send for the doctor to close his wounds, then wash him and change his clothing. When word falls upon the clan that their Chieftain has fallen, many will want to visit and pay their respects."

These orders had been hard for Brady to issue, for he knew it would be a laborious task to expect from Mary. But he was Lord of Kelly's keep now, and this was his duty – to send his predecessor to the after-life with honour and modesty.

"Aye, Lord Brady. As you wish," Mary whimpered. Liam grabbed Brady's arm, stopping him in his tracks.

"Where the devil are you going?" he asked.

"There's a killer among us, Liam. He'll pay for what he's done. Ye're to stay here, an' help Mary 'til I return. Jack will be mindin' the door. No one is to come in or go out," Brady ordered, with a flame in his eyes Liam had never witnessed before. Brady knew he'd not be disobeyed.

As Brady hurled past him and into the hallway, he came face to face with a bonny young red-head, wearing nothing but a pale blue night shift and a smile. He loath to think she was pleased to see him

He vowed to change that.

EIGHT

Violet's heart thudded in her chest as their eyes locked. This was not the same man she had fallen for – the man she'd spent an entire lonely night dreaming about. He had the eyes, and the thick burning aura of a monster and he was coming right for her. Fear clawed its way through her bones, an inferno of pure, all-consuming dread.

"Br…Brady, what's wrong?" she whispered, barely able to control the trembling.

Grabbing her arm, Brady hauled her back down the hallway to her room, pushing her inside with enough force to send her head and body thrashing about in all directions.

"Brady? What have I done to offend ye?" she cried, heart breaking.

"Shut the hell up, ye Ryan bitch. Don't ask questions ye already know the answer to," Brady barked, loudly and close enough she could feel his hot breath – almost taste the liquor he'd been drinking. "Ye'll stay here. Ye'll not roam the grounds. Get used to this little room. 'Tis the only thing you'll see for a while." Brady threw her down upon the bed so hard she thought her innards would shake all around inside her. He tossed the tiny sliver of Ryan family tartan alongside her quaking form. "Ryan filth," he spat.

She called after him as he stormed out of the room, "Why Brady? Why?" she sniffled.

Seething, he turned and faced her. "Ye will have a chance to ask yer father, when he's shackled and, in the dungeon, – that is, if I decide to spare 'is life," he said, slamming the door shut in one quick pull. His words chilled her to the bone with paralyzing agony, although she hadn't quite yet grasped what they meant.

She sprang from the bed, racing to the door when she heard the key turn in the lock. She hammered her fists against the hard wood barrier until her hands turned red and hot, screaming for her father – for salvation – until her throat was hoarse and dry.

NINE

Brady stormed through the stronghold like a savage bear, brooding and in search of its prey. Robert Ryan wouldn't be hard to locate – or so he thought. His only obstacle would be the men who'd accompanied Robert on this so-called business trip. Despite the fact there were six of them in all, and only one livid Brady, he was unafraid.

"Robert Ryan!" he roared. "Robert Ryan! Show yerself, ye fuckin' bastard!" He searched every room on every level starting with the guest chambers assigned to them. Robert and his men were nowhere to be found. Brady's frustration was mounting, and he was losing his patience when he came across a very drunk Morgan staggering through the hall.

Brady's gaze narrowed, his blood thickened. While the slovenly and disorderly man staggering toward him was much larger than himself, and could most likely kill a man with one blow, Brady's fury fuelled him beyond the realm of reason.

"What's all yer hollerin' 'bout, Kelly?" Morgan slurred.

Without a thought, Brady grabbed the Ryan dock-boss and slammed him against the wall, holding him in an unforgiving grip around the man's throat.

"Ye'll tell me where Ryan hides tonight. An' ye best spit it out quickly b'fore I lose what's left o' my patience and decide to squeeze the life out of ye right here an' now," Brady growled, teeth bared.

The man beneath his grasp buckled at the knees, but Brady held firm until he managed to choke out a few low but audible syllables.

"Brothel," Morgan croaked.

"Explain," Brady demanded, loosening his grip to allow the words to spill from Morgan's lips.

Morgan pulled on his shirt collar and cleared the bile from his throbbing throat before he tried to speak.

"When we left the tavern, me and the others wanted to end the night with the pretty whores promised to be waitin' at the brothel down the road. When Lord Ryan left the tavern, he came to seek us out, kick us all in the arse and to send us to bed. I'd had me fill anyway, so I came on back," Morgan watched cautiously as Brady released him. "Might 'ave took the others a little more convincin', but I'm sure they're all on their way, milord."

Cursing, Brady pushed past him, down the stairs and out into the courtyard, where he would be the first to *greet* the murderous Ryan.

Brady lurked in the shadows, fury simmering from every facet of his being, waiting for the neighing of horses and the faint glow of lanterns to appear through the morning mist.

Despite his thoughts being scattered and tangled by grief, he had to work out a strategy. Somehow, he'd have to get the Ryan lord alone. Avoiding an altercation with the rest of the convoy was paramount to his cause, for he was undoubtedly outnumbered.

Putting himself in Ryan's shoes, Brady knew, were it his men off gallivanting until all hours, he'd take up the rear, guaranteeing none of them wandered back to the pleasure house. If that were the case, he'd have the ability to seize the filthy bastard without notice or commotion.

He crouched there, leaning against the cold stone of the gatehouse, calculating every possible scenario, but the longer he was forced to wait, the angrier he became. His thirst for vengeance nearly had him mounting his steed to meet them along the way.

Good sense gnawed, chewing on his already weakened intellect. He couldn't risk going after them, but that didn't mean it wasn't killing him to wait.

What's takin' 'em so long? Could Murtagh 'ave slipped past me to warn them?

Even though the papers for the merge had been signed, Morgan had not taken his new position as foreman on the Kelly side of things, and had no loyalties toward the Kelly's yet. There was a slim chance the drunkard, even in his sloppy state had set out to warn them of what they'd encounter upon return.

Brady bit his lip. His fists balled at his sides until half-moons dented the flesh. And then, the emerald-eyed beauty, whose window still glowed a warm amber, penetrated his heart.

'*Violet*!' he thought regretfully. '*Curse her for being a Ryan!*'

"Augh!" he growled, raking his fingers through his already wild hair. "No fuckin' doubt, they'd been planning this the entire time," Brady muttered aloud, though he just couldn't figure out why. He shook off the infinite questions and silently repeated his father's dying words, telling himself that the *why's* didn't matter. What was done was done, and Robert Ryan would pay for the crime committed against the Kelly clan.

Just as dawn approached, Brady's heart began a rapid thumping as he readied himself for what was yet to come – for the possibility of Robert's men interfering in attempt to protect their lord. Some small part of him wanted the fight – knowing he could annihilate anyone or anything in his path, but he also knew that waging a war with another clan would end badly. For everyone.

Just as Brady's blood reached a bubbling firestorm, five ghostly figures materialized through the fog, hot steam blasting from the nostrils of their beasts, slowly making their way up the road.

Then suddenly, a faint echo of someone bellowing in the wind caught Brady's attention and the party stopped dead. A rider came from the left – from the forest, with a bright lantern in hand, meeting Robert and his men. There was no way to hear the exchange, but to Brady's horror, all six of them abruptly disappeared into the forest from which the messenger came.

What the fuck just happened? Someone had tipped them off, preventing the impending attack – spoiling Brady's right for revenge.

From the depths of his belly, an agonizing moan formed and escaped his throat. "Morgan!"

He stalked toward the keep with unbridled rage and fierce determination. He could see nothing in his vision but blood. *I'll get mine!*

When he reached the upper level, Jack met Brady's alarming scowl with wide eyes. "Where's Morgan? Did ye see the little wretch leave?" Brady snarled, his gaze shifting up and down the vast hallway.

"Nay, you put the brute in 'is place, and last I seen, he was stumbling t'wards the kitchen mumblin' somethin' about ye havin' a foul temper."

"Aye, and they'll all suffer my wrath when I get my hands on 'em."

"I take it, ye didn't find Lord Ryan?"

"Nay, I waited. And just as I seen 'em all headin' in, a rider met 'em just up the road. I assumed 'twas Mr. Murtagh. In any case, someone sounded a fuckin' alarm, and the dastardly cowards fled."

"Brady?" Jack carefully began, "*If*, and I mean '*IF*' Robert Ryan killed yer Da, why would he or any of 'is men return here?" Brady had thought about that as well, but he couldn't forget Sean's last words. They'd haunt his dreams until the end of his days.

"I know what Da said, Jack! Why would the knife used have a Ryan tartan attached if he was innocent?" Brady slammed his fist against the wall. "You weren't there. He wanted me to warn Liam! To protect 'im from the murderin' Ryan's!"

"Aye, so ye said. It still makes no sense to kill your Da and then return here," Jack said in a low calm voice, but there was no way in hell Brady's mind could be swayed. The Ryan's were responsible and now there was a debt to pay.

"It makes all the sense in the world, Jack. He couldn't just leave behind his most prized possession, now could he? The fire-haired lass in the room down the hall is reason enough to come back here," Brady growled. "Perhaps he thought Da wouldn't be found 'til morning...I don't know. All I *do* know is what I seen and heard."

Jack dragged his fingers through his blonde hair, cursing his annoyance. There were long days ahead. Typically, Jack would serve as Brady's moral compass, preventing an attempt for vengeance – at least until they sorted through the facts. After that, what Brady was capable of, no one would want any part of.

"I'll stay here. Liam needs me; at least, he deserves an explanation. Go and bring Morgan down to the dungeon if he's still here. It'll do no good to go after 'em now, they could be anywhere. I'll be along as soon as I can."

∞

Jack didn't hesitate. He made his way down the rear stone steps which led to the kitchen, where he found Morgan sprawled atop a pile of furs next to the hearth. It was obvious he was still drunk when Jack noisily motioned toward him. The slumbering giant made no sign that he was even conscious, so Jack pushed his boot into Morgan's gut, rousing a groan from the sleeping dog.

"Git on yer feet. Lord Kelly waits fer ye in the bastille," Jack commanded.

"Huh? Oh Jesus, can't a fella get some sleep after a long night o' drinkin' and screwin'?" Morgan complained.

Jack wasted no time in getting the half-asleep, still intoxicated Morgan to his feet, hauling him up by his shirt collar. He practically dragged him out of the kitchen, down the back steps leading into the dark abyss below.

"Where are ye takin' me?" Morgan seemed to sober when his surroundings changed from warm and cheery to dark, cold and ominous.

He began a futile struggle as they neared the bottom of the steps, but Jack held him in an unyielding grip, even when Morgan flailed his arms about in attempt to escape. Morgan Murtagh was no small adversary. In fact, he most likely could have tore Jack's head off with his bare hands – had he been more lucid and not taken part in the night's merrymaking. Luckily for Jack, the liquor still tore through his system, leaving him in a debilitated state.

When they reached the bottom, a long hallway with barred cells on both sides, stretched as far as the eye could see. Torches were lit on either side, but being able to visualize what lay in store, would offer no comfort.

Jack opened a heavy gate to a small room and pushed Morgan inside.

"I think ye will stay nice an' cozy right here," Jack mocked as he closed the door, twisted a large key into the lock and fixed the heavy, noisy loop to his belt.

Morgan stared in disbelief but held his tongue until Jack was almost lost to the darkness.

"Lord Ryan will hear of this!" Morgan shouted. "Where is Lord Kelly? Let me talk to Sean!"

Jack's ears prickled at Morgan's ignorance concerning the fate of the Kelly lord, but he said nothing. It was his duty to the Kelly's to serve and protect them. If Brady or Liam asked to have the Devil himself locked up, then he was only obliged to do so – no questions asked. "Nay, the new lord of this stronghold is Brady Kelly," Jack blandly stated with a sombre expression. "Your clan made bloody-well sure of it, didn't ye?"

Morgan slinked down onto the stone floor and brought his knees to his chest. No doubt the cold would soon sink in, causing him great discomfort. Perhaps, enough that he might offer some sort of confession to Brady when he arrived. If there were no explanations, Jack prayed to his gods for mercy upon the man's soul.

When Jack returned to the master chamber door, he knocked twice and then quietly entered the dark sombre space without a word. Even though dawn had broken, and the sun had begun eating through the fog, the room remained gloomy. The unmistakable stench of death lingered in the stagnant air, mingling with kicked up dust motes.

Mary sat next to her deceased lord, holding his hand in her right, while her left stroked the lifeless digits. She had done a superb job of cleaning Lord Kelly's wounds and dressing him in his Sunday's finest to make his final appearance to the clan.

Brady was perched alongside his brother next to the hearth, with his arm draped over Liam's shoulders in comfort. "So, ye see, Liam, the Ryan clan planned this all along," Jack heard Brady say.

"I just don't understand, Brady," Liam protested. "We only merged yesterday morning. What would the Ryan's have to gain?"

"I don't know, brother, but I aim to find out. All I know right now is, Da named 'is killer as he was strugglin' with his last breath. He wanted me to warn ye. Have you an' Robert made any other kind of arrangements that I should know about?" Brady asked carefully.

"Violet," Liam whispered. "We talked a great deal about Violet."

Brady sighed and thought of the beautiful woman who remained silenced in her room.

"And what of 'er?"

"He thought us to be a good match, and he said that if I proved worthy in business, then he could trust that I would take care of his only daughter. He said that perhaps, if she became smitten with me, that we could marry."

"Over my dead body!" Brady exploded. "Ye can get it out of yer fuckin' head right now!"

"But Brady, she's done nothing wrong!" Liam whined like an errant child. "She's alone in her room, confused, and probably scared. We have to take care of her now. *I* will take care of her, now that the Ryan's have fled. I'll see that she get's home safely."

"Not all of them escaped," Jack interrupted. "Morgan has been secured below the keep as ye requested. But I must tell ye, he is as confused about this as the rest of us. I don't think he had any knowledge of it."

"Augh! Jesus sakes, Jack!" Brady roared again. "I'll find that out for m'self when I see him cold, hungry and afraid."

Then Brady stood and walked to his father's bedside and kissed his cold cheek.

"Thank ye, Mary. Ye may return to yer chambers and get some rest. Ye have a long few days ahead," Brady told her kindly.

"Liam, ye'll have to stay here with Da. Try to get a nap before the whole clan hears the news. These good people will want to say good-bye to their chieftain," Brady instructed, cool and collected. "And stay away from the girl. I'm warnin' ye. Go nowhere near that room."

To Jack's relief, Liam knew better than to argue with his brother. Grief and weariness took over and he nodded in compliance. He then turned back toward the roaring fire blazing in the hearth, as if the flames could lick away the aching loss of his father.

Brady quietly went to Jack and laid his hand on the soldier's arm. "I need ye now more than ever, friend. Are ye up for a little torture in the belly of the keep?" Brady asked softly, as not to let Liam or Mary hear.

"Aye, we'll get the truth out of 'im one way or another," Jack replied with no emotion upon his face. Jack normally took great pleasure in inflicting pain and punishment – not only when interrogating a prisoner, but in the throes of passion as well.

On any regular day, he was happily obliged to force a confession out of a thief or a cheat, but his gut told him that the man in the dungeon would offer nothing to Brady's quest for the truth.

When Brady and Jack reached the dungeon, Morgan was shivering and had already begun to appear a little haggard and small. The remnants of liquor hung in the air. His hair was tousled, most likely from the countless times he'd run his fingers through it in attempt to make some sense of the mess he was in.

"So, Morgan," Brady began, as Jack slipped the key into the hole, letting themselves inside the cell. "If ye didn't ride out to warn Robert that I'd found my father dead in an alley, then can ye tell me who did?"

Brady stirred close to Morgan with movements of a cat – slow and deliberate. Morgan's eyes widened with alarm, as he felt the first of many fisted blows to his face. He tried to fight off Brady's attack, but that only resulted in the men shackling him to the wall.

"Ye better tell 'im everything ye know. I've seen 'im almost kill a man for far less," Jack warned.

"I swear to Jesus! I didn't know yer Da was dead," Morgan pled between strikes. "I don't know anything of a plan to kill 'im either."

Brady didn't talk very much, as his fists and feet said all he needed them to. Every time Morgan regained his footing, he defiantly shouted his innocence, only for Brady to beat him back down again. Amidst the chaos, Jack asked question after question that Morgan refused to answer.

Brady breathed heavily, adrenaline coursing through his veins. Teeming with mighty violence, his fists relentlessly hammered the helpless Morgan into a pulp, until Jack could bear it no longer.

"Enough, Brady!" Jack shouted, grabbing Brady's swinging fist before it could make contact with Morgan once more. "He doesn't know anything."

"Christ! Someone knows somethin', Jack!" Brady shouted, pulling away from Jack's grip.

"'Tis not him. Leave 'im be. After yer Da's been properly laid to rest, we'll ride to the River Shannon in Clare and finish what they started," Jack reasoned.

"Nay! I'll not go there. Robert Ryan will come to me. I'll make sure he suffers for what's been done!"

"How are ye gonna get him back here? Ye say he's fled, and ye're pretty sure of the accusations against him. He'll never return."

Brady took the key ring from Jack's belt, went to Morgan and began unlocking the restraints. He pulled a kerchief from his pocket and threw it at the man's feet.

"Clean yerself up, Ryan scum! You'll no' be foreman for my crew. I've a better use for ye," Brady spat.

"What are ye gonna do, Brady?" Jack quietly asked, pulling Brady to the side of the cell where Morgan couldn't hear.

"No sense in hidin' my intentions, Jack," Brady blandly stated loud enough for Morgan to hear anyway, and strode back over to the trodden-down half-man. "Tell me, what would make ye return to the scene of a crime?"

"To get something left behind?" Just as Jack suggested it, a window into Brady's mind opened up, burdening him with gut-wrenching concern.

"Aye, something of great value left behind," Brady grinned the evillest smirk Jack had ever seen. If he could actually see inside Brady's head, he would witness the spinning of a wicked and immoral web.

"Get to yer feet, ye lame bastard!" Brady commanded Morgan.

As Morgan started to stand, Brady's hands grasped both sides of his face and forced him to stare into the steely depths of his own. He could crush the man's head in an instant if he was so inclined, but Morgan was needed for a more important role.

"You'll take a message to yer lord," Brady began, his voice as cold as ice, his gaze never leaving the blood-shot eyes peering back at him. "Ye'll tell Robert Ryan the grief and torment he has caused my clan can't be un-done, and that his precious daughter will feel my wrath until I feel the debt has been paid."

Jack's head fell, utter agony consuming him. *Brady, ye can't be serious.*

"Brady? Let's talk outside." Morgan was quickly re-leased from Brady's grasp as Jack spoke.

"Nay, time for talkin' has come and gone. 'Tis time for action. The murderous coward left her here and fled. When he realizes what he's done – that he has to return to his home and people without her, he will feel the in-tensity of our loss," Brady fumed. "And when he learns of her *situation* he will grasp the enormity of what he's done."

Jack was worried now. He had witnessed Brady angry and fierce before, but never thought his friend could be a monster. But, he would do as was commanded. Brady was lord now, and Jack, but a soldier.

"Aye, as you wish *M'lord,*" Jack sighed, using Brady's new title, hoping it would indicate his displeasure over the entire situation. Brady ignored his friend, treating Jack every bit of the soldier he was.

"Get 'im ready to ride," Brady instructed and then turned back to address Morgan. "Ye will ride to Clare and give my message directly to Robert Ryan. He will not send anyone here to rescue her. I will take from him, what's most precious, and when he can't withstand another moment of heartache, anguish and misery, I'll send 'er home. Although, I can't predict her future condition."

Brady stepped past Jack, leaving the cell. Jack knew better than to even utter a word in protest and done as he was ordered. A sickness in his stomach crept over him and he fought the urge to wretch. The notion of Brady harming a defenceless maiden in an attempt for vengeance was more than he could stand. He steadied his composure, and helped Morgan get cleaned up.

TEN

Brady took the stairs two at a time. The retribution he sought was so clear now. Keeping Violet from her father would torture the man into submission. Robert and his clansmen would never forget what it meant to take something from a Kelly.

When he'd finally reached Violet's door, he stopped for a moment, remembering what he had felt for her only a day before. How her emerald eyes sparkled when she looked up at him. The softness in her voice when she spoke. He drew in a long breath and fought with his emotions for a girl he hardly knew.

'*I could have loved her, in another time, in another place,*' he thought with a pang of regret for what he must do.

When Brady opened the door, he noiselessly made his way to the bed where she lay. He watched as her chest heaved up and down with every slumbering breath. He studied her face and took note of her tear-stained red cheeks. He wondered how long she'd cried, weighted with confusion and isolation. He shook his head to rid himself of unwanted emotion and cleared his throat loud enough to wake her.

Her eyes fluttered open, and as if it was instinct – that the night before had been just a dream – she smiled up at him. His heart hardened instantly, as he grabbed her arm and pulled her off the bed with enough force to send her thrashing into his chest. Her breath caught in her throat and a whimper escaped her lips.

As if completely possessed, Brady pressed his mouth to hers, and lingered there until he became dizzy. She fought against his chest, beating her fists into the hard, bulging mass of muscle, but he was unmoved by her efforts.

When he finally released her, and took a small step backwards, he caught her open hand in mid-swing before she could slap his face.

'*I'll tame that temper*,' he thought, cocking a sideways smirk at her, masking his building fury.

"How dare ye?" she shrieked, bringing her other hand up in one swift crack, this time catching him square across his stubbly jaw.

Brady didn't even think about it. He turned ever-so-slightly away, and then countered with a back-handed whack that sent her whirling onto the bed. For the briefest of moments, she held her cheek in her hands, sending waves of victory throughout him. Brady loved to win – and he was winning, until Violet got to her feet and fought him with every ounce of determination and tenacity she could muster.

She pounded and pushed and thrashed about, until he caught hold of her and steadied her face in his large calloused hands. *I could squeeze the life out of ye,*' he thought, restraining the evil lurking inside. He bent a little, forcing her gaze to lock with his. He searched her eyes for a sign of surrender but all he found was hate. *And Ryan.*

Her breath quickened against his face, creating an appetite for soft, supple lips. *That'll have to wait.*

"Pack yer things, ye spiteful wench."

"Where is my Da?" she screamed, still entwined in his merciless grasp.

"Ye'll not ask questions! Ye'll not speak unless ye're told to. Now pack yer things." As if she bore the plague, he cruelly shoved her away.

"Nay! Not 'til ye tell me where my father is. What have ye done, Brady Kelly?" She continued her shrieking, seemingly undaunted by his wrath, infuriating him for being so insistent on defiance.

Brady grabbed her around the waist with one arm, lifting her into his arms. He carried her to the bed and sat down, stretching her out across his knee, face down. He pulled up her skirts and down her under-things. She fought with all her might to be free of the humiliation, pounding his trouser-clad legs.

The first sting of his hand across her bare arse made her visibly angry. The second, she winced. By the third and forth, the room had filled with blasphemies that would make a sailor blush, for the punishment had become harder and more deliberate. Brady spanked her like a child until her arse was red and fleshy, and tears sprang from her eyes uncontrollably. Only when her body went limp, and her sharp tongue had been silenced, did he stop.

"Gonna be a good little girl now, aren't ye?" he asked derisively, lifting her from his lap. He laid her on the bed, forcing her to look up at him. "If yer gonna act like a child, I'll treat ye as such. Now get yer things ready or we'll leave without them."

Violet pulled her clothes back into place and righted her dress, as to regain some composure. She peered up at the giant standing before her, remembering the affection she had felt for this monster, now a fading memory. "Yer nothin' but a merciless beast!" she snapped, sobs wracking her to the bone.

Brady's gaze fell to the floor, for but a moment. Remorse engulfed him like a smothering hot inferno. He had to temper that useless emotion – and fast. He steeled himself again and raked his fingers through his coal-black hair.

"Ye ain't seen nothin' yet, little girl. Now git movin'!"

Violet moved quickly to the chests of drawers and began folding garments that had been hanging on the back of the chair at the white wicker vanity. She snatched up all her things in one swoop and threw them into her trunk. She wasted no time. Brady assumed her haste may have had something to do with the burning sting in her bottom, and not wanting a repeat of such pain and degradation.

She turned to him. He was rigidly standing next to the window, arms crossed, watching every move she made.

"Can I ask where we are going?" she quietly asked, searching his expression as if looking for some sign that the Brady she knew was still in there somewhere.

"I'll forgive that one," his tone remaining icy, "Ye'll find out when we get there. I have much to tell ye – some I presume ye may already know. Shut up and get it done."

"Aye," she whispered with no other choice but to yield, glancing up from beneath thick dark lashes. Brady beamed with domination, leaving Violet utterly helpless.

When she had packed the last of her things into the trunks she waited for instruction next to the door, holding her coat between clasped hands.

Brady led them down the hallway where he met Jack walking toward them.

"'Tis done?" Brady asked.

"Aye. He rides to County Clare. Lord Ryan will get your message with the mere sight of 'im," Jack replied.

"Good man," Brady grunted.

Jack eyed the pair of frightened emerald pools, his expression softening. Brady sensed his friend's displeasure. "Don't worry, I'll only show 'er the same treatment her people have shown ours. Take care of Liam. Don't tell 'im where I've gone, though I'm sure he'll guess. Keep 'im and everyone else away! Tell 'im he is in charge 'til I return."

"Brady? What about yer father's funeral?" Jack asked, overstepping the boundary from soldier to commander, into friend to friend.

"What about it? Jack, I can't take buryin' another parent when they've been ripped from me, senselessly, and so young." Brady's voice wavered for just a moment, and he cleared his throat, keeping his emotions at bay.

Violet sniffled at Brady's side. "It's become clear to ye now has it? My father is dead. Yer father and his men have fled. An' all ye have left in this world is me, my dear," Brady growled through clenched teeth, towering over her shaking form. "What happens to ye now will be purely in service of punishing yer father and yer clansmen.

"Think me a savage if ye like. Ye've only begun to know what I'm capable of." Then Brady returned his attentions back to the interloper lurking awkwardly beside them. "Jack, when we've safely left the courtyard, and ye're sure no one has followed, load her things onto the carriage and have them sent to the cottage." Not waiting for Jack's reply, Brady led them through the keep and out to the stables, where he lifted her onto Thunder's back and then mounted behind her.

They swiftly rode through the courtyard into the afternoon sun.

Brady waited for the brazen wench to cry out for help. Not much good it would do, for she was a Ryan, an enemy to the Kelly's now. If she knew what was good for her, she'd keep any notions of that nature to herself. But shamelessly enough, Brady's blood surged, and his pulse quickened at the mere thought of having to punish her yet again – watch her cheeks redden beneath his palm once more.

∞

Brady held possessively around her tiny waist as they rode for what seemed like forever to this unknown location.

Through the pink velvet material of the stylish tunic she wore, she could feel the hardness of his muscled chest against her back, and felt his hot breath on the back of her neck. The sensations nearly made her ill.

Every time she shifted in the saddle – due to the burning sensitivity in her arse, his hand around her tightened. She could feel every sinewy muscle in his arm flex to keep her firmly tethered, dashing her ideas that she could somehow just jump off and make a run for it.

Their jaunt had slowed to a sleepy pace ever since they lost sight of the keep and they'd disappeared into the forest. And without a word spoken between them, Violet was alone with her thoughts.

Someone will find me. I know it! Da will send someone! She lifted her head in defiance, giving herself a much-needed shot of reassurance, but as if Brady could sense her insolent musings, his grip became tighter with each jut of her chin.

The winding path that seemed to go on and on was beautiful, and even though Violet was fearful of what lay at the end of it, she noted that on any other occasion she would have enjoyed a ride in the country such as this one.

There were patches of wild flowers, beaming with bright oranges, blues and yellows, spreading across every clearing, and then when the forest became thick again, the trees seemed to offer their arms in protection, nearly kissing the tops of their heads as they rode.

The sun had risen high in the sky some hours ago, and was now starting its descent back behind the earth, marking the end of another day; an exhausting day for them both.

Violet was lost deep in thought when she felt Brady's chest suck in a deep breath, and then exhale sharply behind her. In the distance, a modest cottage and its surrounding lands came into view. The acres of green behind the lonesome dwelling made it look puny and out of place. But although small in comparison to its surroundings, it was welcoming, and sweet. Her mind then, shifted back to the reason why she was there in the first place. Suddenly, the cottage lost all its appeal and wonder.

Brady dismounted quickly and pulled her down from Thunder's back with one swoop of his arm. She stood frozen to the ground for a moment, unsure of what to do, waiting for instruction from her captor. She nervously examined his movements as he went about leading the horse to a small barn on the side of the cottage.

When he returned, she quietly waited as he went to the cottage door and pushed it open. He seemed to hold his breath as he went inside. Violet's thoughts flew to the day in the garden where they'd walked side by side, talking and laughing without a care of their own. In this moment, with his furrowed brow and scornful scowl, Brady was not that light-hearted man, and she found herself longing to be reunited with his carefree, youthful side. Somehow, she doubted that would happen.

She was aware of his attachment to this place and although she was there against her will, she almost felt sorry for him. *Not as sorry as I am for my own plight.*

Brady disappeared further inside the cottage, leaving Violet outside in the evening chill. She rubbed her arms vigorously in attempt to keep the frostiness from touch-ing her bones.

'*I could run*,' she thought, scanning the grounds, not-ing every single detail about her surroundings. The small barn where he'd taken his horse was shadowed by a much larger one just behind it.

Between the cottage and the two barns, lay a path flanked by wilted flower beds, trimmed with stones set in a straight line. Someone had gone to great lengths to perfect the landscaping once upon a time. Violet pre-ferred to think it were Brady's late mother who had touched this place with such artistry, for she was certain Brady wouldn't be capable of this kind of elegance.

The path led to acres of land behind the cottage, all open for as far as the eye could see; there truly was no-where to hide. Her only chance of escape was to go back from which she came, wander through the thick forest beyond the beaten path in a foreign land, exposing her-self to God-knows-what. No matter how hopeless things seemed for her here with Brady, she was certain she would not endure it.

She was shaken from thought when Brady finally spoke in a low, snarling Irish baritone that she found nearly unrecognizable.

"Inside," he growled, standing to the side of the doorway, allowing her entry. She walked in slow, uneasy steps toward him as he glared down at her. Averting her eyes to the ground, she tried her hardest not to make eye contact for fear of what she might see behind his unyielding, threatening glare.

Brady slammed the door behind them and turned the key in the lock. She darted around, facing him when she heard the loud distinctive 'click'.

"How long are ye gonna keep me here, Brady?" she whispered with teary eyes. When he didn't answer, she sighed loudly and watched him move about the cottage, removing linens from the furniture and lighting candles in holders placed on decorative shelves all around the small room.

He put a fire in the stove in the main room, which was also shared with the kitchen. This was truly a humble home, but under different circumstances she would have thought it pretty in design and décor.

'*A woman's sanctuary,*' she thought. It was everything Brady had said it was, when he'd described it with enthusiasm that day in the garden – so long ago, yet just days before.

He disappeared into a bedroom just off the main room, only to reappear with a machete hooked onto his belt, a quiver strapped across his back, and a bow in hand. Her heart thumped a furious gait.

"I'll be back with tonight's supper," he blandly stated.

"How long will ye be gone?" she softly asked, suddenly ignoring the weapons he held. Instead, she panicked at the thought of being left there alone in this strange place.

Brady quickly approached her, cupped her face in his brutal hands with no gentle touch, and searched her eyes. If he'd been attempting to dredge up fear inside her, his tactics were remarkable. When he smiled, she suspected he'd found what he was looking for.

"Be not afraid of what may happen while I'm away. Ye best fear my return." He pushed her face from his grasp, causing her to stumble, and left the cottage again.

She ran to the door, but as she reached it, she heard the familiar tick of the locking mechanism. She hurried to the window and watched as he hiked into the forest. Pushing her face to the glass until breath and tears fogged her reflection, she watched him disappear.

She paced the cottage, fear engulfing her like the flames of hell, until she became weary with worry. She searched every cabinet, looked under the beds, opened and scanned every closet, hoping there was a door to the outside world – a world where freedom taunted. She even lifted the heavy door in the kitchen floor to find a root cellar. Shelves lined with jars of berry preserves, and empty apple barrels lay beneath. She imagined one time the dark space might have housed all sorts of vegetables and perhaps a small hoard of cured meats. The mere thought brought about hunger pangs which were nearly impossible to ignore.

The longer he was gone, the stronger the knots in her stomach became.

With the cottage explored and nothing left to do but wait, she went to the chair next to the window and curled up, resting her head against the back. She drifted in and out of sleep, every noise of the wilderness shaking her awake, adding to the foreboding trepidation.

Just as it seemed exhaustion had claimed her, she was alerted by the sound of footsteps and the key in the lock. Her heart started to wallop so loud it rushed in her ears. She curled into a little ball in the chair as unease paralyzed her.

'*Fear my return.*' She dreaded his words for they now echoed in her brain, forcing bile up her throat.

When the door opened, Brady's gaze fell upon the petite Ryan cuddled into his mother's favourite chair. And for a split second he forgot *who* she was. The sight of her there stirred a desire he'd had all his life – to have a woman he loved enough to share this part of his life with. Then, as fast as the haunting reverie entered his mind, it was ripped apart; reminding him that Violet was the daughter of Satan reincarnate.

He dropped two foul smelling rabbits onto the kitchen table and went to her side grabbing her arm, forcing her to her feet.

"Ye'll cook our supper t'night, wench," he snarled hauling her to the table to peer down at his kill. The death that lay before her caused her face to screw with repulsion, sending shivers of pride up his spine. "There's a good sharp knife in the top drawer. Clean them well."

Violet done as she was told, going to the drawer and retrieved the knife. Tears welled up behind her lids as her gaze met his. No doubt she'd like to drive the razor-sharp point into Brady's gut, ending all the madness, but he knew she wouldn't. She may be a Ryan, but he knew she wasn't capable of cold-blooded murder.

He also guessed she had never gutted and cleaned a kill before. Those gruesome tasks were most likely done for a girl of her station and breeding. She'd probably never even thought about who killed and prepared her food until now. She looked at him wide eyed, questions hanging in the air.

"I c…can't," Violet trembled.

"Aye, lass. Ye will," he grunted in return.

"I can't, Brady! I don't know how. Please don't make me do it."

Brady leaned in, placed his hand over hers holding the knife, and squeezed. He struggled to control her shaking hand as he guided the knife into the belly of the first little creature. Its blood spilled across the table as he made a long slice up through it.

"Stop, Brady! Stop! I can't," she cried, turning her head away from the gruesome sight.

Brady released her hand causing her to immediately drop the knife onto the table and sink to her knees. He pulled her to her feet, only to push her backwards, sending her to the other side of the room, landing on the hard, cold floor.

"Yer good for nuthin'!" he roared, annoyance slithering through his veins. What had he expected? Had he really thought keeping her here would be easy?

Violet crawled to the side of the settee against the wall, and pulled herself up, crying into an embroidered throw pillow.

He cursed under his breath and finished preparing the meal, trying to ignore the whimpering coming from the other side of the cottage. His patience was wearing thin.

"Ye'll stop that blubberin'! Ye hear me?" he shouted.

Her gaze shot up, pinning him to the spot. She dried her face with the back of her hand and stuck out her chin in the stubborn way that drove him to madness.

"Bring me back, Brady!" she howled. "Ye'll not get yer revenge like this." She bit her bottom lip and paused as if considering her next words. "And how do ye know my Da is even responsible for what happened to yers?"

"'Cause, as I watched the life being sucked from his body, he spoke your father's name! Now shut the hell up! How many times do I have to tell ye not to speak unless spoken to? Are ye daft, girl?"

"Aye! I must have been. Stupidity is what caused me to believe ye were a kind and gentle man. Ye're no man at all! You're a filthy beast! Heartless and uncivilized!" As quickly as she'd screamed those words, she shook her head, anticipating his savagery, and wishing she could take them back. He was on her in an instant, hovering over her, red-faced, fists balled up at his sides.

He picked her up over his shoulder. She fought against his hard body, kicking, screaming, and thwacking her fists into his back.

"I'm sorry, Brady! I didn't mean it! Please, put me down!" she cried.

"Aye, lass! I'll put ye down. Down in the cellar. 'Tis where ye'll learn to watch yer tongue," Brady snarled, unable to cope with her insolence, or the manner in which it quickened his heart and boiled his blood.

"Nay! Ye can't leave me down there! Please!" Her fight diminished, but she took up sobbing as a replacement, tears leaving fat little droplets on the back of Brady's linen work shirt.

"Not another word or you'll have another spankin' to cry about!" he said, whacking her arse in mid-air as a reminder.

She stifled her cries and accepted her fate as he opened the hatch door and stepped down the three-rung ladder, depositing her on the sod-covered floor.

"Ye'll learn to not dare speak to your lord in this way. Don't forget ye place here, fair Violet. I am yer keeper now – yer saviour even. Ye *will* show me respect. I demand it!"

She shook uncontrollably, and nodded with frightened wide eyes. Brady smirked at her compliance, but her next words would be his undoing.

"Aye, my lord," she whispered.

ELEVEN

Robert's guts were knotted as they approached the family home on the mighty Shannon River. No one had spoken the entire trip, making it the longest journey of his life.

Although he couldn't make sense of what had happened in Galway, all he did know was that he'd left his beautiful, most prized possession there, in the hands of the Kelly's. He was confident that it would get sorted out eventually, but for now, he'd have to somehow explain it to his wife.

Upon arrival, the entire party was ushered into the study, where Robert hoped he would be filled in on the details of what had happened.

As Seamus, James, Patrick and Martin took their seats on the chairs placed against the walls around the study, Robert took his place behind his desk, Gregory flanking his right side, still standing.

"Move yer chairs closer, men. We've a lot to discuss. Has anyone seen Morgan?" Robert asked, clearing his throat of the culpability threatening to snuff out his air supply. "Someone better have some answers."

"Morgan returned to Kelly's as soon as he'd heard ye were looking for us. I can't say what happened to 'im after that, Robert," Patrick replied, shame for leaving his friend behind evident in the way he wrung and twisted his cap in his hands.

All of the men done as directed, placing their seats around the front of Robert's desk, where they could be eyed and scrutinized by their lord.

"We'll sort out Morgan's whereabouts in due time, but right now, there are more important matters to discuss.

"Gregory, you may also take a seat," Robert stated in a tired tone, without turning around to look at the man, and continued, "One at a time, ye will tell me where ye were and what ye were doing at the time of Sean Kelly's death."

Robert watched each one of them, as their weary eyes widened, and jaws dropped.

"Ye can't be pointin' the finger at us, M'lord. We were all at the brothel," James started, slightly embarrassed. "Kelly was slain long after we'd left that tavern."

The four other men looked to each other and nodded their agreement.

"Aye, 'tis true! I was balls deep in a plump, raven-haired whore – that is, 'til ye arrived to bring us back to the keep," Seamus explained, his face turning red with discomfiture.

Patrick, Martin and James, all gave similar stories, each one feeling a little ashamed of themselves. Ashamed that their chieftain had sought them out when he needed them the most, only to find them all to be drunk and screwing anything that moved.

Robert's head was spinning. In order to call his wife from her sleep, sending her into an unavoidable frenzy over her absent child, he would have to have some kind of explanation.

Sombre grief as thick as the morning fog washed over him. How was he going to tell Beth of Sean Kelly's death and then inform her that sweet Violet had been left behind? Beth would be devastated. He feared more than anything that she would hate him for all eternity for allowing such a tragedy to fall upon their happy little family.

Gregory cleared his throat. "My lord, I think I can put an end to the inquisition of your men."

"Oh? Ye can? Well out with it!" Robert barked. "And then ye can tell me why ye were in Galway in the first place!"

Robert had never given Gregory cause to fear him, until now that is. It hung in the air with the ability to smother all six of them sitting in wait for answers.

Gregory's throat worked rapidly, hesitating to reply. He straightened his cravat and began, "I was in Galway to meet with Professor Baker. I was supposed to have a meeting with him yesterday afternoon concerning Violet's progress. If I am to grade her and give her a certificate of a proper education, her progress thus far has to be looked over by my mentor," he explained. "With Violet away and no one else to tutor, I decided to travel a few days early so I could be there for the ship launch as well."

"Well? I didn't see ye there. Where were ye, then?" Robert narrowed his gaze, unsure of whether to buy the tale he'd spun.

"I would have been there, but I found misfortune on the road. In fact, Robert, I was robbed." Robert's cold gaze softened to compassionate.

Robert came to his feet and went to Gregory's side. "Were ye hurt, lad?" he asked, searching the young man's face for bruises, cuts and scratches.

"No, Robert. Thankfully, my life and body were spared. I cooperated with the bandits, and gave them everything I had, including my grandfather's pocket watch.

"I continued on to Galway, for I knew if I could get there, I could count on you for a salary advance to get me home again," Gregory explained. It was common knowledge that Robert Ryan would do anything to protect the men in his employ, and Gregory was no different. But something was off about the young fellow's story. Something in Robert's gut niggled at him.

"I'm glad ye were unharmed, but how did ye come upon the knowledge of Sean Kelly's murder? How were ye able to warn the rest of us before we arrived back at the Kelly's?" Robert probed, he and the rest of the men watching suspiciously. Perhaps Gregory had seen it as an opportunity to visit with Violet and woo her on neutral soil – away from Robert's watchful eye. If such were the case, Gregory's secret ulterior motives would be frowned upon as well.

"After the brutality I'd suffered, I went to the Kelly's stronghold to find you. A kitchen wench told me where you all had gone, so I sought you out at the tavern. Only, what I stumbled upon was a young fellow screaming over his father." Gregory shifted in his chair as if he didn't quite know what to say next. He recalled in detail what he'd witnessed while lurking in the shadows. He spit the story out like flames off a dragon's tongue. "I waited out of curiosity and concern for him. But then I heard your name, Robert. Of course, that piqued my interest, and so I listened closer.

"It became obvious that the young man crying over the old man's body was a Kelly, and the old man, Sean Kelly himself. But I can't fathom why he named you. I didn't see anyone else in the area. So, yer boys are in the clear."

Robert drew in a deep breath and wiped his face with the palms of his large hands, clearly exasperated.

Just then, a vulgar howl coming from the back of the house resonated. Things were being knocked over, crashing to the floor.

Morgan bellowed in agony, making his way through the manor.

All the men stood and waited for the man who resembled the crew foreman, came staggering through the study door.

"Morgan!" Seamus thundered, hurrying to his friend's side to help him into a chair. "What's happened to ye?"

"Brady Kelly happened. They've got 'er, Robert. *He's* got 'er, to be exact. He's sent me home like this to let ye know he means what he says, and he does what he wants," Morgan slumped over in a chair, exhausted.

"What are ye sayin'? He's keepin' her there? What does he want?" Robert trembled, struggling to stay strong in front of his men.

"Vengeance, Robert. I am sorry, 'tis all I know," Morgan despairingly replied, holding his battered ribs, hissing with pain.

Robert inspected his crew chief, and found that he had, in fact, been beaten, severely. Morgan was covered with bruises, and blood stained his tattered clothing. Robert laid his hand on Morgan's shoulder, but was quickly forced to retract. "Augh! Please, Robert. Don't touch me. I'm in more pain than I ever t'ought possible," he pleaded. Robert scanned the faces of his friends standing around the study, noting concern etched in every crease of their hardened features. He'd have to douse the flames of retribution, for a need to go and take Violet home by force hung all around him.

"Men, ye may take yer leave. Go and get some sleep. I have nothin' else to ask of ye right now. When I've had time to tell the lady of the house what's happened, we will come together and hatch a plan to get sweet Violet back. Patrick, go fetch the doctor. Seamus, please help Morgan to one of the guest rooms." All the men stood at once and made for the door.

"Gregory, I'm glad yer alright, lad," Robert added. It was the smallest of sentiments, but it was all he could offer.

Robert quietly entered his bed chamber with his head hung low, his shoulders slumped in defeat, and the most guilt and self-loathing he'd ever felt, threatening to crush him entirely. He knew Beth would be sleeping without a worry or a care in the world – she hadn't expected them to return for another week or so. He sank to her bedside and knelt there watching as her eyes flitted in peaceful dreams.

He held her delicate hand in his, causing her to stir. Her eyes fluttered open just enough for her to focus on him. She smiled as she always did when she woke next to this man. Then as quickly as it danced across her face, her happy expression drained. She had to know something was terribly wrong.

"Robert?" she asked in a whisper, "Darlin', what's the matter? Why are ye back so soon?"

His head fell to the bed, heavy sobs devastating the very essence of him. His body writhed in agony, sadness and regret. He felt her hand on the top of his head and it seemed to calm him instantly. He looked up into her troubled eyes, tears flowing down her pretty, pink cheeks.

"The unthinkable has happened, my love. Sean Kelly has been murdered and I am in question for it." Every word that managed to escape his lips was blown out between heavy, suffering moans. When Beth failed to speak, he raised his head and took her face in his strong hands. "I swear to ye, with all my love and devotion, I had naught to do with any of it."

He knew she believed him. His wife, while tender and innocent in some ways, could sense a lie from a mile away. It was her gift – the ability to see people for who they were, not who they alleged to be. Through teary eyes, Beth smiled her sweet smile which always comforted him. He thanked the heavens for the gift of this woman.

'*Now comes the hard part. Will she still look at me the same when I tell her of Violet?*' he thought, trembling. Then, he began to make an attempt at explaining further no matter what the cost. '*She has to know.*'

"There's more, my love," he licked his lips, his mouth parched. "Sean Kelly was killed in an alley outside the tavern where we were celebrating the merge and the launch of the new ship. From the bits and pieces of what I'm hearin', *he* named me as the assailant...'though I can't imagine why." By now, the words were coming a little easier, as he tried to put it all together in his mind. "Apparently, his eldest son, Brady held his father's lifeless body, while Sean warned him of me."

"Oh, Robert!" Beth shot up straight, holding the covers to her bare breast. "What are we gonna do? Are the authorities comin' to lock ye away? Oh! I don't think I could live!" Beth sobbed. Then, as if it had just dawned on her, a shrieked punctured the silence, "Violet?". She searched Robert's face for the answers before he'd had a chance to reply. "Where was she durin' all of this? She must be traumatised! I must go to 'er!"

Beth quickly rose from the bed, donning a plum coloured satin robe and tied it tight around her slender waist. When Robert made no motion to move with her, she froze at the door, like the frost of the morning prevented her from turning the knob. Robert's head fell back onto the bed, and his sobs began again, more audibly than before, his entire body shaking with despair.

"Where is Violet, Robert?" she carefully asked. "Has she been harmed in all this? Robert? Tell me. Where is my sweet girl?" Beth was at his side again, standing coolly over him, with her fingers combing through his red and white peppered hair. Her heart plummeted when he hesitated to answer, and she fisted a mound, pulling so tight the harshness made him wince, but he finally continued.

"They have her, Beth," he cried. "They won't let her come home to us."

"Who? Who's keepin' her? Where are they keepin' her?"

Robert drew in an exhausted breath and exhaled slowly.

"Brady Kelly, that's who. I left Violet safely at Kelly's keep durin' the celebrations. We hadn't even reached the keep when Gregory met us on the road and told us of the fate that befell the Kelly lord. Beth, I just wanted to keep her safe. Had I only known, she would 'ave been safer with us." Robert wiped his tears away, trying to regain his composure. "Gregory explained that back at the keep, the Kelly clan were searching for us all. Even though I am suspect, they were out for blood, Beth. Gregory narrowly escaped to warn us, and Morgan was beaten half to death. So, ye see, we couldn't return to get her out of there.

"Forced to head home without her, every rider we met on the road told different accounts of Kelly's vengeance. Ignorant to who we were, some said he'd locked her in the dungeon, another laughed and said Brady had been seen ridin' early that mornin' with a girl upon his horse, headin' into the countryside," he explained, shaking his head, helplessness from within.

"You must get her back, Robert! You have to," Beth cried, relinquishing her hold on her husband, throwing her hands up into her own sleep-frenzied locks.

"We don't know his demands yet or even where he's taken 'er. He may be willin' to make a trade – her life for mine," he reasoned. "For now, we have to wait and see. I can't leave here, leavin' you and the clan unprotected. The Kelly's may be workin' on a way to get their revenge, or to get to *me*. We'll have no way of gettin' her back if I'm captured or killed." Robert's tone was more serious now; now that he'd successfully broken the news. He had to keep a level head if he was going to safely get Violet back, and guard his homestead in the process.

"What if there *are* no demands, Robert? What if he never lets her come home to me?" she tearfully asked.

"To us," he corrected, "and that won't happen. We must give it time. A few days at least. I don't think he'll hurt her. He might be the less refined Kelly, but he's a gentleman. He and Vy seemed to hit it off at the feast on the first night. Hopefully, he will remember she's an innocent in all this and try to negotiate a trade or a deal.

"If he thinks I had something to do with his father's death, he will first need to deal with Lord Kelly's passin', then he will surely seek revenge. But I don't think he will use her to get it." Robert took his wife's tiny hand in his, kissed the back of it, trying his best to reassure her, and maybe convince himself too. She pulled away quickly and shot daggers at him.

"A gentleman ye say? What kinda gentleman steals an innocent young maiden with the purpose of torturing and tormenting the girl's family? If anything happens to 'er, Robert, ye'll regret the day ye ever said *'I do'* to me." Beth left their bedchamber, slamming the door upon exit. Her venomous words were felt in the pit of Robert's stomach and he knew she'd make good on her promise.

Exhausted, he lay motionlessly staring up at the printed canopy of their marriage bed. Cherubs floated amongst blooms of every color on a backdrop of green rolling hills. He and Beth had chosen the design together as a reminder to live a life of serenity, love and protection. A reminder that no matter what became of the business, their family and their home was to be protected and cherished, always. Where once this scene offered great comfort, it now grieved him terribly.

'Dear Angels of mercy…keep 'er safe for me,' he prayed, weary sleep engulfing him.

Two lonely mornings had passed when Robert was startled awake by the crash of his chamber door swinging open. Quickly sitting upright, he swung his legs over the side of the bed, trying to focus in a sleepy haze, on what had disturbed him so abruptly.

Beth was standing at the side of the bed, panting and red-faced. She was holding an envelope with an outstretched hand, waiting for Robert to reveal its contents. Peering behind her, he spied a stranger watching from the doorway.

"Who the hell are you?" Robert barked.

The man without a name remained as such, merely shrugging his shoulders and *harrumphing* his reply.

"*That* is a messenger from Galway. He was sent to make sure yer eyes were the only ones to read this letter," Beth said, enraged.

Robert stared the stranger up and down. The young stag didn't flinch.

'*Clearly a Kelly,*' Robert thought, furiously.

The man was dressed in plain but shiny silver armour with a black tunic and breeches underneath, and his breast-plate bore the Kelly and Son's insignia.

Robert hastily snatched the letter from Beth's hand, regretting his cruelty instantly when he caught the pained expression it had caused. He gave a long sigh, patted the bedside next to him, and urged her to sit while he began to silently read. She waited patiently for him to finish.

To the man responsible for the murder of Lord Sean Kelly, my father. I hereby sentence you to a life of misery. You have taken from my brother and I, the only family we had left, the anchor that steadied our clan. By fleeing Galway, you have seen to your own demise, and the demise of your daughter. You've removed your-self from justice, but I will see that justice is served.

You need not worry though, I will not be sending authorities to detain you until a trial can be held, and I will not dispatch my soldiers to rain hell down upon your kin folk.

Through Violet, I will have my revenge. Every day she is in my care, rest assured, she will feel dejected, used, and utterly downcast.

I make no offer of returning her to you until I decide she has paid your debt – if I decide to send her back to you at all.

I take from you, Lord Robert, the one thing you cherish most. An eye for an eye.

Brady Kelly

A tear trickled down Robert's cheek, his face turning bloody-red crimson. He fisted the parchment in his hand as if he was choking the life out of those horrific words. Beth's body trembled with worry beside him.

"Why are ye still here, ye filthy bastard?" Robert shouted at the stranger in the doorway.

"Lord Kelly wishes me to stay 'til ye've read the letter, gauge yer reaction and bring back to him my findin's.

Yer house will receive me every fortnight, onward 'til this ordeal has concluded. He insists that I be treated with the utmost respect. Respect that ye would extend to any esteemed guest, I'm sure. If ye refuse or fail to comply in any way, ye'll not receive word of yer daughter from here on in," Jack spoke with calm, calculated words, barely making eye contact with the lady of the house.

"Well ye've seen what it's done! 'Tis tearin' the heart out of my body in front of yer eyes! Ye can go back and relay *that* to the vile beast of Kelly's keep." Robert leapt from the bed and quickly closed the distance between Jack and himself. Beth gasped in horror as Jack knocked Robert off his feet and onto his back with one swift thwack of his sword hilt. Jack shook his head at the stupidity of the older man and stood directly above him. Robert held his bloodied nose, staring up, disbelief glistening in his pupils.

"Lord Ryan, I wish not to bring harm to ye or yer lady, and no matter what ye may think, I do not enjoy knowin' yer daughter will be beaten to a pulp if I tell Lord Kelly of your intent to attack me. So, 'cause ye are new to all this and I can clearly see yer not thinkin' with a rational state of mind, yer attempt will be forgiven.

"But I warn ye, obey Brady Kelly's wishes in every small detail and she will suffer less for it," Jack warned. When Robert quickly nodded that he understood, Jack reached down and helped him to his feet. Robert couldn't choke out another word, a sense of defeat shrouding every inch of his being.

"Will she be alright?" Beth asked quietly, fearing breaking the rules even by asking. "Will he mistreat her? Is he a cruel man?"

"If she can hold her tongue and do as she's told, he might be able to control his temper," the soldier replied, gravely.

Beth began to weep uncontrollably; loudly, quite nearly groaning in agony. Her gaze landed upon her husband with blood running down both sides of his face. They exchanged the same sickened look.

"What is yer name, lad?" Robert growled through clenched teeth.

"The name's Jack. Jack Manning. But ye'll not be callin' me lad, no matter how old ye think ye are. Jack will be fine, as we'll be seein' quite a bit of one another."

Beth moved to the wash basin and soaked a soft cloth with cold water. She hurried to her wounded other half, and tended to his injury, but no amount of water and tenderness could repair his wounded pride.

"So ye think Kelly will keep her a long spell?" Robert asked, fighting to remain steady as his wife inflicted more pain upon his already throbbing nose.

"Aye, I do. Brady's not the type to forgive easily or to forget quickly. I shouldn't be havin' this discussion with ye, but I think your daughter is an innocent in all this. And if I can prevent ye from doin' somethin' foolish, she just might live through it.

"Why did ye do it? Why did ye kill Lord Kelly?" Jack's eyes went wide, as if he were about to uncover some great mystery.

"I didn't. I was nowhere near Sean Kelly when he was murdered. He spoke my name as he lay dyin', pointin' his finger at me, though, I can't tell ye why," Robert explained. "I'm as innocent as Vy is. Ye can take that back to yer lord, and tell him I'll stand by it 'til my dyin' day. But, God help me, if he harms one hair on 'er head, he'll rue the day he drew his first breath."

Jack snorted, "I don't know if I believe ye, Lord Ryan. But what's for sure is that Brady will not. And he *will* see this through. Ye just best let it play out 'til the end," he added. Beth sighed and sobbed at hearing those words, '*the end*'.

"Fine, fine!" Robert shouted. "If yer done here, ye'll leave me and my lady in privacy. She's not well as ye can see. Just tell me what's to happen next."

"Tonight, I will be ridin' back to Galway. Ye may have time to write a reply to Lord Kelly, but I warn ye to choose yer words carefully. Brady is not a man who possesses much of a conscience. And even less sympathy.

"Once yer message is in his hands, I will return again. Expect me in a fortnight or so."

Beth fell to Jack's feet. "Please sir, ye seem to be a nice fellow, and if ye have a heart, ye'll help rescue 'er. Ye can't let her stay alone with him. He'll break her.

"She won't hold 'er tongue, and she certainly won't do as she's told. I fear for her safety and 'er life. Please, Mr. Manning! Please bring her home to me." Jack didn't flinch at the outrageous display of emotion.

Robert rushed to her side, plucking her from Jack's immaculate leather boots, and held her tightly in his arms. He pinned Jack with pleading eyes, but no compassion rested in Jack's baby blues. '*This man is a true soldier*,' Robert thought, woefully.

TWELVE

Violet screamed at the closed trap door overhead. "Please, Brady! I can't stay in here any longer. Ye can't just leave me down here. Ye just can't!" She didn't know exactly how long she'd been down there. It might have been days, or it might have only been hours. Time dragged on and on, but she slept when she could.

Some solace could be found in the fact that locking her in there also served as protection from his castigation. As long as she was in that cellar, he wasn't punishing her – well, not physically anyway. The darkness and isolation had the ability to cripple her, if she succumbed to it.

Although she despised when Brady used brute force to humiliate her, she couldn't help the lingering, wicked attraction that slithered its way into her mind. It seemed she had two enemies here in this strange place – Brady, and her own body. His footfalls across the floor above, awakened something deep inside of her. Was it fear?

Baffled by her emotions, discerning fear from something more primitive, tested her resolve. Was it lust perhaps?

Her heart nearly skipped a beat with every sound he made. Every grunt escaping his lips with item after item he'd destroyed upstairs caused the rushing of her own pulse to echo in her ears. He had to be wrestling with some vicious inner demons of his own.

Violet considered how he'd lost his mother only a short time ago. From their conversation in the garden, she knew he'd cherished the Kelly matriarch dearly. And now to lose his father, just as they'd found a common ground between them, was a crime beyond all imagination. Her lonely heart wept for him, regardless of her own situation.

With too much time to think, her memory clung to that day in the garden and the night of the celebration ball. He had been so handsome, charming, and a real gentleman.

'His father's death has driven him to madness,' she thought with equal amounts of sadness and empathy.

Despite her conflicting convictions, she simply couldn't understand how keeping her there would make up for the wrongs he'd suffered, or even serve as vengeance against her father. Why Brady was convinced her father was even responsible for Sean's death was beyond her comprehension. Violet knew in her heart that her Da would never hurt another living thing. The idea that he'd murdered another man – a fellow Irishman and business partner, was utterly ridiculous, no matter what Brady thought.

The head-strong Ryan in her wanted nothing more than to fight him at every turn, but she wasn't sure how that would serve her. Would he remain this cruel and callous? Would he go beyond merely giving her a good spanking for her brazen tongue? What was his ultimate goal in holding her against her will, anyway? Those questions hung in the thick sour air of her prison until her head spun.

∞

Brady tried to ignore the cries from below. He paced the floor back and forth, struggling with his own decision to put her down there. An impossible task it was – making sense of his own actions. He'd been so distraught when Sean was killed, it was a small wonder that he hadn't seriously harmed the girl. But while only a little time had passed since that dreadful event, his thinking had cleared some. Regretfully, stubborn pride would never allow him to concede or release his prisoner.

'*I've kidnapped this poor, sweet lass. Now what?*' he cursed under his breath. Brady's cruel streak had been screaming and clawing its way to the surface since he was a boy, but he'd never harmed someone who hadn't deserved it, and certainly not a woman. It had never occurred to him to do such a thing. He was, for the most part, kind and oft-times a gentleman with the ladies; apart from the brothel wenches. But this hatred toward the Ryan's had something sinister inside him slithering to the surface – something even he couldn't get a grasp on.

With Violet tucked away, her father was surely suffering the loss, as Brady too had been forced to suffer. Yet, with her trapped just beneath the floor boards, so damn close, the guilt he inflicted upon himself became almost unbearable.

He remembered how it felt. Recalling the nights he'd spent in the bitter dark prison beneath the keep in his youth, played against his sense of even-handedness. He knew what it meant to be trapped like that, and now questioned if there was another way to deal with bringing Robert Ryan to the justice he so deserved. Yet, if all he'd wanted to do was to hurt Robert Ryan, he'd already accomplished that, but without hurting Violet? Impossible.

Brady stepped quietly toward the cellar door in the kitchen, lowering his head to try to hear her. She was so quiet again, and he wondered if she had fallen asleep.

He had put her down there just two days ago, but the first day had been the worst. After she'd ceased yelling and cursing him to hell, he'd crept below with a bowl of the rabbit stew he'd cooked. He'd found an exhausted heap, asleep in a pile of old quilts that his mother had left down there in hopes of someday mending.

'*How could I hate her this much, when she looks that beautiful?*' he thought, creeping about, quietly making her a temporary privy, gathering some preserves his mother had made, and trying his hardest not to wake his little captive. He'd left her supper next to where she slept. *I can't be that horrendous. I'm still feedin' 'er, after all.*

Brady instantly knew when she awoke, for her anger bellowed up again, and the smashing of the clay bowl containing her supper against the stone walls beneath, nearly rattled his teeth.

"Damn you, Brady Kelly and damn yer filthy rabbit stew! I'll die before I eat what ye prepare for me. Ye hear me? I'll wither and die!" she shouted.

Even in all her fury, Brady still continued to leave her meals on the first step of the small staircase. He'd wait until peace and quiet filled the cottage, then quickly open the door, and shut it again, wary of waking a sleeping dragon. Each time, he'd have to remove the cold and dried up meal from before, untouched. At least she'd stopped breaking all his mother's dishes.

"How long can she go hungry? Spiteful wench," Brady chuckled. But in truth, he was beginning to worry on the third morning. Hours had passed since he'd heard a sound from the cavity below.

He crept to the door, opening it carefully and cautiously. He hoped that three nights were long enough to break her high spirits – to make her yielding and obedient. Each night as he sleeplessly lay in his mother's bed, that word haunted him. He would demand her *obedience*.

In the days that had come before, he'd tried his hardest to come up with perfect retribution. Kidnapping Robert Ryan's daughter –heir to the family fortune, next in line to run the company, his prized, sweet, virtuous gem – it should have been the ultimate revenge.

When Brady was finished with her, his intent was to send her home, unfit to rule the clan and unfit to run the company. Not to mention the repercussions of living with a man, alone, unchaperoned for an extended period of time. No man in his right mind would seek her hand in marriage now, not when she'd be regarded as nothing more than used goods. She'd be forever ruined, her dreadful plight torturing the Ryan lord for the rest of his days.

It seemed like the perfect plan, until that is, his conscience unexpectedly stepped in, allowing regret and even shame to come calling. The two emotions took residence in Brady's psyche, despite being uninvited.

He descended the steps, careful not to startle her. All he could hope for today was that she wouldn't pitch another fit. He didn't like leaving her down there, but he would, if she forced him to.

He watched her resting upon the patchwork pile and his heart melted in an instant. The way the sunlight crept down to the corner of the cellar and reflected off her long, disheveled locks, illuminated her in a glow of strawberry red. She slept so soundly that Brady feared she'd slipped into unconsciousness.

Then, as if she'd felt his presence, she slowly opened her eyes. Too weak from hunger and spent emotion, she failed to make a move.

With tender arms, he lifted her from the make-shift bed and carried her up the steps, careful not to jostle her too much. She hadn't the strength to hold on, and her head fell against his brawny chest. He was certain she could hear his heart thumping inside his ribcage, for it hammered in his own ears.

He brought her into his old room – a masculine space with deer antlers and animal furs, from slaughters both big and small, decorating the four walls. This was to be Violet's room now, even though his mother's space would have served more comfortably for a woman. Caitlyn's room would have suited Violet nicely, but he couldn't bring himself to share that part of his life with the Ryan wench.

He gently sat her at the end of the bed, then reached up and pulled down the covers. He picked her up again and gingerly placed her into bed, pulling the blankets up to her chin.

"Now, wee lass, that'll teach ye to eat yer meals when they're sent to ye," he scolded, but Violet's gaze fixed on the window, without acknowledgment that he'd even spoke. He'd broken her. Strangely enough, satisfaction was not born of her acquiescence.

Within minutes, Brady left, returning with a bowl of steaming hot soup. He helped her sit up in bed, laying a tray across her lap and urged her to eat. She silently eyed every move he made, as if he was a starving mountain lion, ready to pounce on its prey, or just a wicked, evil man, waiting to mete out another punishment. She must have been a smart lass, to be cautious and watchful, for he was both the animal, and the man.

Violet did as she was told – obeyed him to avoid suffering his wrath. He held the steaming spoon to her lips, and she suspiciously sipped the flavourful brew until it warmed her down to her toes. She wanted so much to ask the questions that needed answering, but feared his temper would rear its ugly head, resulting in another lonely night in the cellar.

Mutely, she watched as he appeared more like the Brady she'd first met and had liked very much, and less like her monstrous captor who was hell-bent on earning her hate.

"That's right. Eat up. We can't have ye gettin' weak like this again. I'll have none of that," Brady scolded, but not entirely unkindly. Violet merely nodded.

Every instinct in her wanted to throw the bowl of hot liquid right in his face and run for her life. But as she pictured it in her head – Brady covered from head to foot in his own soup, she had to choke back a small grin and the laughter that would surely accompany it.

When her meal had been devoured, '*like a good little girl*', she thought, she found the courage to finally speak.

"Brady?" Violet asked sweetly, praying she'd not anger him, "May I speak freely?"

"Aye, Violet. Ye may," he replied, removing the serving tray from her lap and setting it on the table next to the bed.

"Why am I here? And please don't get angry, I just need to know why," she pleaded, looking up, searching his steel-blue pools for the first time since the dance they'd shared.

"Because, my sweet Vy, yer father needs to know what it feels like to lose everything. He needs to feel my wrath every day of his life."

Her heart sank, and she felt the urge to vomit. Her mother and father called her *Vy*, but hearing it roll off Brady's tongue sickened her.

She watched closely as he made his way around the room, opening the curtains to let the sun filter in. His sinewy body moved with purpose and she marveled at the cut of him. He appeared so strong, and she couldn't help but feel that familiar attraction welling up inside.

"Then, he's already lost me, Brady. Does that mean you're going to keep me here...forever?" The thought of being forced to stay there with him for the rest of her days both exhilarated and terrified her beyond thought.

"Nay, not forever, sweet Vy. Just until I think he is at his breakin' point. And then, ye will return to him, reputation sullied, worked to the bone, unsuitable for marriage. His dreams of handin' over that jest of a company to ye, will all go up in smoke." The way he chuckled was pure evil, causing Violet to see through the tenderness and kind exterior. She had better tread very lightly.

"And what are yer intentions then? Do ye think that my Da won't send his men here to rescue me?" she asked, a delicate brow raised in question.

Brady sneered at her question and stalked toward the door. "I intend to do exactly as I like...don't forget it. And as for yer father sendin' anyone here...he'd be an eegit to take a chance like that. I've made sure he feels as helpless as I did," Brady grinned, unaffected by the silent tears tumbling down her cheeks. "Ye'll find yer chests in the closet, along with all yer things. I will give ye a few hours of rest, and then yer to get cleaned up and changed. I expect ye to be out of this room before supper time, as this will be the last time I prepare it for ye. I will have a list of duties for ye, so dress comfortably and accordin'ly."

Brady left her room, pulling the door closed with a gentle *tick*. The need for a safe barrier between them screamed at her sensibilities, and so Violet wearily rose from the bed to check for a locking mechanism. She damned his very existence when she found none.

However, she needed rest if he was permitting it. She lazily stripped and discarded the three-day old dress into a heap on the polished wooden floor. She went to her chest and pulled out a clean night shift, brought the garment to her nose and inhaled the sweet scent. It still smelled like home. As she pulled it over her head, it brought a small bitter-sweet smile to her face, and she crawled into bed again.

With a full belly, and a little more understanding of why she was there, she refused to worry about the day ahead, and easily awarded herself with peaceful slumber.

∞

A sense of pride rose from within the depths of him, casting his shame and regret to the wind. This fiery, free-willed pain in the arse had actually asked permission to speak. *Progress.*

Sitting at the table, Brady began to ink a harsh and lengthy list of chores, pondering over what he could possibly have her do. But, irritation settled, as he kept adding things, then scribbling them out again, thinking they were too callous and severe for her delicate body to endure.

He found himself becoming aroused thinking about her scrubbing the floor, her wild red hair sweaty and in disarray. He pictured her on her hands and knees with a brush in hand, a bucket of soapy water at her side, with her blouse falling enough to reveal her lush breasts.

'Jesus! I gotta stop thinkin' this way. The bloody bitch is a Ryan! Come on, Brady, get yer head straight,' he cursed under his breath, shaking his head as if he could shake the thoughts of her out. But he couldn't. Just knowing she was a few breaths away, tucked into his

bed, made him crazy with desire. He could have her if he wanted her. She was, after-all, his captive, to do with as he pleased. Picturing their bodies entwined, his massive form pounding into her soft flesh, nearly sent him over the edge.

Instead of giving in to his raw, dark desires, he chose to let her sleep and went outside to seek Thunder's companionship.

He leapt up onto the steed's back and rode hard, all the while obsessing over the innocent maiden back at the cottage. He could only imagine what she must be feeling.

"AUGH!" he cried into the wind. "She's a filthy Ryan for Christ sake!" And with that, he dug his heels into Thunder's haunches, picking up the pace as he vowed to hate her for vexing him so.

When Violet awoke, the sun was still high in the sky. She was grateful she hadn't missed supper for she knew she'd be punished. He'd already informed her that it would be the last meal he'd prepare for them, drawing her to the conclusion that she'd have to learn to cook – and fast. It was a good thing she was a quick study.

She stretched and yawned, feeling like she'd been asleep for hours. The wash basin had been filled with water, although she didn't know when that had happened – most likely while she slept. The thought of Brady entering her room while she was asleep unsettled her, but she tried not to think about it.

The water had gone icy-cold, but she washed with it anyway, and then made a speedy repair of her chaotic hair. Eyeing the chest peeking out from the closet, she pulled from it, a yellow day dress. Something in Brady's gaze earlier, had alarm bells clanging in manic mode inside her, so she'd chosen a modest cut; careful not to reveal too much.

Quietly inching the door open, afraid he would be sitting, waiting for her to emerge, her own heart thumping in her chest nearly deafened her, as fear and anxiety caused her to shiver.

She poked her head out, scanning the cottage. She blew out a breath of air, relieved to find she was alone.

Her reprieve wouldn't last long however, when it dawned on her, '*Now I have to anticipate his return,*' she thought nauseatingly.

An idea struck her. *If I'm stuck here anyway, might as well make the best of it.* She wandered into the kitchen, noting that Brady had not yet started preparing the evening meal. *Won't hurt to try.*

She'd seen a few jars in the cellar labelled apple sauce, and quickly went about fetching one. Leaving the door wide open, she ran as quickly as she could down the steps and back up again with the jar in hand.

In the kitchen cupboard, all she found was flour, sugar, oats, and some other sacks containing coffee and loose teas. *He certainly wasn't prepared for company.*

Because she held no talent in the culinary arts, the porridge would have to do. She'd seen the cook at home prepare it, how hard could it be?

When Brady returned from his 'diversion excursion', he opened the cottage door, finding Violet perched quietly at the table, hands clasped in her lap, a bowl of goo steaming before her. Directly across from hers, another bowl of ghastly gunk taunted him.

He couldn't deny that she'd set the table nicely with his mother's silverware and some napkins she'd most likely found in a drawer of the hutch. '*I'd forgotten about those*,' he thought thankfully. A plain blue linen cloth covered the hardwood table.

Brady was only half impressed with her efforts but most astounded by her composure. *She can hold 'er tongue, after all.*

For once, Violet was silent, watching him with wide innocent eyes. He knew she wanted nothing more than to please him. When their gazes met, she lowered hers. '*She's finally yielded*,' he thought ardently, satisfaction adding to his many layers.

Brady cleared his throat. "What have we got here?" he asked, kindly.

"I…I don't really know how to prepare a supper, Brady, but I tried with what I could find. I hope ye'll find it satisfactory," she politely replied.

Suppressing a laugh, he eyed the bowl of apple sauce sitting in the middle of the table with its large serving spoon listing to the side.

"'Twill be fine, Violet," he said curtly, hiding his amusement. "What's in here?" He pointed at the gooey bowl.

"Umm...porridge. With apple sauce to drizzle on top," she replied, cheeks aflame, obviously embarrassed by her efforts.

Without a word, he eyed it cautiously, dipped his spoon inside and forced himself to ingest the most horrific bowl of gruel he'd ever tasted. Yet, he said nothing negative.

In fact, the entire time they sat facing one another, not a word was exchanged. The ache to beat the beautiful wench, just for being beautiful and trying so hard, vibrated through him like an explosion.

Violet secretly wished Brady would choke on his supper.

After they had suffered down her first attempt at a meal, she rose from the table and tended to the dishes. She didn't know where to get the water, or even *how* to wash dishes, but she knew it was expected, and she was up for the challenge. Her survival would depend on her willingness to learn.

"Ye're catching on pretty quickly, sweet Vy. Ye'll find the well out back. There's a wash pan under the counter. If ye bring in enough fire wood, which ye'll find in the wood shed, ye should be able to stoke the fire hot enough to warm yer dish water." He was mocking her, and she knew it. Her revulsion took on a new and heightened form. *I could stab him with…what? A spoon?* Her situation was almost comical.

"Aye, Brady," she replied, passively. She wanted to scream and yell in the beast's face. *'Oh, so you've brought me here to be your slave, did ye?'* But she refrained, hoping that he would grow tired of her in time and let her return to Clare. If he didn't, she held on to the hope that her Da would find a way to rescue her from this…this purgatory.

In the meantime, she vowed to keep a level head and do what was expected. Keeping him from losing his temper and subsequently dishing out another insufferable punishment was her main objective at this point.

His eyes bored into her as she lugged two large pails of water into the cottage, transferred the liquid into a massive pot and lifted it onto the stove top to boil.

A sense of accomplishment stunned her. She'd done it! It seemed like a menial task in theory, but the buckets were heavy and now she was rather proud that she'd done it without his assistance.

"Vy, did ye get the fire wood yet? Ye can't boil water on a cold stove," he laughed. *Yes! A spoon just might do!*

For a split second, the fury that had been brewing deep within her reared its ugly head.

"Christ Almighty! The stove's still warm from cookin' supper! I'll bank it up when I'm ready. Ye can't expect me to do it all at once!" she shouted back at him. He'd managed to diminish her new-found sense of triumph with one contemptuous question.

His stare turned to stone at her outburst, causing the butterflies in her stomach to squirm in protest.

"My apologies, Brady," she quickly recanted, lowering her eyes to the floor again. "I…I've never done these tasks before. Please, be patient with me." He was standing over her in that imposing manner which made her blood boil and her adrenalin gush.

"Be patient? Ye're here 'cause I always get what I want," he spat through tightly clenched teeth, "and I want ye and yer bastard father to suffer. I'll not need patience, Violet. Ye'll need to learn yer place and know when to hold that bloody tongue of yers."

Grabbing her arm in a bone-crushing grip, he led her to the door and pushed her outside. "Don't have me warn ye again, Vy. Fetch the fire wood and be quick about it," he growled. "And I'll be watching ye, so don't get any ideas of runnin'. Ye'll find more harm out there on yer own than in here with me. Imagine that," he snarled.

Her bottom lip trembled, but she refused to cry in front of him. He'd already earned enough of her tears to flood the River Shannon. Never again would he witness her wretchedness.

'Stupid little girl, why can't I just keep my mouth shut? Perhaps, he wouldn't be so cruel,' she thought as she deliberately weighed herself down with as much fire wood as she could carry.

She set it all in a wood box next to the stove and wiped her brow. Poking at the flames like she'd seen the help at home do, the smouldering embers within came to life.

While exhaustion threatened to hinder her efforts, Violet managed to get the dishes and the kitchen cleared away. It seemed she knew no other way to go about her tasks than to do them the hard way. '*It'll get easier…it has to,*' she told herself, optimistically.

A small miracle it was, that Brady never spoke the entire time and rarely even looked in her direction. He'd retreated to a wooden rocking chair, ankle hooked atop his knee, fixated on a piece of parchment draped across his leg. With quill in hand and a furrowed brow, his incessant scratching out and adding in, nearly drove her to insanity. *The list*.

When the sun had finally begun to set, her body screamed almost as wildly as her mind, insisting she retire to the cozy bed in Brady's room. Not even her repugnance for the vile creature could keep her from sleep this night. Despite his masculine scent still lingering on the bedclothes, causing her heart to betray her head, she desperately needed to rest.

Brady felt her presence before he actually looked up at her. She stood before him unwaveringly, a pink tone tinting her fair complexion – an indication of the fatigue she would never own up to.

'*Beautiful,*' he thought. He pictured the flushed hue of her cheeks if ever thoroughly satisfied by a lover. A groan built in his chest at the thought of *him* being that man.

Silent and motionless for what seemed an eternity, Violet's weary gaze never left his. Was she waiting for further instruction? Permission to retire for the evening perhaps? Her sweet honeyed scent mixed with a pleasant musk of perspiration, tickled his senses, forcing him to imagine making her sweat between the sheets of his bed.

Mechanically, he placed his hand on her hip, his gaze roaming the length of her trembling form. Again, a deep satisfaction that he'd inflicted enough fear upon her, that her body betrayed her stubborn exterior, engulfed him. *Aye, tremble in fear, ye little traitor.*

In Brady's show of tenderness, his hand burned a hole straight through her, searing the flesh beneath the fabric of her dress. She longed to run her fingers through his thick black hair, desire blazing inside her like never before. Her mind raced, but her body responded to his touch involuntarily; as if the last three days hadn't happened.

Traitorous body.

Her right hand dove into his wild hair, while the left found his brawny shoulder. *Such strength.*

As if the contact seared his scalp and the skin beneath his linen shirt, he slapped her hand away, cursing under his breath. Nodding his head in the direction of her room, she took the hint, and wobbled away, insulted and deflated.

When she was safely behind the bedroom door, tears flowed in torrents down her face; the sobs in her throat aggressively suffocating her.

'*What was that? Why does he have to confuse me so?*' she thought, his scorching hand print still warming her hip.

Mud beneath one's boots would be held in higher regard than Brady after that slip. Why couldn't he just stick to the plan? *Why the fuck can't I just despise the wench*? He had been so close to letting basic and natural desires take over, allowing him to make love to her until she was spent with affectionate exhaustion.

He couldn't fathom what would happen if she fell in love with him, all because the need in his trousers had shamelessly seduced her. He couldn't let himself get this close again. *But she looks and smells so divine.*

'*I'll fix that*,' he thought, rushing to his mother's room, pulling out the chest hidden under the bed. He rummaged through some old clothing his mother had saved over the years, most likely with intentions of using it to make yet another patchwork masterpiece. Sadly, she'd never gotten around to it.

Pushing the heartbreaking memory from his mind, Brady pulled out a white blouse, a dark grey vest and the trousers to match. They would be a little big on Violet, but they would do just fine. If he couldn't control his urges, at least he could manage the source of said urges.

'*There! She won't be lookin' so damn temptin' in these. Have to stay focussed. At least 'til Jack returns,*' he thought, quite proud of his bright idea.

Without even the courtesy of knocking, he flung her door open – hard and fast. This was his home and he refused to ask permission to enter any part of it.

"Here. Put these on tomorrow," he said, tossing the hand-me-downs onto the bed. "I'll not be havin' ye paradin' around here barely covered in yer fancy dresses. Ye think I don't know what ye're up to?" Violet stared back at him in wonder.

"Brady, I…I'm not up to anything. I swear," she whimpered, nearly giving in to yet another crying jag. He had to remain heartless. If she broke out into a fit of bawling, he'd damn-well give her something to cry about.

"Aye. Stately and regal, as all Ryan's are," he snarled, sarcastically. "I'll be wakin' ye bright an' early. Yer to wear these, and only clothes I provide. And no more of that perfume. Makes my eyes water." Without giving her a chance of rebuttal, he slammed the door, rattling the mirror on the wall outside.

Brady fought so hard in that moment not to barge back in and ravage her right then and there. He'd just shattered her spirit, yet again.

'*Dammit, Jack. Where are ye? I need a distraction.*'

THIRTEEN

Jack pounded on the cottage door until his fists were throbbing. Oddly, no one answered, and he heard no movement from within. Since the sun hadn't yet begun to rise, the eerie morning air sent chills straight through his bones.

"Brady! Jesus b'y! Unlock the door, 'tis me," Jack hollered, continuing his torrent of wallops upon the wooden barrier.

After his third round of assaults, he finally heard Brady cursing and fumbling around inside.

When the door swung open, Jack's eyes grew wide. "What's happened to ye?" he asked, cocking his head to the side, a smirk tugging at his lips. "Ye look like shite! Has the little imp been givin' ye a hard time?" Jack laughed, sauntering in, sensing Brady's aggravation. Removing the armoured breast plate and weapons, he relaxed in a chair next to the wood stove in attempt to free himself of the frosty tremors wracking his body.

"Augh," Brady groaned, rubbing the back of his neck. "She's provin' to be a real pain in the arse – more than ye know," he added, raking his fingers through his wild, raven hair. He attempted to repair the disheveled state of his slept-in clothes, but his efforts were futile. His linen shirt was wrinkled beyond recognition.

Jack could see that Brady was wrestling with intense misery, and said nothing else to tease or provoke him. It was apparent that the situation had reached frightening heights, and he couldn't have it on his conscience if he were to make matters worse. Despite the need to tread lightly, he reached into his leather bag, retrieved a letter and handed it to Brady.

"The girl's mother is very upset. This will destroy her," Jack said, bracing for Brady's temper to respond.

"I don't give a good God damn about her mother, Jack!" Brady pounded his fist on the tabletop, sending the sugar bowl crashing to the floor. '*Here it comes*,' Jack mused. "I'm glad they're all sufferin'! If her mother weeps for her, as sure as hell, her father is takin' the brunt of it."

This wouldn't be Jack's first acute encounter with the beast within Brady. He had a responsibility to show Brady how senseless this was, how cruel he was treating Violet, and how innocent the girl truly was. Perhaps Brady could be convinced of her father's innocence as well.

"Brady, we've been friends for as long as I can re-member. But, this is not who ye are!" Jack raised his voice, hoping his words would penetrate Brady's thick skull. "I've seen ye be as mean and intimidatin' as an ornery bull. I've watched ye beat a man to a pulp fer nothin' more than a snide remark. I've witnessed ye at odds with your own brother *and* father. But an innocent girl? Brady, 'tis low, even for you.

"As yer faithful friend and officer, I vowed to stand by ye, but I don't know if I can uphold my promise to ye in this." Jack shook his head, his expression turning sol-emn as he waited for Brady's judgement.

"You know what? Yer criticism of *me* is a little com-ical," Brady half-chuckled. "'Tis not me who takes to bed every wench in the village, sometimes two at a time. Nor is it I, who's been known, on occasion, to knock one around 'til she begs for mercy. Nay! 'Twas you, wasn't it, '*Sir Nobility*'? So, before ye go on a tirade 'bout how I treat my women, ye'd better take a good look at yer own misdeeds. Ye'll find ye're no less of an ogre than I am!"

With that, Jack was on his feet, solidly standing face to face with Brady, fuming. "Ye forget, *friend*. The Ryan girl ain't yer woman!

"And, yer not gonna turn this around on me, ye self-righteous bastard! What yer doin' to Lady Violet has nothin' to do with me or how I choose to live my life. 'Tis you who has to live with yerself.

"Keepin' that poor lass from 'er home and 'er family is inexcusable. Did it ever occur to ye that her father is innocent? That he had nothin' to do with Sean's death?" Jack could see Brady's demeanour change at the suggestion. Instead of anger, Brady's face clouded with uncertainty.

"Why would he say it then? If Ryan had nothing to do with it – if he wasn't connected somehow – why would Da say the man's name, for Christ's sake?" It wasn't a mere question. Brady beseeched Jack to make sense of it, as if he had all the answers.

Drained of all fortitude, Jack fell back into the chair, kicked off his boots and rubbed his cold aching feet.

"I don't have the answers ye seek, my friend. Just read the damn letter."

With a deep sigh, Brady broke the Ryan seal, carefully unfolded the parchment and began.

Lord Kelly,

There are no words that can convey how deeply sorry I am for the loss of your father. We would have been great partners in business, and perhaps even friends if the union between your brother and Violet had come to pass.

But now, I can only plead and beg for you to return her safely to us, as she is an innocent in this, as am I. I vow upon her life that I had no desire to harm your father, and would like to help you in any way I can, to find the fiend who did.

Despite the torture and pain you are inflicting upon my family, I will co-operate in any way I can until you see the grave mistake you have made, and decide to make it right.

   Sincerely,
   Lord Robert Ryan

Crushing the letter in his fist, Brady shook his head. *'The union between your brother and Violet,'* he seethed. It was as if that statement alone stood out above the rest. He would have preferred to have been beaten within an inch of his life, if it could've saved him from reading those seven dreadful words.

The thought of Violet with another man sent him into a rage. The thought of her with *Liam* nearly consumed him. The need to take complete possession of her took over.

With no regard for Jack's presence, Brady heatedly threw Violet's door open and yanked her out of bed. The fierceness in him made her flinch and whimper. He forced her out to face Jack, wearing nothing but a pale pink night shift. Her cheeks and nose were rosy from terror, and already shed tears. No doubt she'd been listening to the entire exchange since Jack arrived.

"Does this look innocent to ye?" Brady roared, shaking Violet until she fell to her knees, sobbing. "She is but a temptress, with a murderous father. They *will* be taught a lesson."

Brady fisted her fiery hair, mercilessly pulling her to her feet. But before he could deliver further punishment, Jack had placed his body in front of hers, shielding the lass from a maniacal Brady.

"Stop!" Jack yelled, holding his friend at bay with a sturdy forearm. "Stop this, now!"

He gave Brady a quick shove backward, but only enough to remove Violet from danger. He draped his arm around her shoulders, sending Brady a warning glare, and then led her back to her room.

"Now, lass. Fix yerself up and get dressed. I'll calm the beast, no' to fear. Come out when ye're ready." Jack's voice soothed her fragile nerves and she done as she was told, without a whimper of protest.

"Aye," she quietly nodded as Jack closed the door, directing his fury back to Brady.

"Ye've lost yer bloody mind!" Jack fumed, examining Brady while he paced the floor like a rabid, caged animal. There was something deeper to his anger. Something written in that letter had set him off and Jack had to know what it was. "Ye can't be of a sound mind and still treat the girl like this. Ye can't hate her father this much, can ye? What got ye all wound up? What did ye read in that letter?"

Brady halted his frenzied stride, taking a long look at Jack, but no acceptable answer came to mind. Not one he could share anyway.

'*Aye, I hate 'im. I hate them all,*' he thought, violently. '*A union between she and Liam would come to pass over my dead body.*' Without another word, he left, slamming the door behind him.

Jack gently wrapped his knuckles on Violet's door.

"Lady Violet? Are ye ready to come out yet? He's gone."

Violet already knew that. She'd heard the door slam so often that it was the one noise she could now depend on. All other sounds still made her nervous.

Not quite trusting her new protector, she opened the door cautiously. She really had no choice. If he was going to be an ally, she would at least have to talk to him.

"Where is he?" she asked, not daring to meet Jack's gaze.

As if he sensed her trepidation, Jack smoothly closed the distance between them, and pulled her chin up with his finger. She refused to let their eyes meet.

"Look at me, girl," he coaxed gently.

Violet found herself looking into the palest blue pools she had ever seen, reminiscent of the sun bleached blue-eyed-grass her mother had cursed last year when it had taken over her immaculate garden. She stared into them as seconds ticked by, waiting – searching for the monster behind them to emerge. Instead, kindness and understanding poured into hers, soothing her frayed nerves.

This stranger was quite the opposite of Brady in every way possible. Unlike Brady, he stood almost nose to nose with her, his fair complexion contrasting Brady's dark mysterious skin tone. Even from this first impression, their individual personas were like night and day.

He seemed to be more laid back and casual, while Brady proved to be a rogue and a tyrant at every turn – with the exception of their first few days of meeting.

'Had that man ever existed?' she wondered, reflecting on the moments when they'd talked and danced and how he'd been the most fascinating and captivating creature she had ever set eyes upon.

"'Tis nice to finally meet ye, Violet. I'm Jack." He smiled, revealing a dimple on the left side of his face. "'Tis a shame I wasn't able to have a dance with ye at the ball…meetin' me now might not be so dauntin' for ye."

Jack was quite different, indeed. Even though he wasn't making her stomach somersault with butterflies, or her knees weak at the mere sound of his voice, he was pleasant enough to talk to, and easy to be around. For the first time in days, she almost felt safe.

"Won't he be returning soon? He can't be gone far," Violet trembled.

"Aye, yer right. He's not gone far. Probably gone to the barn to cool off for a minute," Jack chuckled. "What is it about a wee little thing like you that makes his blood boil over?"

He swaggered about her, looking her up and down, obviously disgusted with the boy's clothing she'd donned. His scrutiny hit her like a ball of lead.

"I don't know," she whispered, hands clasped tightly in front of her, fighting her mounting humiliation. "I'm behavin' like he said I should. He just gets so angry at everything I do."

Jack wiped a fat tear from her cheek with the back of his fingers, then reached into his pocket for a kerchief and handed it to her.

"Well, the only thing I can tell ye, lass, is to ride it out. Brady's like the tide. He comes in fast and unyielding; high and mighty. When it's his time to retreat, he will bow out gracefully, yet unapologetically."

"I just wish I could make him believe my father is innocent. Then he'd let me go home."

"Aye, to yer mother," Jack agreed, but with the mention of her mother, Violet began to sob uncontrollably.

"She must be in pieces worried about me," she hiccupped.

"Aye, she is. She misses ye terribly, and wants nothing more than to see ye safely returned. But she does worry about your stubborn disposition." Patting the space next him, Jack urged her to sit with him in the window seat. Instead, she placed herself in the rocking chair on the other side of the room. She might be a little more at ease with this man, but she couldn't say she trusted him already. From overhearing Brady and Jack's argument earlier, she knew they were the best of friends and for all she knew, he could be another wolf in sheep's clothing. Having already learnt that hard lesson, she dared not risk getting too close. However, with regards to her family, she yearned to know everything.

"So, you've talked with her in person? My mother?" Violet asked wide-eyed, drying her tears with the piece of lacy linen he'd offered.

"I thought ye knew what my role was, Violet," Jack shifted uncomfortably in his seat. "I'm Brady's messenger. I will be returning to yer lands every fortnight to give your father Brady's correspondence."

"Correspondence? Is he ransoming me?" she asked, mind racing. Despite being a complete rake, she couldn't imagine Brady demanding payment for her release when his family oozed with old money.

"Nay. He asks nothing of yer family. And that is all I can say about it," he replied curtly.

Violet sighed. She sensed that he was a loyal man, loyal to the Kelly's first and foremost. Still, she wondered if she could get close enough to him that he might divulge Brady's secrets. Most importantly, tell her exactly what Brady's purpose in keeping her was. That hope went flying straight out of her head when Brady returned from his cool down.

She held her breath, waiting for him to lash out with fury upon her. But he didn't. He gaped at her exasperatingly, then to Jack, then back to her again, saying nothing. His annoyance and intensity radiated throughout the entire room, bouncing off every wall and every piece of furniture.

"I see you're ready to start your day, sweet Vy," Brady snarled, showing his teeth like an angry dog. "Get up."

She stood, frozen in one spot, hands firmly at her sides while he inspected her attire.

She was wearing the plain trousers, and utilitarian white work shirt he had provided, but she'd obstinately refused to don the vest. He seemed pleased enough when he chuckled at the sight of her in men's clothing. No doubt he'd enjoy seeing her flounder in the masculine boots which were much too big, as well. Her hair was pulled back into what she thought an unflattering pony-tail, fastened with a piece of knitting yarn at the nape of her neck. She felt no more like a lady than she deserved in this get-up.

The fact that he'd taken so much pleasure in her dis-comfiture was infuriating. For a fleeting moment, she pictured him slipping on a pile of horse dung out in the yard and brutally landing on his arse. *That's better than ye deserve!*

Brady plopped down at the kitchen table and dug into his pocket, bringing a piece of wrinkled parchment into view.

He held it in his outstretched hand, glaring at her until she moved to retrieve it with shaky fingers. He held it tight in his grip, making her eyes flicker to meet his cold stare.

Unfolding the hand-written note with a furrowed brow, she studied his words closely. The first few tasks hadn't seemed too difficult – *fetch water from the well any time it was required, fill the wood pile next to the stove, cook all three meals for the day, clean the floors, wash the clothes, and clean the dishes after every meal.* But as she continued down the list, the tasks became unfathomable. *Feed the horse, hitch him to the plough, clean his stall every day, and feed the chickens and pigs.* She stopped reading, gaping at him with questions swirling in her head.

"There's nothin' on here ye can't do. I've decided that until I determine yer fate, you and I will turn this place into a runnin' farm again," he bitterly stated, the ice in his gaze sending chills down her spine.

"Ye don't have any animals *to* feed," she quietly said, pointing at that particular item.

"Nay, not yet, but he will see to it that they are delivered by next week. Isn't that right, Jack?" Jack nodded his approval and Brady continued, "Ye may begin, Vy. Jack and I have some business to finish," he said, shooing her away with little to no regard for her feelings. With a wave of his hand, she'd been forced to feel the enormity of her situation. *I am slave. He is master.*

Hanging her head, she ambled out to the well to fill the first pail with freezing cold water to begin the morning's duties. Strengthening her resolve, she vowed to overcome this travesty. *He will no' break me. I am a Ryan, dammit!* She would prepare his breakfast. She would indeed feed that blasted horse – Thunder, if she recalled correctly, and she'd certainly scrub that little cottage until her hands were raw and every surface shined. Her nearly forgotten stubbornness and determination would see to it that she done her tasks well. *Who knows, I may accidentally poison the monstrous lout.*

Jack had silently examined the exchange between them, studying how she trembled in fear with the mere sound of his voice. The fact that Brady celebrated it did not go unnoticed either. And in complete contrast to her bodily responses, Jack couldn't miss the shimmer of lust in Brady's gaze as it swept over her quivering form. His observation brought about a staggering conclusion. *'He's not only keepin' her to punish 'er kin. He's keepin' 'er for himself.'*

Before now, he'd been apprehensive about leaving her there to endure Brady's petulance and cruelty, but knowing his friend's secret affliction, set his mind at ease. Brady was falling in love with her – hard and fast.

'*I'll keep this secret to myself I think,*' Jack thought wryly. Recognizing what lay beneath Brady's brutal facade could cause more harm to the girl than necessary if Brady felt threatened by his old friend's knowledge. Brady would go to unthinkable lengths to prove Jack wrong – to prove his own heart wrong – and Jack couldn't have the demise of such a bonny lass on his conscience.

"What shall I tell Lord Ryan when I return?" Jack asked, desperate to get the hell out of there. He knew Brady's temperament and how quickly he could be provoked in a brawl, but lusting after a woman? This was a first. Jack hadn't the stomach for it.

"Aye, I have a letter ready, but it is to remain sealed until Ryan reads it himself. Did ye have any trouble with them on your first visit?" Brady cocked his head as if Jack were about to tell him a tale of an immense battle between him and the Ryan clan folk.

"Nay, they were hospitable enough, and have assured me there will be a room ready when I return. I've informed them that my next stay will be an extended one," Jack said, nonchalantly, slipping back into his boots.

"Stay? Why would ye do a thing like that?" Brady asked, brows knitted.

"Because, if ye must know, Brady, I am of sound mind and judgement, and I can't believe Robert Ryan had anything to do with the crime ye accuse 'im of. And for that reason, I will, however, stick around and find out what I can."

Brady scrubbed his stubbly chin and sighed. "Very well then. Just keep yer cock in yer pants. And don't go knockin' around any of them Ryan wenches. I won't be around to bail ye out this time," Brady gave a small smile, pat his friend on the back, and handed him the letter. "When will ye be bringing the livestock and other provisions?"

"Ye can expect 'em in a few days. Ye think ye can play nice 'til I return?" Jack mocked, letting Brady's jibe about knocking around the Ryan wenches slide. There were some things even Brady couldn't understand, and Jack hadn't the time or patience to explain them.

Brady sent him a warning glare. "Aye, I can behave as long as she does as she's told. If she doesn't, I'll be forced to take the switch to 'er," he replied, narrowing his gaze, gnashing his teeth. *He'd enjoy that, wouldn't he?* This situation was far worse than Jack had thought.

Jack remembered what her mother had said – Violet was doomed if she was expected to behave herself. But as far as he could see, she'd been doing just that. Her mother would be pleased to hear it. But he couldn't help but wonder how far Brady had gone with his punishments to achieve her surrender of will and spirit. *I'll have to hurry.*

Brady sent Jack away with a friendly wave and sat back in the swing on the porch. It instantly reminded him of his mother, and of simpler times.

Beneath a thick quilt, she'd cradle him for hours while they waited for the sun to peek out over the green field beyond.

Caitlyn had always loved the sunrise. She'd said it was nature's way of starting fresh – a new day, a new way of thinking. He supposed she'd been right, as he watched Violet tending the well, struggling with two heavy pails. She appeared physically stronger today, yet more compliant. However, that obstinate streak lurking inside her was yet to be eradicated. She still held her head high, with her nose in the clouds. Brady couldn't help but admire her tenacity.

As per usual, this spirited little imp had Brady's mind reeling with impure thoughts. *Why does she have to look so beautiful, even in my old clothes? I need to taste her.* The plumpness of her berry-red lips taunted him. The longing to throw her to the ground and ravage every part of her was nearly all-consuming.

Trying to remain gentlemanly for the sake of Jack's request, he refrained, causing unimaginable discomfort. '*She's an itch I can't scratch,*' he reminded himself.

It wasn't common-place to take young ladies prisoner, making farm hands out of them, but he couldn't help the joy that tickled his insides with the notion of Violet toiling in the field, or harsh, burning calluses forming upon her delicate, lily-white hands. When he determined her father's debt had been paid, no gallant, young gentleman would want to marry a lass who'd been so unceremoniously used. It wasn't lost to him that he, himself didn't fall into either category. He was neither a gentleman, nor chivalrous.

As suddenly as his lust had waned, a pang of guilt gushed in the pit of his stomach. 'Twas only a short time ago when he'd rushed to Mary's side to aid her in the very same task. But he wouldn't help Vy – he couldn't. *I must remain strong.*

Contradictory cravings forced him to retreat inside the cottage, and leave Violet to her day. It was the only way to save her from him – and save himself.

Despite Jack being the only friend she had in her present situation, Violet hadn't the opportunity to wave her goodbyes, with her arms weighed down with sloshing water. Losing herself in thought, she pictured herself scratching Brady's eyes out and screaming after Jack to take her with him – but of course, she couldn't. Instead, she immersed herself in her work, trying so hard to be patient and do as she was told. That alone was exhausting.

Her heart told her that Jack wouldn't turn back to help her; his loyalty to Brady prevented it. If she'd made even the slightest noise of distress, she'd certainly suffer Brady's wrath – that possibility alone terrified her beyond words.

With Jack long gone, Violet went about her day, checking off each task as she'd finished them. And despite her fatigue, pride of what she'd accomplished shrouded her like a warm blanket.

Living in Shannon, daughter of a wealthy ship builder, the need to learn to do such menial tasks had never emerged. It was difficult for her to understand then, just what the folks who'd kept the house running like clockwork went through daily. Now, she knew exactly what she'd taken for granted.

Sinking into the window seat, where Jack had occupied only a few hours ago, she reflected on the days duties. The breakfast she had prepared was edible enough, although the bread she'd attempted to make refused to rise. To her surprise, Brady hadn't said a word about it. No scowls, no ridicule.

For lunch she'd chopped cheese into little chunks, and sliced unripe apples she'd picked from the tree out back. When Brady merely ate them without a word, despite their tartness, and then returned to his work in the field, she'd been mighty pleased with her new talent – feeding the beast. *At least he's quiet when he's eatin'.*

Between lunch and supper, the cottage was scrubbed from top to bottom, Violet figuring it all out as she went along. She'd seen the maids doing these chores all her life, so she had some inkling on how to do them. *I think.*

When Brady returned from the field, he had with him, three plump fish that he'd caught in the river which ran alongside the property. He'd been in a better mood since this morning and he'd even had the patience to show her how to gut and prepare the catch for their supper.

"I'll only show ye this once, so ye'd best pay attention," he said, but to her relief, not exceedingly callously.

"Aye, Brady," she answered obediently, biting her bottom lip. "I'm watchin'."

"Aye. Tomorrow, I'll show ye how to saddle, feed and hitch Thunder to the plough."

"Aye, Brady." She'd forgotten to do those tasks, as she'd been so busy learning how to do the others. But to her relief, he hadn't chastised her for her neglect.

'*How am I ever going to keep up with all of this?*' she sighed.

When the meal of over-cooked, pan-fried trout had been cleared away, Violet went out to the porch where Brady was lounging in the swing, finding that he was quietly swaying, sipping his amber liquid.

"Will that be all for today? May I retire for the night?" she asked, amiably.

"Sweet, Vy. Come and sit for a moment." The words fell from his mouth with a familiar tenderness that caused her heart to flutter. He shifted to make room for her, but she didn't sit. *I can't.*

"I-I'd like to go to bed, Brady. I'm awfully tired," she whispered, praying that he remained pleasant and she would get her wish to retire peacefully.

"I said sit, Vy. I'll not tell ye again," he slurred, the ice in his tone returning. She eyed him warily, as he swallowed another gulp.

'*Oh, this is drunk Brady. I haven't met this side of him. Proceed with caution,*' she told herself, the frost surrounding her heart forming the protective shield once again. She complied and sat in the swing beside him.

"Ye know, my ma and I used to spend all our free time out here, watching Mother Nature in all Her glory," he began, "We talked a lot about the future. About *my* future. She always knew I didn't want to take over the business. She knew I wasn't cut out for it. But *he* never understood."

Brady turned and met her silent gaze. His eyes filled with water, tears he no doubt ached to shed.

I refuse to give him my pity.

"Do ye know what it's like, Violet, to have yer whole life mapped out for ye? To have everything yer heart could desire, but *want* none of it? Do ye understand what that's like?"

"Aye, I do," she replied, impassively. She couldn't tell him her complete existence felt much the same. That the pressures of being torn between two worlds – one, to take her father's seat within the company or the other, to marry a nice lad and have lots and lots of little children – nearly struck her down with ferocious severity most days. Nay, she refused to give him her inner-most secrets and desires. Brady Kelly had already taken enough. Still, the weight of his anguish threatened to crush her stubborn restraint and caused an aching inside her, a yearning to ease his pain. Until he continued.

"I'm so sure ye do," he scoffed sarcastically, rolling his eyes. "I know all about ye, Violet Ryan. Ye were to be married off to my brother, make little Kelly-Ryan pups and live in *my* grand house, bein' waited on hand and foot by people I employ. Ye were gonna' live happily ever after. 'Twas all ye ever wanted, wasn't it?" He searched her expression, pushing her to say the words, provoking a reason to lash out. "Ye knew all along about your father's plans to give yer hand to Liam, didn't ye? Even after the spectacle ye made, moonin' over me at the ball, you knew it even then, didn't ye?"

"Nay! I've heard no such thing 'til now, I swear it." Horror welled up inside her, fearing the direction this conversation had turned. The weight of his words hammering at her resolve. *A marriage contract? With Liam?*

"Ye knew it, aye, ye did." He downed the rest of his glass, her eyes glued to his every move. "When ye were wrapped in my arms, dancin' and laughin', makin' my blood boil for ye, ye were playin' a foolish little-girls' game," he growled, his piercing glare cutting her down where she sat.

The accusation hit her hard, reaching the deep pit of her stomach. But with her pride still intact, she rose from the swing and started toward the door.

"And where do ye think yer goin'?" he drawled, grabbing her arm.

"To bed, Brady. Exactly where ye ought to be goin'!" she shouted, unable to keep her temper from flaring up. It was high time she'd given him a little taste of his own medicine.

"Aye! If that's the way ye want to play it, sweet Vy, 'tis the way it'll be!" he shouted back, taking her into his arms, holding her tightly in his grasp, while she pounded his chest in attempt to break free. "Be still, wench. I'll make ye see that ye ended up with the right Kelly brother. Ye'll never lust for Liam after this night, I swear it," he roared.

Alarm bells chimed in her ears so loudly she thought her ear drums would burst. She fought against him with every step he took. But with each long stride, he grew angrier and more intent on ruining her.

Violet knew very little about the intimacies between a man and a woman, save the stories she had over-heard while the house staff went about their chores, unaware of her eavesdropping. Now, suddenly, her head was blank, like she had never heard anything on the matter before.

Fear and desperation took hold, causing her body to still.

When will I learn to keep my mouth shut?

Finally noticing she was no longer putting up a fight, Brady stopped cold in his tracks. He looked down into her unsure emerald gems and his heart instantly melted.

"Brady, I'll do whatever ye say." That one small hushed statement – spoken so softly he strained to hear – tore his heart out. "Please, not like this."

He brought her into her room and set her down upon the bed. He stood back and merely watched his little captive in silence – so accepting, yet so strong-willed. She amazed him. Her hair had fallen from its hold and spilled down around her shoulders. And despite looking quite ridiculous in his old clothing, there was no denying that an exquisite woman lay beneath.

Brady lusted for her in a way he'd never imagined. He longed to taste her lips, caress her firm breasts and discover each and every part of her. He yearned to covet the flesh that no other man had ever known.

Then, she'd done the unthinkable. Slowly, she began unbuttoning her dirty work blouse, apprehensively sliding it down her shoulders, revealing the fullest blushing breasts he'd ever set eyes upon. His trousers became uncomfortably tight and he shifted where he stood to ease the surging ache.

He realized then, that underneath her hand-me downs, she had been keeping the greatest secret. The thought of Liam ever unveiling this gift made his senses unfurl. All rational thought left his mind.

Before she could continue to undress, Brady closed the distance between them in two long strides. He pushed his body down on top of hers like a bear mauling its prey.

Cupping her breast, he caught her mouth against his in a furious crash, drinking her until his senses all ran together. It didn't matter that she hadn't returned his violent kiss; he was hell-bent on ravishing her until she screamed his name.

Damned if I need her permission!

A whimper escaped her when his teeth tore at the tender flesh of her neck. A scream garbled in her throat when his fingers dug into the soft crevasses of her hips. Only when he tasted her salty tears, did he take pause, gazing down into the pure innocence shimmering back at him. She closed her eyes, the fat droplets sliding into her hair.

Brady snapped himself back to reality.

'*Jesus sakes. What are ye doin', Kelly? She doesn't deserve this,*' he thought, shaking his head.

Rising from the bed, he pulled a blanket from the chair in the corner and quickly wrapped it around her. Shame tearing at his insides, he studied her for a moment.

Her hair was wildly disheveled, her face wet from silent tears, yet she dared not look at him.

Disgusted with himself, he left her room, gently closing the door behind him.

Hearing her sniffling from behind the door, guilt wracked every inch of his being.

'*Maybe Jack's right. What I've done to punish her father, is only punishing myself. I should 'ave let the authorities sort 'im out,*' Brady thought, regret consuming him.

For the first time since he'd taken her, Brady was filled with self-loathing, remorse, and uncertainty. It sobered him instantly.

He would have to rely on Jack to get close to the Ryan's now. Hopefully, Jack could shed some much-needed light on the situation, before something like this happened again. It was only a matter of time, and he knew it.

He briefly considered letting her go, but as stubborn as an ox, he vowed to never show weakness.

However, the time had come to stop treating her like a prisoner. The realization that she had nothing to do with his father's death was bashing him with full force.

What a fool I've been.

He was still as captivated by her as he'd been the first time he'd laid eyes upon her, and instead of making her his, he'd made sure she hated him. He vowed to change that.

∞

Violet sighed in relief when the door closed behind him. The scene played back over and over in her mind, leaving her confused and unable to rid herself of conflicting emotions. No doubt, Brady suffered as she did. His torment and shame washed over him in waves, radiating from every word he spoke, and through every erratic movement of his body. When he'd ceased his assault, she found his deepest apologies glistening in the cold eyes staring down upon her. What had he seen in hers, to force him to stop? Had he found her humiliation too much to bear?

Or had he recognised an emotion so completely identical to his own? Had he found her wanting? Could he feel the lust bubbling just beneath her brittle surface?

Violet shook her head at the ridiculousness of it all. Why did any of it matter? Why was she beginning to care so deeply for a man who'd been so cruel?

I can save him from his demons. I know I can.

She quietly wedged the chair beneath the door knob as a make-shift locking device, then washed and dressed for bed while fresh tears still emerged. Only now, she cried for *him*. Sinking into her pillow, the inner turmoil had become down-right overwhelming.

Brady was nowhere to be found when Violet arose the next morning. The only proof that he'd awoken early and had left, was a bouquet of fresh flowers tied together with the scraggly piece of yarn that had fallen from her hair the night before, neatly placed on the kitchen table. A white leaf of folded paper was laid against them, simply saying, "No work for you today, sweet Vy."

FOURTEEN

When Jack returned to the Kelly's stronghold, he was met in the study by Liam. The funeral had clearly taken a toll on him, as did trying to run the business, the household and addressing the clan's concerns about the future of their lands. With a permanent crease furrowing his brow and a scowl to match, the youngest Kelly appeared well past his years. Jack had wondered if the lad was capable of handling his father's obligations, but the evidence lingering in Liam's hazel eyes screamed that he indeed was not.

The upheaval amongst the clansmen was the most taxing. Some wanted a war to be waged between Kelly and Ryan, the less civilized clansmen contemplated setting out to seek vengeance. To kill, pillage and rape the Ryan kin folk. Liam tried his best to set his people's minds at ease and keep the peace, but it was becoming more and more difficult, especially with the absence of the new Kelly lord, Brady.

"Jack, I just don't know what to tell them? They're all looking at me for answers, but I have none. I can't even guarantee the business will survive.

"Even without the merge we could have kept it going, but without father's contacts and savvy business sense, I just don't know now," Liam moaned, tearing at his cravat. "And where is Brady when our people need him? Off hiding at the cottage, as usual." Jack nodded in understanding, but despite Liam's desperation, he had to set the lad straight.

"Nay, ye've got it all wrong. Yer mistaken if ye think he is in hidin'." Jack wanted to tell him that Brady was in perpetual torment, that the young lady who kept him company was also holding him hostage. But he feared he would say too much, causing Liam to run after his would-be bride. "He's got his reasons, and ye best respect his decision."

"Why is he keeping her? What purpose will it serve? You know Da had arranged it with Lord Ryan for Violet and I to be married?" Liam said, his gaze drifting off into nothingness.

No doubt, Liam imagined what it would have been like to marry Violet. Having the two families merged would result in a powerhouse of ship manufacturing. His knowledge and ability, matched hers. There would have been nothing they couldn't have accomplished when the time came to take over. Now, he'd been left with no wife, and no brother. Jack couldn't help but pity the lad.

"Well ye know Brady's a hot-blooded and temperamental fella, his actions precede his rational thinkin' sometimes, but he's got good intentions – or at least, he *had* good intentions," Jack said, trying to make Liam understand.

"Good intentions? What good could possibly come out of this?" Liam pinned Jack with a disbelieving scowl, waiting for an answer. When Jack offered nothing further, he pushed, "And what do you mean, he *had* good intentions? Has he changed his mind on the whole thing? Has he realized that keeping her prisoner will solve nothing?"

"Well," Jack began, "no, not yet. And if you're wonderin' if he's hurt her, I don't think so. But he doesn't want her family to know that. As far as they're concerned, Brady's mistreating her in unfathomable ways."

Liam shook his head, clearly unable to grasp the logic behind it. Jack knew Liam needed his brother, and for the first time in their lives Brady wasn't there for him.

Jack explained what he could about Brady's planned vengeance. They talked for hours but no matter how Jack spun things in attempt to mollify the distraught lad, the conversation kept coming back to the fact that Brady was the clan lord now, and an absent one. Jack also thought it strange, that Liam hadn't seemed at all upset about Brady keeping his almost betrothed holed up at the cottage.

'Doesn't he care about her being with another man?' he wondered silently.

"Liam, what exactly did Robert Ryan promise ye with regards to Violet?" Jack dared to ask.

Liam rose from his chair and paced the floor. "The night of the ball, he had watched Violet and Brady dancing, talking, laughing, etc, etc," he rolled his eyes and fashioned hand gestures to make his point. "Her father didn't like it one bit. I mean, everyone knows Brady's reputation of being a rake and a rogue, and an ill-tempered one at that. So, the night of the merge at the pub, Robert and I talked in great detail about what he expected from his daughter."

"Which was?" Jack cocked his eyebrow.

"Violet is his greatest accomplishment and he had no mind in telling me so. She has been bred and tutored since she's been old enough to walk and talk, not exclusively for marriage, but to take over for him when he became too old and feeble to build great ships."

"And what of it? He hadn't had any sons, so of course he would ready his only heir," Jack added.

"Well yes, but she's twenty and two, still unmarried, with no prospects. Sure, she'd had some suitors come to call upon her, but her father hadn't let her meet any of them."

"So, he's prevented her from marrying all these years?"

"Of course. Robert had hoped that one day, he would find a lad much like me – level headed, intelligent and business oriented. That way, if she turned out to be incapable of running things on her own, she would have a husband to help her along," Liam paused for a moment and then exploded. "That's why I know Robert didn't kill Da! There was too much at risk! It just doesn't make sense!" he blew out, finally collapsing into his leather chair, obviously exhausted.

Jack went to his side, and laid a steadying hand on his shoulder. He couldn't help but notice that Liam looked so child-like in his father's seat, despite aging ten years in the past few weeks.

"I know it doesn't make sense, Liam, but I promised yer brother I'd do all I could to find out what happened that night. If, for any reason it was in fact Robert, wouldn't ye like to know what his motives were?" Jack tried his best to calm the weary youth.

"Yes, I would, but…"

"Leave it to me. I am returnin' to Clare in a few days' time, once I've handled some things for yer brother. While I'm there, I intend to learn as much as I can about the clan and unravel this mess."

"What have you to do for Brady?" Liam asked wide-eyed.

"Oh, don't concern yerself with such things. He just needs some provisions. Supplies and such. He's tryin' to make it a workin' farm again. Ye just stay here and keep doing what yer doin'. Yer people need ye right now, don't fail them," Jack said light-heartedly, and then gave him a cheeky salute good-bye.

"Wait!" Liam quickly rose. "How long do you think he'll keep her out there?"

"Why? Are ye finally concerned that yer brother is closer to your betrothed than ye'll ever be?" Jack chuckled. He hadn't meant to sound callous, but the snarky reply just kind of fell out of his mouth. When Liam didn't answer, Jack knew the answer.

Business. 'Tis all business with this one.

Jack went about his duties the very next morning, trying not to get stopped and questioned along the way by any of the house staff or Kelly kin folk. Guaranteed, everyone was wondering what Brady was up to, and most probably thought he was a cruel bastard for taking Violet prisoner in the first place. Jack didn't have time to deal with such opinions, so he took the corridors less travelled, avoiding as many people as he could.

When he reached the massive kitchen, Mary was working away with her hands down into a huge pan of dough. Her hair was clinging to her plump round face with sweat, and her cheeks were as rosy as ever. Jack made his entrance known, clearing his throat.

Her eyes instantly lit up when she noticed him in the doorway.

"Little Jack!" she said, hauling her hands from the sticky mess and wiping them in her apron. "Ye've returned!"

"Aye, Mary. But not for long. I've come to rob the kitchen of some necessities for Brady. What can ye spare?" Jack smiled and gave her a tight squeeze.

"Brady!" she blew out. "What am I gonna do with that boy? Keepin' that poor wee thing up there against her will. I hope he's ashamed of hi'self. I'd send nuthin' if 'twas only he, but I guess I'll have to come up with the grub, for the girl's sake."

"Now now, love," Jack laughed. "'Tis not as bad as ye think. B'tween you an' me, there's more goin' on than people think."

Mary put her hand to her mouth in shock.

"What do ye mean, Jack? He's not been inappropriate with her virtue, has he? I'll whoop 'em m'self."

"No no, Mary, he thinks his only motives are to punish the Ryan clan, but he's really doin' himself in." Jack knew he could trust Mary like no other; she'd been like a mother to him his whole life. "I think he's sick with himself over what his temper allowed him to do. All the time they're spendin' there together is only pushin' them closer. He'll never let her go…he loves her. He just doesn't know it yet."

Mary laughed at the suggestion, for she had never known Brady to love anything or anyone, aside from his own mother.

"Is that why ye've been goin' along with this plan of his? I must say, I'm quite surprised at ye for havin' anything to do with it," Mary scolded, crunching her brows together, waggling a doughy finger at him.

"Well, I admit my role has become a bit of a nuisance. Once I deliver the supplies to Brady at the cottage, I'm travellin' to her home again. He's tasked me with keepin' Lord Ryan informed about her well-being, lyin' through my teeth I might add to make them suffer.

"I am *supposed* to be carryin' correspondence back and forth. But I've decided that I'll not cause further distress by giving them Brady's letters – no matter what my orders are. I'll give them my own assessment instead. If I must tell a few white lies of my own to keep her mother's heart from breakin', I will," he explained, tearing into a fresh biscuit. "I'm extendin' my time in Clare to sort the whole thing out. Who knows, I might learn more about what actually happened that night.

"Rest assured, Mary, I'll look in on them before I leave for Clare. I won't leave 'er there if things have gotten out of hand."

"Honestly, Jack, is there no other way?" Mary tsked her disapproval and shook her head, pushing another tasty treat his way.

"Not in Brady's mind there's not. Time…this entire mess needs time to work itself out." Jack's gaze fell from hers, to the biscuit he was mangling between his fingers. "Mary? How did the funeral go? Is Liam gonna hold it together 'til Brady returns, ye think?"

"The funeral was a beautiful send-off, love. The entire clan was 'ere to pay their respects, and said such good t'ings about Lord Kelly." Mary wiped a tear from her cheek and sniffled. "Liam will be fine, lad, ye have no worry 'bout that. He's more like his da than he knows. A strong boy, a born leader."

"Glad to hear it," Jack said affectionately, resting his hand upon her shoulder. "Now! Those provisions for Brady…here's a list. I'll go and hitch up the wagon. I'll be back to load it all aboard soon." Mary nodded frantically, still dabbing at the corners of her eyes.

Jack disappeared into the stable and was grateful not to run into any of the hired hands out there. He hitched up two of the finest stags to the sturdiest wagon. He loaded the wagon with feed for the horses, feed for the pigs and chickens he'd not yet acquired, and four heavy bags of seed for Brady's summer crop.

'*I hope these horses prove to be good on a plough. Thunder's not built for such hard labour,*' he mused, looking over the sturdy beasts with approval.

Then, a nicker and blow caught his attention. "Hmm, what a beautiful mare. Violet will love 'er," Jack whispered deviously, spying the majestic animal. The sleek, dark brown filly was Liam's newest purchase, bought only a few months before life had become much more complicated. Jack smoothed his gloved hand along the length of her forelock to her muzzle appreciatively.

The late Caitlyn Kelly's mare whinnied competitively in the stall beside him, but there was no way he could gift that particular horse to Violet without angering Brady. Instead, Liam's latest addition to the stable would do quite nicely.

He tied the horse to the wagon, and then moved the cargo to the rear of the kitchen, where he and Mary finished loading up the supplies.

When Mary noticed the tethered mare, her eye cocked suspiciously. "What are ye doin' with Liam's new mare?" she asked with a slight waggle of her salt and pepper brow.

"Violet's new mare," Jack corrected. "She needs a friend."

"Lord Brady's not gonna like this one bit, ye know. What if she uses it to escape?" Mary fretted, wringing her apron into a mangled mess.

"Then, either she would find herself lost in the middle of nowhere and *want* to return to Brady, or he would certainly seek 'er out and bring 'er back. Either way, I'm unconcerned," Jack laughed.

"What are ye up to, Jack Manning?" Mary kissed him quickly on the cheek before he climbed into the buggy seat. Glancing down at her, he smiled devilishly and winked urging the team onward with a *'tck, tck'*. "Just make sure they don't kill one another. I do hope ye know what ye're doin'," she shouted as he pulled away ignoring her warning.

Jack's next stop was to a small farm on the outskirts of the village. There, he purchased three of the fattest pigs he'd ever seen, a dozen hens and two hefty roosters. The old farmer gave Jack a great deal on the entire package when he learned who they were for. And to Jack's relief, the haggard old man never asked any meddlesome questions concerning the new, and absent lord of Kelly's Keep.

Jack took his time on his way back to the cottage, stopping to make camp for the night in a heavily wooded area along the lonely road. He imagined Violet making her great escape, how scared she would be if caught out there all alone. He almost regretted taking Liam's new horse as a gift for her.

'Perhaps Brady won't even let her accept it,' he thought, curling up next to a tiny fire.

No matter how much his body protested, his mind kept him from blissful slumber. His thoughts were of the Ryan's – Violet included.

He'd be returning to her people, staying in her home to learn as much as he could about her family. Something about the entire situation niggled at him, tormenting his psyche. His and Liam's discussion came to mind. He couldn't help but agree that if Violet was set to be married to the youngest Kelly, then Robert would gain nothing in killing Sean. *'Why would he sever ties that hadn't been bound yet?'* Jack grunted in annoyance and pulled his quilt up and over his head.

The next afternoon, Jack arrived at the cottage, and surprisingly, found Brady in the field, reins wound about his back and neck, sweating bullets, red-faced, and roaring at Thunder.

"Move, God damn ye! I said move!" Brady's foul mood and abominable temper had gone from bad to worse.

"I'll fix that!" Jack hollered, approaching his friend with instinctive caution. "'Tis not his fault. He's no work horse, but I've brought ye two that's used to it."

"Thank Jesus! I was about to shoot 'im myself," Brady snorted, although Jack knew he'd never do such a thing. Thunder was as much as Brady's friend as Jack was.

"Come on down to the cottage. I've got the supplies ye ordered. I'll help ye unpack 'em over a cup of ale," Jack offered.

"Nay!" Brady yelled, making Jack flinch and regard him with curious apprehension. "I mean, I can do it my-self. Or I'll have the wench do it later."

"Oh, still callin' her the wench are ye?" Jack mocked.

"Aye, and she's not fit for company today. So ye can just leave it, and be on yer way," Brady snapped.

A familiar queasy feeling formed in the pit of Jack's stomach. He knew Brady's rotten temper, and had even witnessed firsthand what he was capable of when forced. Something was very wrong.

"What have ye done, Brady?" Jack probed, grabbing Brady's arm, anchoring them to the soil beneath their feet. Jack studied the sullen face before him. Regret, sadness, and self-loathing gazed back, glistening in pools of oblivion. While Brady could attempt to mask his feelings with animosity and violence, Jack could see right through him. "Sit. Start talkin'."

Brady slumped onto the half-ploughed soil, pulled off his dusty cap, and rubbed his sweaty forehead with the back of his shirt sleeve. Jack sat down next to him, like he had when they were boys – when Brady had been chastised by his father for God knows what transgression he'd committed.

"Go see for yourself, then. But I warn ye now, she deserved it." Jack faced the cottage, noting the lack of life from within. He had thought it strange when Violet hadn't come out to greet him when the noisy wagon had clinked and banged its way into the yard.

"Nay. I'll not go in there, 'til ye tell me what I'm facin'. Is she alright?" Jack asked, raising his voice, blood and angst rushing through his veins.

Brady sighed and began, "After ye left, we had an argument," he started, leaving out the part where he had been a drunken lout and tried to take advantage of her. "And well, things got a little heated. But I apologised."

"Go on," Jack urged, his gaze still fixed on Violet's stone and sod prison.

"The next day, I'd gone to the trouble of leavin' her some flowers and a note tellin''er she'd not have any chores on the morrow. Ye know…a way of sayin' how sorry I was for…just, how sorry I was. And ye know what she had the nerve to do?"

"Did she shove 'em up yer arse, stem first?" Jack chuckled, trying to ease the air around them.

"Nay. When the spitey wench rose the next morning, she viciously ripped them to shreds and penned me a little reply."

"Well, what did it say?" Jack asked, thinking it couldn't be that bad.

Brady pulled her reply from his shirt pocket and unfolded it. "It said, and I quote, '*Ye should be ashamed of yerself. Yer a scoundrel and a sorry excuse for a man. Liam would have been a better everything than you, includin' a lover. Yer mother must be turnin' over in her grave. Never think that flowers could make what ye did last night all right. I hate ye, Brady Kelly.*' How 'bout that? She hates me. Even when I try to apologise, she hates me."

Jack felt a pang of pride that Violet wouldn't just let Brady away with whatever misdoing he'd committed, but knew that comparing him to Liam and the mere mention of his mother, was the gravest mistake she could make.

"Those are only words, Brady. What happened next?" Concern for the girl had Jack wanting to run from the field and see to her, but he waited to hear the rest of the sordid details.

"Aye, only words," Brady hissed. "She was in 'er room when I read them and 'tis a good thing. I would have choked the life out of her on the spot I think," Brady paused, shook his head and then, "Well, who do she think she is? Comparing me to Liam. Saying Ma would have been ashamed of me?"

"Brady, please don't tell me ye hurt her 'cause of something she'd said in anger. She's every right to be angry. I don't know what provoked the argument the night before, but all else considered, I'd have stuck a knife in ye by now."

"I might have to watch out for that," Brady mumbled, quite shamefully. "When I tried to open her door, to give her a good talkin' to, it was barred from the inside. I hammered on it, but she just cursed me out and refused to open it. So, I broke the bloody thing down. I went to the shed, brought in the axe and chopped away at it 'til there was nothing between us but flarin' hot tempers.

"She missed my ear by an inch when she pitched the water jug at me, but I didn't reach her in time to stop the wash basin from cold clockin' me in the side of the head.

"I was furious by then – and left with little self-control. I s'pose ye could say I went blank…mad with fury. When I finally regained my senses, all I knew was that I had given her a whoopin' she'll not soon forget. And I'm not sorry, I won't apologise. I hope she's finally learned a lesson," Brady lied.

Jack stared at his friend for a very long time, saying nothing. There were no words that could convey how deeply disgusted and ashamed of Brady he was in that moment. He pictured Violet being brutalized by this beast of a man sitting next to him and thought it hard to believe they were ever friends. Then and there, he'd made a decision.

"I won't be returnin' after this trip. I refuse to play messenger in yer game, Brady. When ye were merely spinnin' lies of cruelty, I didn't mind so much, but makin' those lies a reality, is something I refuse to witness.

"I'll find out what happened to yer da as quickly as I can. Not for your sake, but for hers." Jack rose from the ground, and left Brady to sit in his self-inflicted misery.

When Jack entered the quiet dwelling, he could see the remnants of the disaster which had broken out the day before. Neither Brady nor Violet had even cleaned up the broken dishes left in the kitchen, or straightened up the toppled over furniture throughout.

"Lady Violet?" Jack asked softly, "'Tis Jack. Are ye awake?" When Jack reached her doorway, and inspected the destruction of the frame, he was appalled. Looking beyond the opening, his gaze fell upon a tightly wound bundle of blankets in the middle of the bed. She was facing the window on the far side of the room, and he suddenly became afraid of what he'd face when he moved around to the other side.

"Violet? May I come in?" he asked, gently.

"Aye, Jack. But stay over there. Ye can't see me like this," she sobbed. He wondered how long she had been laying there with fear and pain consuming her. Ignoring her wishes, Jack made his way to the other side, where he could examine Brady's handiwork for himself.

He tenderly moved the blanket from her face, concern for the girl clawing its way inside him. He winced at seeing her swollen bottom lip and the smeared blood stains on her chin. Her matted hair clung to her cheek so terribly, that when he tried to free the locks, she flinched at the sting.

"Oh, wee lass, what have ye gotten yerself into?" Jack sighed, disappearing into the kitchen. Returning soon after with a bowl of fresh water, he fished a kerchief from his pocket and soaked it in the frigid liquid.

She tried to sit up when Jack perched on the side of her bed, but began to sob helplessly at the mere effort. No doubt, her injuries went deeper than the surface. Wringing his cloth, shaking his head with disapproval, Jack gently wiped the blood from her face, revealing a bruise beneath.

"Now now, don't cry. I'll fix ye up, no fear. Can ye tell me what else hurts?" he asked, sweetly.

"Just achy. Though, nothin' hurts as much as my pride," she replied, forcing a small smile.

Jack washed her as gingerly as he possibly could. He was beside himself with guilt for having left her there; knowing full well that Brady's rage could rear its ugly head. He despised the thought of having to leave her yet again, but what other choice did he have? Duty dictated he'd do as Brady commanded…but to what end?

"Now, what possessed ye to inflame 'im in such a way? Ye know he's ill-tempered," Jack asked, fumbling through her chest of drawers, pulling out a fresh summer dress. Gauging her negative reaction – pitifully shaking her head – he carefully refolded it and put it back. Curiously, she nodded her approval when he presented a set of Brady's hand-me-downs.

Jack understood perfectly. *Eliminating the temptation.* Yet he was unsure of whose idea it had been for her to take such measures.

Carefully and chivalrously, Jack helped her dress, then led her from the room, where she could see for the first time, the damage Brady had inflicted upon the cottage after she'd lost consciousness.

"Oh, Jack. I must've made him so angry. I didn't witness any of this," she whispered, a shaky hand covering her lips.

Jack was a little relieved to know she'd only received a few blows, that her body hadn't been the battling ram which had caused the chaotic state of the rest of the place.

"Aye. He was livid, by the looks of things," Jack said, setting a chair back up on its legs. "Ye know I can't stay, right?" he asked regretfully, as if each syllable would haunt him until the end of days. "Rest assured, I am not with him in this anymore, so I don't mind tellin' ye what I'm up to. Ye have to listen carefully. Understand everythin' I say and tell Brady nothin' of this conversation. Ye think ye can do that?" he asked, bending down to help her pick up large shards of glass; the remnants of the sugar dish.

"Aye. I'll do whatever ye say. Whatever *he* says," she replied, wretchedly.

Hearing her say it like that was nearly his undoing. *Whatever he says*. He remembered how her mother had described her. She'd been a free-spirit who rarely conformed to conventional society rules, and now, that feisty, strong-willed girl no longer existed. '*Damn him,*' Jack thought, furiously.

"Good, because he won't let ye go, Violet. He'll never let ye go. At least, not until I prove that yer father is innocent."

"Ye believe he is, don't ye?" she asked with hope glistening in her red-rimmed eyes.

"Aye, I do. I just have to prove it. But, I can't stay in Galway and still accomplish that. So, you'll remain here with his mean, ill-mannered disposition, for just a while longer. We have no choice.

"I wish there was another way, but sadly, I can't just snatch ye away from 'im and take ye back to yer kin. He'd have me hunted, and most likely gutted for such a betrayal." That fleeting moment of hope disappeared from her eyes, replaced with despair. "Ahh, now, don't worry. Ye don't know 'im like I do. He's been through an awful lot this past year, and he's still workin' through it. Losin' his ma and his da has kinda pushed 'im toward madness. He might be in a dark, dark place, but there's still good in 'im too. I promise. Ye just have to be on yer best behaviour, 'til I get back."

"I know, and I will. I don't think I'll live through another punishment. I can't endure any more," she trembled. Jack held her in his arms for a quick moment and then looked tenderly into her eyes.

"I don't think ye'll have to. Ye see the bruises he's left on your pretty, fair face?" Jack asked, turning her toward the glass hanging on the wall. "This is nothing compared to what he feels right now. There's never been a guiltier conscience. He may not admit it, but I know 'im. He hates himself for what he's done. But more importantly, he knows everything ye said to 'ím was the truth."

"I should 'ave never wedged that chair beneath the door knob to keep 'im out. I knew it would incense 'im. And I had no right to write what I did. I knew how his father pushed him to be more like Liam. I knew about the closeness between him and his mother, and I used it all to hurt 'im," she cried, throwing her arms up with exasperation.

"There, there, wee lass, 'tis all said and done. Hopefully ye'll not repeat the same mistakes. And one more thing. Because he practically never apologises for any-thing, *when* he does, cherish it. Brady really gotta dig deep to admit he's wrong."

Violet nodded, but Jack suspected that she couldn't quite comprehend the weight of his warning. He hoped with all he had, that Brady would swallow his damn, foolish pride and make things right.

"See ye soon, Mr. Manning," Violet replied with a dead-pan expression, no doubt exasperated about how Jack seemed to be siding with Brady. He understood how it might look like that, but he couldn't tell her that noth-ing was further from the truth.

Jack left her to finish putting things right and went outside where Brady was still sitting in the field, immo-bilized, deep in thought and wretchedness. The last time Jack had seen his friend cry was when they were chil-dren, but as Jack approached him in the dusty field, the sight of Brady's shoulders retching, and the echo of faint sobs filled him with fear and unease. The situation was precarious, at best.

Jack quietly came upon Brady and sat down beside him. When Brady didn't speak, he draped his arm around his friend for comfort.

"'Tis quite the mess ye've made," Jack said, softly. "She'll live, but that can't happen again, ye know it can't. She'll behave too, and so will you."

"I…I don't know what happened, Jack. I snapped. Like a powder keg exploded in my mind and I couldn't think straight. All I could see was father's scolding face, mother's disappointed eyes, and Liam. Liam holding her instead of me. Everything she said was true and I punished 'er for it," Brady sobbed. "Ye know what started the fight the night before? 'Twas the reminder that she was promised to him. I was drunk and almost forced her into bed. I almost violated her, Jack. What's wrong with me?"

"Yer jealous. Ye don't want to admit it and I know it didn't start out that way, but ye care about 'er more than ye know. But if ye care for her, like I think ye do, ye'll not hurt her ever again. Just look at what ye've done to yerself."

"Care about her? Jealous? I've never been jealous in my life!" Brady seemed wounded at the accusation, but in the depths of his being, he had to know Jack was right. "She's the only retribution I have against 'er father."

"That all stops here and now, or ye can consider me retired. Ye'll be nice, ye'll treat 'er with respect. I'm not sayin' she can't help out 'round here, but if ye feel ye need to keep 'er here 'til ye know what happened between Robert and yer da, then so be it, but on my terms, Brady. Mine.

"If I find one hair harmed on 'er pretty little head when I return to fetch 'er, I'll hand 'er over to Liam myself."

"Return for her? What do ye mean?" Brady had ceased snivelling, by now and seemed to be finally heeding Jack's words.

"I'll not see ye 'til the identity of the murderous bastard's been revealed. And because I know in my heart, it wasn't Robert, Violet will be returned to her kin, unharmed, virtue intact." Jack rose and held out a hand to Brady, but instead of accepting the offer, he glared at Jack with seething venom. It was the first time since they'd been friends, that they *weren't* friends. When Brady got to his feet of his own volition, Jack added, "Go unpack yer provisions. I've brought a gift for 'er, as well. And ye *will* let her enjoy it. I think she's earned it."

They strolled into the yard quietly, side by side, without a word exchanged between them.

Brady's eyes widened when he spotted the filly still tethered to the wagon. Turning to Jack, his lips parted in protest, but slapped them tightly shut when Jack met his cold glare with a warning.

Jack freed the mare, then led her to the barn while Brady watched on, brooding and disgruntled.

"She'll run," he whispered.

FIFTEEN

Brady cursed Jack for bringing her such a gift. The conniving, miserable bastard hadn't even stayed long enough to give it to her himself.

'*Now she'll think it's from me,*' Brady thought, pigheadedly. While his feelings toward Violet and his own behaviour were teetering on the brink of insanity, he flatout refused to let her think the horse was an extended olive branch. He'd be damned if he'd give her the opportunity to tell him to shove it up his arse.

The night of the row, he'd slept in the barn to avoid facing what he'd done – to both Violet and his mother's home. He knew the fallout would be dreadful, he knew he'd feel the pain and regret of his actions. Truth be told, he already did, even without seeing the chaos he'd created. And he *was* sorry, no matter what he'd said to Jack, he hadn't meant to hurt her – not to that extent.

Scare her into behaving, yes. To make her imprisonment unpleasant, absolutely. But to physically hurt her? Never. He truly did care about her and somewhere deep down, he knew he was falling in love with the hotheaded little minx.

Was this what love felt like? A bone-crushing anguish eating him from the inside out? The dark, ominous place his thoughts seemed to go to, when another man became his rival, sure didn't feel like love. Even if that other man was his own brother. *Because he's my brother.*

He tried to reason with himself, tried to convince his own psyche that it was merely jealousy; that she was nothing more than his possession – a toy to use in his wicked game of revenge. But there was no denying he'd rather die than see something happen to her, especially now and especially at his own hand.

Even if he couldn't admit it aloud yet, Brady's actions spoke volumes. Why had he become so enraged when her betrothal to Liam was thrown in his face, if his feelings didn't run deep?

The saddest part of the entire conundrum was that because of all he'd done to make her loathe him, she'd never return his love. The realization made his skin crawl, made him want to throw himself to the wolves; he deserved nothing less.

'*Time to face 'er*,' Brady sighed, urging himself into the cottage, petrified of what he might find.

He slowly opened the door, half expecting another flying projectile to come floating across the room. Instead, he found Violet softly humming a tune, sweeping the floor. He stood frozen in the doorway, as if his presence should evoke some type of reaction, but she carried on with lacklustre indifference.

The angry red welt on her chin and the blue tinted lump on the side of her forehead caused his head to spin, as he tried to remember how they got there. Had he backhanded her? Was it a full-on fisted punch? *God, please…tell me I didn't strike 'er with a brutal fist.*

And then it hit him.

All the memories of his cruelty and violence came flooding back like a torrent in a monsoon.

The instant her first weapon had hit its mark, he'd leapt to the other side of the room like a hungry panther; quickly and deadly. He'd shaken her with massive hands until he could hear her teeth rattle and her bones crack, but it wasn't enough to silence her venomous tongue. She'd cursed him to hell, called him the cold, heartless bastard that he really was.

With a steely backhanded whack across the face, he'd managed to temporarily shut her up, sending her flying backwards into the corner. Spitting the oozing blood from her mouth, she rose and roared, "*Ye thought I'd lay with the likes of you? You'll never have me. You'll never control me! To hell with you, Brady Kelly*!" Hearing those words spewing from her lips was the strangest thing he'd ever heard at the time, for the Violet he'd grown to know would never shout such profanity. Her vulgarity elevated his fury, causing the palm of his hand to strike mechanically and reflexively, making contact with her cheek again. The second violent blow sent her flying, banging her forehead against the dresser, and then her lifeless frame slid down in a heap onto the floor.

Violet didn't move. She'd finally been silenced.

'Jesus! Open yer damn eyes. Is she breathing?' he remembered thinking as his lungs seemed to crush beneath his ribs.

Then, panic set in. Blood trickled down the side of her head. She lay perfectly still and silent. He immediately picked her up, laid her on her bed, listening to her chest to see if she was breathing. With his ear nearly touching her breast, he watched for a sign of fluttering eye lids, for a quivering lip, for the rise and fall of her chest. Something…anything.

Brady let out a howl and shook her limp body. "Wake up, damn ye!"

Finally, the gurgle of a shallow intake of air filled the room. He waited for the exhale with fists of his own hair tangled within his fingers. When what felt like an eternity had passed, Violet's breaths steadied. What he wouldn't have given at that moment for her emerald eyes to flitter open, but he didn't suspect that would happen any time soon. Regardless, Brady silently thanked his long-forgotten Gods that she'd survive.

Relieved and completely exhausted, Brady covered her with a thick blanket and left her room. That's when the unrelenting self-disgust took hold, resulting in a path of destruction left in its wake. Broken dishes, upturned furniture…nothing had been safe from Brady's vehement shame.

After he'd ravaged the place once regarded as a safe haven, he'd gone to the barn and gotten thoroughly and completely drunk, refusing to think about her or worry over her well-being.

Even despite his throbbing head the next morning, he'd never worked so hard in his life. He'd stayed out in the field the entire day and into the night, without even a bite to settle his queasy stomach.

Standing face to face with her now, he couldn't help but marvel at her strength and resilience. If he was even half the man he aught to have been, he would have had the cottage cleaned from top to bottom, instead of having fled the scene to drown himself in a tankard of moonshine. If he'd been a better man, none of this would have happened to begin with. So many regrets, so much he couldn't take back.

Amongst the rubble, she dutifully went about putting the cottage back in order, heightening Brady's sense of self-disgust. Making things worse, she refused to meet his steely gaze. What would she find behind his eyes? Would she see remorse and sorrow there? Was her indifference a sign of forgiveness? How could she pretend it hadn't happened when she was cleaning up the mess *he'd* made?

"Evenin', Brady," she said with a stale, yet cordial tone. He still couldn't find the words to even reply to her forced pleasantries.

He watched her as she worked, marvelling at the way she moved – this simplest task somehow more provocative than it should have been. He wanted nothing more than to bury his face in her satin red hair and breathe in the light scent of her – show her how sorry he truly was.

Now that he had come to terms with his feelings for Violet, there was no denying that he'd probably loved her from the first day they'd met. Brady had never believed in such miracles as love at first sight, but he'd almost lost her, and now those once disregarded sentiments were confirmed. He just couldn't forsake them any longer.

Silently and uncomfortably, he strolled to his mother's favourite chair by the window, taking a seat, watching in awe, this wonderful creature before him. His heart ached remembering the pain he'd caused. Yet, just as quickly, his loins began to throb when his mind wandered back to her sitting on her bed, so willing to surrender to him and his savage male need.

He shook those thoughts from his mind, struggling with the man-beast within him. Jack was right, he'd have to be on his best behaviour, or else he'd lose her forever. He'd come so close already.

But now, all he wanted to do was make up for each and every misdoing he'd committed, make the best of each and every moment he was fortunate enough to spend with her.

"Are ye hungry, Brady?" she sweetly asked. She noticed him watching her for a moment, and then repeated her question. He still said nothing. "Brady?"

Finally finding his tongue, he replied in a deep, low baritone, "Aye?"

"After ye've had supper, will ye teach me how to tend the animals Jack brought?"

He blankly stared at her without a reply, noting the change in her expression. Her eyes became glassy and her cheeks burned crimson, waiting for him to respond. *'That's fear, right there,'* he thought, disgracefully.

The time to repair their rapport was now. No more would his presence turn her into an anxious, scared little mouse.

"Aye, Violet. We can start that as soon as I've had time to wash and eat. We also have much to discuss," he replied gruffly and then disappeared into his room, surveying the damage he'd done to her room and to her door along the way. That door had offered the only privacy she'd have, and he'd even robbed her of that. *'A damn, jealous fool ye are, Kelly,'* he mused, shaking his head, slamming his door shut.

When Brady emerged from his room a short time later, Violet was patiently waiting at the table for him to join her. She had made quite a lovely meal of boiled eggs, and fried pork rashers. Flanking the chipped plates set out before them was a pot of piping hot coffee.

Brady was pleased with her efforts, and amazed that with little or no instruction, she'd managed to learn this all on her own. *Bright little vixen.*

"This looks tasty," Brady praised, relieved when she accepted the compliment with a graceful smile. "But before we sup, I've got somethin' I gotta do." He turned on his heels, taking a few long strides toward her demolished door. It was beyond repair. "If ye've got no privacy, then neither will I," he said, picking up the axe, still laying amongst the splintered rubble.

Shooting her a wicked grin, Brady heaved the iron into the wood, chuckling under his breath with each slice, at how she flinched and gaped at him like he'd lost his mind. *Perhaps I have lost m'bloody mind!*

When there were no barriers left for either of them to hide behind, Brady returned to the table, sat and laid a napkin in his lap, quite proud of his handiwork. "There! Dig in."

"I can't believe ye did that," she whispered, pleasantly, yet undoubtedly more than a little shocked, marked by her wide, curious eyes and gaping mouth. He vowed to find more reasons to please and surprise her.

Struggling to find the courage to say what needed to be said, Brady shifted in his seat. *Coward! Ask her how she's feelin', for Christ sakes!*

He cleared his throat. "Ye look well. I'm happy to see it," he said through a mouth full of meat.

"Aye, I am. Thank ye."

Nearly losing all patience with the small talk, he forced himself to remember that she feared him now above all else, and he shouldn't expect too much by way of in-depth conversation. It would take time to mend all he'd torn down. Some part of him though, wished she'd send him to hell on her tongue again, but the spirited girl that he'd brought to the cottage had become a stale, frigid woman. Knowing he was the cause of such a travesty nearly unravelled and ruined him. He shifted in his chair uncomfortably once again, and drew a long deep breath.

"Things will be changin' 'round here," he blurted out. Violet blinked twice, laying her napkin on the table, alongside her knife. Brady's tone softened, noting how close her hand remained next to the inadequate blade. It might not kill, but it could certainly draw blood. "I mean, what happened here the other night will never happen again." When she didn't reply or react, he knew he'd lost her to mistrust and fear. How could he expect any different?

The Violet from days gone by, would have slapped him, and petitioned the Devil to make a ladder out of his spine. At the very least, she might have sneered and declared her refusal to trust a single word he said. But the mute woman before him seemed unaffected by his words, and so she simply nodded.

"No, no, I mean it." He rose from his chair and rushed to kneel at her side, looking up at her with tough determination. "We have to change everythin' we've been doin'. Mostly, I have to change."

"Are ye lettin' me go home?" she murmured, hopefully, peering down, searching his expression. When he quietly shook his head, tears welled behind her eyes.

"But, it won't be like b'fore. Ye're not gonna be my prisoner, Violet. I want ye to stay here with me…help me." Could she not see how utterly burdened he was? Couldn't she recognise his inner chaos? While he knew she couldn't forgive him, might she be ready to forget for just a little while, and try to live in harmony?

"Whatever ye say, Brady," she sighed, defeated. "If I'm not permitted to return home, then I'll do whatever is asked of me," she added, gloomily.

Although she was being agreeable, it was like he'd just lost a battle. He had wanted her compliant and obedient, but she was without thoughts and wishes of her own now. Frustration mounted, making him second-guess his decision. He would rather have a sliver of the girl he'd met, than the ghost of her. '*What do ye want, Kelly? One minute, ye want 'er obedient. The next, ye want the lass to fight.*' Brady's own thoughts seemed to sound a lot like Jack Manning.

With the reminder of his best friend, he was hit with a bright idea. Rising quickly – a little too quickly – Brady stood, making Violet flinch, raising her arms to shield an impending attack. Knowing her fear ran that deep, Brady became heart sick. '*I deserved that,*' he thought, gently lowering her arms, taking her by the hand and leading her outside.

"But Brady, the dishes," she objected.

"We'll do them later," he laughed, bringing her around to the barn. "Stay here," he said, with a forced smile. Changing his thinking, altering his brooding, foul disposition would be a challenge, but by God if it provoked her to smile, he'd do just about anything.

Brady disappeared into the back of the barn, leaving her frozen to the spot. No doubt her nerves were in tangles, for even he recognized how unpredictable he'd been. When he came into the light, he was holding the reins of a magnificent, russet brown mare. A lovely creature to be sure.

Passing her the reins, Brady waited for her to gather them. Instead, Violet ogled him curiously and shook her head, perhaps assuming his sudden kindness to be a deception of some sort. He really couldn't blame her for her mistrust, could he? Still, it perplexed him as why she wouldn't jump at the chance to ride again.

"Nay?" His brows knitted, confused. "I know ye ride. And I'll have a side-saddle sent for ye soon," he explained with hopeful eyes, praying hers would mirror his own delight.

"Nay, I mean, aye." *Huff.* "I love to ride, but no side saddle. Is this trick'ry?" she asked, suspiciously holding his gaze.

"Nay, no tricks. She's yers to do what ye wish with," he replied, kindly.

Obviously still unconvinced, Violet pushed, "Ye mean I can ride 'er...whenever I want?" she asked, a shaky hand reaching out to smooth a caramel mane.

"Aye, ye can. She's yers. But I have to be honest with ye." He looked at the beast, then at Violet, his eyes screaming for acceptance. "She's a gift from Jack. He thought ye'd like 'er."

Violet lovingly stroked the long silky neck of her new mount. Brady sensed her happiness, yet she refused to show it. Until that is, she unexpectedly wrapped her arms around Brady's middle in appreciation, knocking him back a few steps.

"Oh! Thank ye, Brady. Thank ye so much," she giggled, obviously forgetting herself *and* the misery he'd inflicted.

"No need to thank me, Violet. 'Tis Jack who gets the credit for makin' ye happy today," he replied with a small tight smile, yet, he daren't reciprocate her embrace. His skin had already begun to sizzle with her nearness and he worried about instantaneous combustion, were he to throw his arms around her.

Violet broke his frustrated reflection. "But ye wouldn't present her to me, if ye weren't gonna let me keep 'er, right?" she stated, as she inspected the animal.

"Right ye are. But there has to be rules," he added, trying his damnedest not to make her feel like his captive, choosing his words very carefully. "The forest beyond, is full of terror and horrors unimaginable, so I don't want ye ridin' out there alone. Yer to stay within the fence line; preferably, where I can see ye.

"Who knows what's out there? I don't wanna have to go out lookin' for ye," he scolded.

"I won't cause ye to worry. Promise," she vowed through spirited, batting lashes. "Can I go now?" Violet's eyes were as wide and bright as he'd ever seen them. He wondered how many opportunities he had missed to make her as happy. He silently vowed not to make the same mistakes again. The shattering regret was too much to bear. He'd sell his soul to the Devil if she'd look at him like that again.

"Aye, ye may. Go!" he laughed and helped her upon her new friend.

Violet took off quickly, kicking her heels into the horse's haunches. Her laughter mingled with the breeze, stirring contented and cheerful emotions within him. He could watch her all day – so carefree, without fetters or restraint – exactly how he pictured her as a child; how Jack had said her mother had described her.

Sendin' 'er home would make 'er happier.

The thought entered and left his mind in equal measures of lightning speed. He had to try to make her happy with him first.

Violet felt as liberated as she ever had. Somehow everything that had happened vanished from memory and all she knew was freedom. For the first time, she was really able to survey the land, to marvel in the beauty surrounding her. She completely understood why Brady loved it there so much, for even she'd been able to find peace.

On her way back to the cottage, she caught sight of Brady ploughing the far north corner of the field. She halted her mare and watched as he painstakingly drove the two stags onward, pulling on their reins, shouting and cursing them to move.

These new workers were proving to be an asset to Brady's mission of making the land farmable again. Amazed by his determination and knowledge, and the way he worked the land, a small familiar twinge smouldered within her. What she'd found so attractive before all the murder, death and violence was still there. He was truly cut from a different cloth than the other Kelly men, and she even pitied him a little, for having lived in their shadows.

It was crystal clear that this farm was where he was meant to be. Destiny dictated that Brady become a farmer; not a shipbuilder like his late father, and certainly not a stuffy business man, like Liam.

'*Such a simple life*,' she thought, noting the hard sinew of his biceps and forearms, which seemed amplified with the leather straps wrapped tightly about them. Despite the cussing, and the sweat wetting his linen shirt, he appeared happy. Watching him in his element was like getting a glimpse into his soul, and Violet finally understood what made this man tick.

Even though the work was hard, he wasn't bothered with meetings and merges. He wasn't trying to calculate books and figures. She was beginning to see what Brady loved so much about this place and the life it provided. He worked the land to feed them. Nothing was handed to him on a silver spoon. Everything he'd possess in this life, he'd earned with the sweat off his back and calluses on his hands. So completely opposite from Liam. *Brady's mother has certainly raised him right.*

Thoughts of the Kelly boys' mother made Violet miss her own mother and father dearly. But she was determined to just wait out her captivity, putting what had happened between herself and Brady behind her. To do that, she knew she had to trust that he wouldn't slip up again, for next time she feared the outcome would be much worse.

She'd start by conducting herself as a lady should, which meant not letting her brazen tongue run off, and most certainly never speaking Liam's name again. Accepting the fact that Brady would not let her go had been difficult to swallow, so she turned her head to the sky and said a little prayer for Jack Manning. The length of her imprisonment depended solely on him.

With Jack in Clare, searching for answers, she knew it was just a matter of time when Brady would permit her to leave. Jack would clear her father of Sean's murder and Brady would have no choice but to send her home.

'*Home*,' she reflected, as she continued to watch the monster she knew, driving the horses to plough the north field. But for some strange reason, home didn't appeal to her as much as she would have once thought.

With the small freedom she'd gained, and his promise to change, she was more hopeful that the beast within Brady wouldn't rear its ugly head again, leaving her somewhat content to enjoy this time in all its simplicity and wait until Jack returned. *I must be daft!*

Butterflies danced in her belly – Brady had caught her watching him. She smiled sweetly, for she was truly happy, basking in the fresh air, with the sun blazing down upon her, entertained by the song-bird's melodies. Not to mention her appreciation for the pure, male form, toiling amongst the rows of upturned earth. She raised her hand ever-so-slightly to wave, but he quickly looked away, returning to his task.

Scarcely acknowledging her existence had hurt.

'*He's merely putting up with me until Jack returns*,' she thought, dejectedly. Incensing her further, she reminded herself that she was supposed to despise this man. What did it matter if he treated her with disinterest or indifference?

Unable to help herself, she still clung to those first few days when she'd met him, hanging on so very tightly, to the memory of a good, caring, and charming man.

When Violet thought her mare had been run in enough for one day, she started back toward the barn. It had been the best day she could remember, and she yearned to share that fact with *him*. Would he even be interested in the steady she'd found up-river? That she'd stumbled upon a patch of wild raspberry bushes out behind the barn? *'Of course he won't care! 'Tis not like he doesn't already know what's on 'is own property!'* she scolded herself for even having such delusions.

Dismounting her mare just outside the barn, she silently thanked God for Jack's generosity and compassion, for she had really missed Daisy. She'd missed days just like this one, where the worries of the world were the furthest thing from her mind.

Pretending not to watch her had been the worst. '*She's so beautiful upon that mount,*' Brady sighed.

He knew he would have a lot of making up to do to win her over before Jack returned. Brady feared that once he did return, he would take her back to her kin, no matter what the outcome of his investigation was. It was no secret that Jack disapproved of Brady's hasty and irresponsible conduct, and it wouldn't be entertained for much longer.

With a taste of her happiness burning into his mind, he became more determined to win her love, and perhaps, when the time came, she wouldn't want to leave. *Do I want her to stay?* Were his feelings that deep? Or was this merely a bi-product of his regret and pity?

She needs time.

He put his head down, focussed on his struggle with the land, instead of obsessing over the way the descending sunlight caught her dark strawberry hair.

Despite his determination to remain absorbed in his work, she'd not gone unnoticed. When she'd disappeared behind a thicket of tall overgrown bushes next to the river, his head shot up, waiting with the hairs on the back of his neck prickling against his shirt until she re-emerged. Somewhere in the back of his mind, he'd had a sinking feeling that she would in fact, run. Surprisingly enough, she hadn't.

Unable to help himself, Brady wandered nonchalantly toward the barn when she disappeared inside.

"How was yer ride? Do ye like 'er?" he asked, startling her, discovering her whispering hushed appreciation in the mare's ear, while she brushed the dust from the beast's coat.

"I do. She rides well and has a mild temperament," she replied sweetly, and then an awkward silence fell between them. Brady couldn't help staring at her battered face. A pink hue crept up her cheeks, no doubt embarrassed by how she must look.

"It doesn't hurt anymore," she said, brushing past him toward the cottage. Brady caught hold of her arm and pulled her close enough that he could smell the fresh scent of the wind in her hair.

He tenderly touched her face, his fingers tracing the set line of her jaw. Then, to where her once velvety, rosy lips were plump and tender, were now bluish, bruised and swollen. He ran his thumb along the bottom edge, examining his latest masterpiece with revulsion.

"I'm glad. I don't want to ever hurt ye again. I hope ye know that," he replied sincerely, pinning her with his steely gaze.

Holding her so close and touching her in such an intimate fashion, felt like the wind had been knocked out of him; light-headed, just like the night when they'd danced. Their heat detonating, like a blade to flint. The initial attraction between them reigniting with all the intensity of a cloudburst. It rained down upon them.

"Aye, Brady. I know," she breathed, with watery eyes and crimson cheeks.

Unable to contain the need any longer, Brady placed both massive hands on either side of her face, leaning in to steal her intoxicating breath.

When their lips connected, the feather-like sensations burned like an inferno in the pit of his gut, setting his heart on fire. He'd never crave any other woman's lips again…just hers. Forever Violet.

With a madness in his mind, and a galloping in his chest, Brady craved more than one chaste kiss. His hands itched to roam her feminine body, to caress the soft perfect flesh beneath his old clothes. *Damn it! I do her such disservice, forcin' her to dress like this.*

Good sense triumphed suddenly, fighting its way through his clouded lust, allowing him to release her, shaking his head in frustration.

He'd not apologise. He felt no regret. Her lips were begging to be kissed, and so he had.

He took her hand in his, and silently led her back inside the cottage. *'One kiss, no more'*, he argued with his inner man-beast. Instead of staving off the intensity of his desire, it fuelled something deeper, darker. He knew she felt it too, in the way her breasts heaved, the way her lithe body leaned into his, and how quickly her hands had found their way into his hair, if only for a moment.

Once back inside for the evening, Violet cleared her throat and said, "I'll get at these dishes right away." She rolled her sleeves to her elbows and seemed to ignore his penetrating gaze piercing her. He could identify with her quandary, for like him, regaining her composure was not a possibility, yet unlike him, she was an innocent; unaccustomed to such tawdry encounters. Their brief, yet intimate moment had left them both staggering like asinine fools. He understood she needed something to occupy her thoughts, and so washing the dishes would serve as a good distraction.

And, he would have offered to help – really, he would have – but that would've required him to be in close proximity again, standing shoulder to shoulder with his unaware temptress, and he wasn't sure he could control those nagging basal desires he fought so hard to temper.

"Aye, I'll get washed up. Perhaps I'll make us a small snack," he suggested with an uneasy smile and then disappeared into his room.

Violet was rendered speechless and very much confused. It had only been days before when she was considered *his* maid and given a list of chores to do on the farm. Now *he* was cooking for *her*? *He must be sorry*!

They nibbled on sausage and potatoes Jack had brought from Galway. Brady poured them both a glass of wine and as they sipped, they politely chatted about the weather, Violet's new mare – who she had decided to name Cocoa – and the price of seed and feed.

Neither of them dared talk about all that had happened in the past few days, and especially not their intimate exchange in the barn. Perhaps that subject was best left alone. Yet, the more commonplace the conversation became, the easier it became for them to share bits and pieces of themselves.

Brady regaled her with tales of his youth here at the cottage. Even when Liam went off to Cambridge and there was no one taking up his father's attentions, he'd preferred being here with his mother – the one person who'd truly understood him.

She'd talked about her many lazy afternoons spent daydreaming on the banks of the Shannon. She'd spend entire sunny days either watching the fishermen with their nets and skiffs haul in their catch, or getting lost inside a good book.

"Ye won't find many books kickin' around, but would ye like to go fishin' with me some time?" Brady asked, almost nervously. "We could go, ye know. As soon as the crop's in."

"I'd love to. I've never been fishin' before," she replied shyly. She'd never been courted by the young men in Clare either, but this certainly felt like something a suitor would ask. She didn't quite know what to make of it.

"Well, then 'tis settled. O'er the next few days, I'll need yer help. I intend on gettin' the rest of the north field ploughed tomorrow. We'll get the crop in the day after, and then, the day after that, sweet Vy, we'll go fishin'." Her heart nearly leapt out of her chest. It was the first time he'd called her '*sweet Vy*' since the first days, when the sentiment had been laced with hatred, anger and punishment. All she could do was nod, and swallow a gulp of wine, which left her head spinning.

That night they lay in their separate beds, divided by their separate rooms without doors, but for the first time, sleep came easily for both of them.

Brady didn't seem concerned by every sound, vigilant of preventing her from running off, and Violet wasn't on guard that he would find some reason to brutalize her. It seemed peace had befallen the little cottage.

The next few days became a blur, as they worked side by side, ploughing the remainder of the hopeful ten

acres with one goal in mind – a day free from labour…
together.

Violet was beginning to catch on, and learn various
new skills such as feeding the livestock, cleaning the
barn and horse's stalls. Brady taught her how to sow a
crop of potatoes, carrots, cabbage, parsnip, and turnips,
and had been an enthusiastic and patient teacher, despite
the budding yearning between them.

The day the seeds had been sown, dusk descended
upon two exhausted creatures, who were contented to sit
on the porch and watch the sun disappear behind the
hills.

"To whom are you going to sell these crops?" Violet
asked, innocently sipping her lemonade.

Brady chuckled, "I won't sell my crops, Vy. I hope
to fill up the cellar to get us through the winter, and then
bring the rest to the stronghold for the clan."

"Get *us* through the winter? Ye don't think Jack will
be back by then?" she sweetly asked, unable to take her
eyes off the sunset.

Fear of finding disappointment and sadness behind
her well-placed mask, Brady refused to look at her.

While the past few days had been a revelation for them both, there was no doubt she still yearned to be returned to her kin. He'd not won her heart yet. The lamented tone in her voice spoke to his conscience on a deep, rueful level.

He understood her grief, but he still fought with his own guilt and anguish. It wasn't a matter of punishing her father any longer. No, this was about keeping her, because he couldn't imagine his life without her.

His first instinct was to become angry and punish her for what she was unable to say. She didn't have to say it, he'd felt it. Her longing for home radiated off her in waves, seeping into his skin, digging its way inside his cold heart.

'*I'm trying so hard. And she still wants to go home,*' he thought furiously, and then took a deep breath, calming himself again. '*I've got to control my temper, or she'll never choose to stay.*'

He leaned forward, resting his forearms upon his thighs, clenching and unclenching his fists between his knees. "Aye, Jack will return with answers soon enough. And he'll get to the truth of it, he won't rest 'til he does,

I assure ye." Brady reclined once again, dragging his fingers through his dusty hair in quiet aggravation.

"So, we can go fishin' in the mornin'?" she asked, obviously oblivious to his prickliness.

Brady stood and took her hand, leading her toward the door. "Aye, I'll wake ye bright an' early. Now go, get some sleep," he said, placing a sweet kiss on her forehead. She instantly melted beneath his touch and he secretly wished he could kiss her again; like that day in the barn. Now that her bruises were almost healed, and they'd found their natural rhythm, he wanted it more than anything. *'Tis not time yet.*

The sun was barely up, poking its fiery face from the clouds when she awoke to clanging in the kitchen. She dressed quickly, and rushed to see what had caused such an explosion of sound.

She stifled a giggle when she saw that Brady was fixing sandwiches and attempting to pack a picnic basket for their outing. When he noticed her standing in the archway, he smiled and waved her forward. As she neared, his expression changed from cheerful, to discontent. Creases formed in his brow and he simply shook his head.

Violet craned her neck, gazing into the basket. "What's the matter?" she asked. "Surely, 'twill be a fine scoff to break our fast."

"Sweet Vy, work clothes simply will not do today," he said, his gaze wandering from her toes to her head. He smiled wide again, "Go put on yer favourite dress."

She didn't pause or question him; she took off as fast as she could, back to her room.

Choosing a pink satin gown with a velvet bodice, matching long boots and white gloves with little pink bows, she gave herself a once-over in the glass. It was the perfect cut, and fit her in all the right places, revealing just a hint of her lush breasts, and accentuated her slender hips. Finally, she felt like a lady again.

Anxiety and nervousness welled up inside her as she reappeared. '*Is this too much? Is he going to order me back into his old garb? Oh, why Violet, did ye choose this one*?' she panicked.

But when she looked into his eyes, the angst and worry dissipated in an instant. He strode toward her and took her hand. Smiling, he led her outside to her mare, helping her to mount.

"Ye look astonishing. I'm sorry I ever put ye in anything else," Brady mumbled, his admission laced with severe regret, but she beamed in appreciation of the compliment.

Brady had her lead the way to her favourite part of the steady that she'd told him about the night before, then set up a blanket and unpacked their breakfast. She couldn't take her eyes off him, as he expertly baited her hook, and then his own. Handing the pole to her, a slight grin formed, pulling at his freshly-shaven lip.

What are ye thinkin', Brady Kelly?

After a considerable amount of time, lines in the water, suspended silence between them, Violet's sweet voice finally shattered it. "I enjoy being with ye like this," she said, refusing to look at him. Was it fear of rejection or her bashful innocence which kept her from meeting his gaze? *'Look at me. See what's in my heart,'* he silently begged.

"Ye're startin' to bring out the best in me," he replied, his voice low, desire mounting, creating a rumble in his chest.

"Oh! Brady, I feel somethin'!" Her fishing pole began to quiver and pull. Her child-like joy and wonder utterly intoxicated him.

Brady jumped to his feet to help her get the fish in. But in his haste to be her hero, he lost his footing on the bank, and plunged into the water with a splash.

"Brady! Brady, are ye alright?" she screamed, bounding to her knees, digging her fingers into the grassy embankment.

Finding his footing, standing in the waist-high stream, Brady was soaked from head to foot. A curled, raven lock of hair fell in his eyes and he pushed it back with a saturated sleeve. With a crooked grin, he held up her line, a thrashing fish dangling from the end.

"I'm alright, but I fear the fish won't get off as easy. He's to be our dinner," Brady chuckled, self-consciously.

Violet flew into a hysterical fit of laughter, but instead of his usual glower at being made a fool of, Brady's shoulders began to shake, and a boisterous roar grew with in him, sharing in her humour.

He awkwardly climbed the bank, still holding her line, and fell into her awaiting arms. Violet wrapped the picnic blanket around his shoulders, rubbing his arms vigorously to stave off a chill, unaware of the repercussions of her kindness. The heat that emerged from their closeness sent them both into a shiver; there could be no more denying what was blossoming between them.

Brady held both her hands in his, and kissed them tenderly. She gazed into his eyes, and he prayed she'd recognize the man behind his fierce gaze. The man shivering in her arms was the man she'd first met, despite all that had happened to prove otherwise. It was as if time ceased to exist. He felt her hunger, breathed in her lust, uncertain of what to do next. Denying her would kill him. This woman would be his undoing.

SIXTEEN

Jacks motives were clearer than ever. He had to find out what happened to Sean Kelly, if not for Brady's sake, then for Violet's. She deserved better than the life sentence of suffering Brady's wrath.

'*If I had me a woman like that, I certainly wouldn't be beatin' on 'er, no matter what she'd done to deserve it; not like that anyway,*' he thought, as he neared the Ryan family home on the Shannon.

Jack took notice for the first time of how beautiful the grounds were. The estate was almost entombed within an apple orchard. All he could see peeping out from beneath the thick green foliage was the tall west tower. Having been there before, he knew this was Lady Ryan's place of worship. He imagined her up there right now, kneeling before a bronze effigy with hands tightly clasped, making deals with the higher powers to have Violet returned safely. *'I'll bring 'er home to ye, but I fear she'll not return the same lass she was when she left,'* Jack thought, morosely.

As he neared, his concerns began wreaking havoc. His mind spilled over with indecision; right and wrong. *Will I tell them what I've discovered?* Or should he tell them that she was in good health and patiently waiting for the whole mess to be cleared up?

Uncertainty engulfed him as he dismounted and wrapped on the large door knocker. When the door swung open, as expected, Robert Ryan stood there, almost as if he were waiting all these days and nights for Jack's return.

Skipping the usual pleasantries, Robert met him on the threshold and whispered, "Well? How is she? Is she ok? Come in boy, come in." Robert frantically wrung his fingers and shifted in his immaculate three-piece suit as if the fabric choked him.

Jack followed him into the house, silently at first, still unsure of how to explain things.

When he finally got up the courage to speak, he decided to forsake Brady and his damn loyalties to the ornery bastard for the time being, and go with his gut.

"Is there somewhere we can go to discuss this matter in private, sir?" Jack quietly asked.

Robert's shoulders slumped as if he'd been expecting the worst. Of course, Jack understood the man's dread. Were it his own daughter being held captive by a man of unscrupulous reputation, he'd feel the same way.

"Aye, come. We'll not be bothered in the study. But can't I call my lady? She's most anxious for ye to return with news of our dear, sweet, Violet."

"Ah, I think 'tis best if we talk somethin' o'er before we involve Lady Ryan," Jack explained, suddenly feeling like the villain, as he followed Robert down a long heavily decorated corridor.

Robert stopped and spun to face Jack. "Oh, Jesus! Is it that bad? Has she been harmed? What's that bastard done to her?" Robert bellowed, but Jack grabbed the arm of his waistcoat, gesturing to keep it down. Robert's gaze shifted up and down the hallway, and then he replied quietly, "Fine, fine. We won't be interrupted in the study. Here."

When they were both seated and the study door had been closed, Jack began. He promised himself he would be as honest as he could, without sending these innocent people into a frenzy of despair. The last thing anyone needed was spontaneous retaliation against Brady, because whether or not people believed so, there was no doubt he'd be ready for it. *Too much blood has been shed already.*

If such a rebellion were to occur, Jack feared Violet would receive the brunt of Brady's aggravation and retaliation. *Is he capable of harming her now*? Would Brady kill her before the truth was revealed? He shuttered at the thought. *Nay! He loves 'er! I ain't wrong about this!*

"Lord Ryan," Jack began.

"Please, call me Robert."

"Aye." Jack nodded. "Robert. Let me begin by tellin' ye that Violet is safe for the time bein'. Unfortunately, I am unsure how long she'll remain as such. Brady becomes increasingly irate and demands too much of 'er." Bewilderment etched creases into Robert's face, but Jack knew holding back would serve no one. These people had to understand that Brady Kelly wasn't to be trifled with.

"Demands? In what way?"

A stitch of guilt for deceiving his old friend gnawed its way through Jack's mind, but what choice had he been given? Brady had been hell-bent on hiding his feelings for the girl. The consequence of that denial caused him to treat her dreadfully...brutally. "First, 'tis important that ye know I believe in yer innocence. I can think of no motive for ye to kill Sean Kelly, as ye had naught to gain. Therefore, if it pleases ye and yer lady wife, I'd like to stay and investigate further. Hopefully, I'll clear yer name."

"Oh! Of course, Mr. Manning. The quicker we can get this cleared up, the better. I just want Violet returned to us safely."

"Exactly my plan," Jack stated with all the intensity of a brewing storm. "I'll have to talk with yer crew, ask a few questions, and take note of everythin' that happened that night. I want no detail left out. 'Tis imperative that everyone is completely honest."

"Aye, of course. I don't know what they'll tell ye about that night, however. I've already questioned each and every one of them. They all have an alibi, and not one of them seen or heard anything. But feel free to have another go at it."

"Good. I'll start in the mornin'. Ye can arrange for them to meet with me at first light," Jack said. "Now, back to Violet. As ye know, the girl has a mind and spirit all 'er own. I fear, she's gotten herself into a little bit of trouble with Lord Kelly."

"Oh?" Robert trembled, eyes wide, concern simmering behind them. "What…what kind of trouble?" Robert's mind had to have been wandering toward total darkness, for he pulled his shaking fingers through his disheveled, greying hair. Jack regretted having to continue.

"As I said, Violet is quite the sassy and brazen lass – pardon me for sayin' so – who has not been able to hold her tongue. So, Brady, bein' an equally hot-headed, ill-tempered sort, has seen fit to give her duties. Chores, if ye will, around the farm."

Robert nodded, seemingly satisfied with Jack's reply. Moving to a small sideboard, he poured himself a drink without offering one to Jack, silence becoming an assailant between them.

"Wait! Farm?" Robert asked, turning quickly toward his guest. "What do ye mean a farm? Is that where he's taken her? I was under the assumption that she'd been confined to a country estate." Robert's eyes widened with utter panic, perhaps picturing his precious, beloved child cleaning stalls, feeding slop to pigs and such.

Jack then realised that the Ryan's had no idea how dire and bleak the situation truly was – that Brady was completely untouchable as long as he was holed up at the cottage.

"Aye, a farm. Away from Galway and the protection of the keep. I must admit, I am relieved ye haven't sent any of yer men after her. That would have inflamed 'im beyond words. He would have taken it out on 'er. Ye heeded his warnings well." Jack shrugged out of his coat and slung it over the arm of a nearby chair before he continued.

"She's to assist him in workin' the land. It isn't exactly a workin' farm yet, and he hasn't bestowed upon her any tasks that are impossible in nature. But she has endured a punishment or two, I'm sorry to say." Jack turned to face the man whose heart he was shredding.

Robert's head fell into his hands. When he looked up, meeting Jack's apologetic gaze, his face turned as white as the driven snow.

"Has he beaten her?" he trembled.

"Aye, but not brutally," Jack solemnly replied. "She bears no scars, I assure ye. Perhaps, she's learned a lesson or two and starts usin' her head before she uses 'er tongue," Jack half-chuckled, but then Robert pinned Jack with a serious, disconcerting glare.

"Has he... has he raped her?" Robert sobbed and stuttered. "I worry 'bout her virtue," he admitted.

Jack could understand how the father of a beautiful young maiden would worry about such things, but how could he tell the man that if Brady lost control again, her virtue would most assuredly be at risk?

I can't tell 'im that.

"Brady Kelly was brought up a gentleman, I assure ye," Jack lied. Brady may have been brought up in a gentleman's home, but he'd grown to become the furthest thing from it. Some things were best left unsaid.

Robert seemed relieved with this news, the quiver in his hand ceasing enough to down the remainder of his drink.

"Her virtue remains intact, but there's a special somethin' brewing b'tween them, which is why I wanted to speak to ye alone. I can't face yer lady and tell her that I believe 'tis just a matter of time before her only daughter is ruined by Brady Kelly." *'There! I've said it,'* Jack thought. Having to explain further would create an uncomfortable situation, especially if Robert Ryan persisted in eyeing him that way.

"What do ye mean somethin' brewin'? You're not suggestin' she loves 'im?"

"Nay, far from it. Right now, she's promised to be on her best behaviour to avoid his tantrums. She's merely doin' as she's told to save herself. But I know Brady. I think he's fallin' for her, and that sir, could be a good thing."

"What in bloody hell do ye mean, a good thing? How could that be *good*?" Robert erupted, slamming his fist onto the desk.

"Calm yerself," Jack warned. "Ye see, if he's got feelin's for her, that'll buy us time to find out who killed his father." Jack stopped in front of Robert's desk, planted two palms flat on top, and stared him down. "If he loves 'er like I think he does, won't it be punishment enough when I return her to ye? Think about that for a moment. There's no worse punishment than losin' a loved one." Jack didn't know if he really wanted Brady to suffer the loss of Violet, but when it was time for her to go home, she would decide for herself. And Jack would make sure it happened, even if it cost him his friendship. His honour depended on it.

"Why do ye think she'll be ruined? Is he capable of forcing himself upon her?" Robert wearily asked.

"Aren't all men, when enticed by a beautiful woman?" Jack cocked his brow at him, refraining from further explanation.

A low growl sounded from the depths of Robert's throat. "Aye. My own father was a mean-tempered drunk, who'd been known on occasion for rapin' the women of our *then* rival clan, the Murphy's. I've never condoned such a barbaric behaviour and I loathe thinkin' about it befallin' my own daughter.

"We need to get this done as quickly as possible, to prevent any more harm comin' to her. In the meantime, I can trust that he will beat her no more?" Robert searched Jack's solemn expression for reassurance, and so Jack nodded again, perhaps feigning his agreement or perhaps trying to convince himself that Brady's brutality was a thing of the past.

"Right. I'd prefer if we kept these details b'tween us. I wouldn't want to upset yer lady any more than she already has been. For now, we'll tell 'er that Violet is unharmed and unaffected, except for missin' you both terribly," Jack said, sticking his hand out for Robert to shake on it, for it was a pact both of them had to keep.

Robert took the proffered hand, but Jack could feel the man's tremors of terror coursing through his own body, causing a surge of determination to bubble within his belly. He would indeed put an end to this chaos, even if it killed him.

"I'll call for 'er now. She's been eagerly waitin' for yer return," Robert offered. In an instant, he was gone. A moment later, loud bellows echoed through the great manor, summoning the lady of the house.

Jack wandered around the room, taking note of ship plans lain about the desk and admiring the paintings on the wall, especially the largest one. It was a likeness of Violet. She was poised in a seated position, wearing a royal blue gown, her red hair spilling down in front of her shoulders. She looked to be about fifteen, and had eyes as innocent as a newborn doe. A heavy, disheartening thought plagued Jack's mind, *'She'll not fare as innocent when all this is o'er.'*

"Mr. Manning! Ye've returned!" Beth exclaimed from the entrance of the study. Jack turned to greet her, but to his surprise, she was on him in an instant, her long slender arms wrapping about his neck. Jack quickly and awkwardly disentangled himself from the fretting matriarch, and cleared his throat, refusing to make eye contact.

"Lady Ryan," he choked out, "ye appear to be feelin' better than the last time I was here. I take ye're comin' to terms with what's happened?" Jack asked, cautiously, yet with genuine concern. Violet's mother was a beautiful soul, and he hated seeing her aggrieved and distressed.

"Aye, Robert tells me to stay in good health, for Violet may need me once she's returned." Beth lowered her gaze for a moment and Jack yearned to ease her pain. When she looked back up into his eyes, it was as if she searched them with something akin to hope swirling in hers. "Has he sent more correspondence? Are we forced to once again, read and imagine the horrors of her plight?" she asked sullenly.

"Nay, there will be no more letters. Nothing more to relay to you, M'lady," Jack replied curtly, putting the letter that he'd used for kindling the night before out of his mind.

When her shoulders slumped, and her pretty face fell, he'd realized his blunder. Certainly, she would assume the worst.

Before he got the chance to correct himself, her small voice quivered. "Is she…has he killed her?" Beth shivered, her bottom lip trembling.

"Nay, nay love," Robert interrupted, rushing to her side. "She's just fine, isn't that right, Jack?"

"Aye, Lady Ryan. She's merely on a holiday of sorts. He's taken her to his late mother's cottage. I assure ye, 'tis a beautiful place, with a lush garden, acres of farm land all about. 'Tis indeed a kiss of nature," Jack lied, trying as hard as he could to make it sound delightful. "She also has a new mare to ride, which means she also has a bit of freedom to roam the lands.

"She misses ye terribly, but she's content for the time bein' and patiently awaits her father's name to be cleared."

Beth's watery eyes dried a little and her panic-stricken features began to soften. Thankfully, she seemed to believe every bit of Jack's tale. He silently appreciated the fact that she hadn't pushed for further details.

"Oh, Robert! Did ye hear that? She's bein' looked after!" she squealed with relief. "Will he let her come home soon, do ye think? And why is he not sendin' us any more letters detailin' her confinement?"

That had been Jack's own doing. He would not concede to bringing these good people tales of horror and dread, watching them fall apart at the seams. He out-right refused to do it – Kelly soldier or not. He knew that one day, this would all come to an end, and when it did, his pride and self-respect would be in tact.

"There really is nothin' to report, M'lady. Although he treats her with indifference, he tolerates her enough and tends to her needs." Jack felt Robert's eyes upon him, the secrets between them safe, and so he continued, "The sting of losing his father hasn't worn off yet, I'm afraid, but his brutality has. He wishes to keep her 'til Robert can be proven innocent. Dare I say as an insurance policy? She will be home in no time, M'lady," Jack explained cautiously.

"Oh! Thank heavens! Can ye get a letter to her for me then, Mr. Manning?" she asked.

"Beth, darlin', Mr. Manning is gonna be stayin' here with us for a while. He's promised to help catch Lord Kelly's murderer, and clear my name. Isn't that right, Jack?" Robert replied. Jack merely smirked and winked at Beth.

"I hope ye find success in it then, Mr. Manning. We just want her back. I'll fetch Kylee to show you to your room. How long do ye expect to stay?" Beth asked, as she hurried to the door.

"I'll stay for as long as it takes," Jack politely replied.

When she was no longer in ear shot, Robert chuckled under his breath. Gaping at him in question, Jack cocked a sideways grin his way.

"Aye, ye've gone an' done it now! I haven't seen 'er this vibrant in weeks…well since before…" he trailed off, the sadness returning to his cheeks.

Jack laid his hand on Robert's shoulder. "It'll be over soon. It has to be."

Jack was led to the guest wing by an attractive young chamber maid. He immediately took notice of her small stature, curvaceous frame and the way her generous, yet feminine hips swayed to and fro in front of him as he followed.

'*What I wouldn't give to explore every inch of 'er,*' he thought, imagining being buried between her full plump breasts. Jacks trousers became so tight, that walking behind her was becoming more of an aching chore than a delight. He was grateful she couldn't see the effect she'd had on him.

She opened the chamber door and stood aside for him to enter. As he walked by, her sweet lemony scent crawled into his nostrils, bewitching him instantly.

"Is yer name Kylee?" he asked courteously, yet lingering in front of her longer than necessary.

"Aye, Jack Manning. M'names Kylee O'Roarke, an' don't be callin' me sweetie, honey, or anythin' else of that nature. Ye'll do fine to remember that," she snapped back with sass.

Jack almost swallowed his tongue. How could this angelic beauty before him have such an abrasive disposition?

He stared silently as she moved about the room. She opened the curtains, allowing the sun to filter in, giving Jack the first glimpse of just how pretty this wicked creature truly was. The way the sun reflected off her long pale-yellow hair, reminded him of newly spun, gold satin thread – soft and shimmering. When she looked in his direction, even with unmistakable distain, he was transfixed by the deepest turquoise green eyes he'd ever seen. *Other-worldly*.

"I shall call ye Ms. O'Roarke then, if it pleases ye," Jack replied so softly that even he had a hard time of hearing it.

"Fine. So, I hear yer gonna get our Violet back? How do ye plan to do that, huh?" She eyed him brazenly and tapped her foot, waiting for his response.

"Aye, 'tis true. I'll return with her myself, but *after* I've satisfied Lord Kelly's inquiry," Jack replied nervously.

This woman was making his head spin in all directions. Her one question had him second guessing himself and his own motives. A moment ago, he could've gotten lost in her mystique, now he wanted her gone. She was a walking, talking contradiction. *The face of an angel, the character of the devil himself.*

"Fine then. If ye need anythin', leave me a note. I can read, ye know. I'll see to it that yer needs are met while yer here," Kylee said in a huff, and then Jack got his wish. She hurried out the door, slamming it shut behind her.

Jack sat on the bed for a long spell, shaking his head, stunned and confused. Lady Ryan was such a lighthearted, delightful and kind woman, and he couldn't understand why she would employ such an ill-tempered little wench.

Shaking the imp from his mind, Jack opened his leather bag and retrieved his quill and ink pot. He looked about the room, and found what he needed – a writing desk, sitting in the corner by the window. There was no chair placed there, so he hauled the leather wing-back from its position next to the hearth, over to the desk and sat, quill in hand to begin his task.

He prioritized the list of people Robert had given him, men he would have to interview, starting with Robert Ryan's crewmen. He knew he had a mountain of work ahead of him, but if it saved Lady Violet from his childhood friend, there would be no stopping him.

The next morning, he was awoken by foul language and the splashing of water into the wash basin. When he was finally able to focus, his angelic demon had returned to curse him conscious. Jack groaned.

"What are ye moanin' about, Jack Manning? I went to all the trouble of makin' the bed fer ye and ye sleep in a chair o'er at the desk?" Kylee scolded, making Jack feel like an errant child, and he was forced to explain.

"My apologies. I must've fallen asleep. I never meant to…" Jack explained, rubbing the sleep from his eyes and stretching the kinks out of stiff shoulders. He looked out the window, finding the morning was brand new, barely dawn.

'Jesus! What time do they rise here? I'll have to talk to lady Ryan 'bout what time she can send the she-devil in to torture me,' Jack thought irritably.

"Well don't ye be thinkin' I don't have enough to do 'round here. I don't need ye makin' unnecessary work for me ye know," Kylee chided.

"Aye, I'll do my best to make *necessary* work for ye then instead," Jack snorted his rebuttal, callously brushing past her toward the basin.

Rendered speechless, Kylee turned on her heel and stormed out the door. Jack smiled at his victory, small as it was, and readied himself for the day.

After breaking his fast, Jack started with the first name on the list. Even though each of them had already been questioned, he needed to delve further, and possibly interview their alibis as well.

He began his morning in the study with the crew chief, *Madman* Morgan Murtagh. He'd intentionally set this one up to take place first, as he predicted it might become intense, perhaps even violent after the not-so-warm welcome Murtagh had received at Kelly's keep.

Morgan entered the study where Jack and Robert both sat behind the desk, and while to some it might appear they were attempting to intimidate, Jack doubted very much the mountain of a man would be.

"Ye may take a seat, Morgan. This shouldn't take very long," Robert instructed with a half-smile.

Morgan grunted and shot Jack a look of complete distain and loathing. Jack understood though, and refused to engage. He'd earned the man's disgust and abhorrence after all that had passed between them.

"Mr. Murtagh, yer boss has told me that you and yer crewmates were all at the brothel when Sean Kelly was murdered. Can anyone back up that story?" Jack asked, refusing to look him in the eye. The guilt for bashing the man to a pulp was still fresh.

"Aye, 'tis where we were. The entire whore house can vouch for us. Go and see for yourself, ask for Maggie," Morgan stated gruffly, turning his glare to Robert. "Can I go now? The less time I spend with this vile excuse of a man, the better. I still can't believe ye let 'im lead up this investigation after the beatin' he and Kelly laid on me."

"Never mind that, Morgan. I'm sure Mr. Manning was only followin' orders. Isn't that right, Jack?" Even if Robert was trying to mediate reconciliation between the two, it would do no good. Yet having them at each other's throats at a time like this, served no purpose either.

Jack nodded, meeting Morgan's harsh brown-eyed scowl and said, "Aye, followin' orders. My apologies, Mr. Murtagh."

Morgan didn't look like someone who'd easily accept apologies, but he shot Robert an exhausted glare and replied, "Fine, if that's all, ye know where to find me. I still have a ship to build, ye know." Morgan stood as rigid and hard as the planks he used to craft his vessels. With his fists bunched at his sides, no doubt he craved the opportunity to inflict the same damage Jack and Brady had, but to Jack's surprise, he resisted. Perhaps a time would come when Murtagh's employer wouldn't be there. A time when it was one against one, fist against fist. Today was not that day. Nonetheless, his was a hate Jack could understand. *Do unto others.*

Jack jotted down a few scribbles as Robert showed the man out. Morgan didn't come off as someone who'd commit murder unprovoked, and for that, Jack ruled him out as a suspect.

After Morgan left, the other crewmen were all waiting outside the study flanking the corridor, leaning against the walls. Each man was called in alone and each one gave the same statement. While some embellished what had happened at the brothel, others looked scared and wanted to be anywhere but there.

Just before noon, and after many interrogations, Jack stood to stretch, and poured up two glasses of whiskey. "Is that all of them?" he asked, the door closing behind the last one.

"Of the crew, aye, but there are two more people of interest I think. I never did get back to the tavern to talk to the barkeep. I don't know what he could tell us, as he was busy slingin' booze o'er the bar, but he's worth talkin' to." Robert stretched his arms and rubbed the back of his neck. It had been a long and stressful morning. "And then there's Gregory. Violet's tutor. He was the one who met us on the road, warnin' us not to go back to Kelly's place. If it hadn't been for that boy, who knows what Brady would have done that night."

Jack silently agreed to that statement, and then something niggled at him. "Ye take Violet's tutor on business meetin's? I don't remember meetin' him. She must be well schooled," Jack laughed, trying to ease Robert's tension with a little humour.

Robert chuckled, "Nay, he was there for a meetin' with his former professor. Do ye know that poor boy was robbed on the road along the way?" he said, shaking his head. "What is this world comin' to when a man can't even make his way from Clare to Galway without bein' assaulted? 'Tis a shame."

"Aye, 'tis a mad world, indeed. So where is he now? I would like to talk with 'im," Jack asked, falling back into his chair, hooking an ankle over his knee, swirling the liquid in the glass he held. The morning had been rough on him too.

"I haven't seen him in about a week, perhaps a little longer. At first, he was as angry as a bull that Kelly had kidnapped Violet, but then when the rumours of how despicable Brady was treatin' her surfaced, he just about lost 'is mind," Robert sighed. "'Tis killin' him ye know; her not bein' here. He thought one day I would agree to let him marry 'er."

"Ah, so he loves 'er. Were they ever gonna marry?" Jack asked with keen interest, the wheels of his mind beginning to churn. He remembered Brady mentioning something about a betrothal to Liam, and recalled how the news of it had incensed Brady to madness.

"Well, I thought long and hard about it at one time, and I almost agreed. But knowin' she could never return his love, I couldn't approve of it. He'd become too much like a brother to 'er.

"Violet needs someone who'll stand up to her, put her in her place from time to time, yet someone who doesn't mind havin' a woman with smarts and respect 'er for it," Robert's eyes became misty and he sniffled, his longing for Violet almost a tangible entity in the room. "Gregory liked bein' her teacher, and had never expected her to be anything other than who she is. But marriage is a completely different affair, isn't it? I knew if she married him, she'd be expected to fall in step and conform. To toe the line with his colleagues, he'd expect her to become a mindless, spiritless twit. I couldn't let that happen. Not to my Vy."

"After meetin' yer lovely daughter myself, I can understand why." Jack smiled. "Where do ye think Gregory's gone? Can ye tell me where he lives? I'll just need a few minutes of his time, like the others," he added.

Robert scribbled down the directions to Gregory's boarding house on a piece of paper and handed it to him.

"Be gentle with him, Jack. He's devastated and fragile."

"I'll try my best," Jack replied sympathetically. If Violet had come to regard Gregory as a brother, then it was possible Robert seen him as a son. Interrogating this man would have to be done delicately.

Jack spent the rest of the day and into the night in his room, writing notes, recording every simple detail he could think of.

'*Seamus was a brazen lot. He seemed uncaring about anything other than the length of time his cock had been beating against a whore named Kitty's backside.*

Patrick was much the same – boasting that at the time Robert had arrived at the brothel, he'd had two nameless tramps entangled into a threesome. One was sitting on his face, while the other was full of every inch of him. The other details he'd described are too crude to write. I don't like Patrick,' Jack had written. Who were these tactless people?

'*Martin and James on the other hand, were married men and they'd only gone to the brothel for the novelty of it, and because they were drunk. They didn't boast or embellish details. I have a feeling they would have preferred it never happened.*

James's wife had given him a beating he'd not soon forget, and Patrick's wife nagged him constantly about it, still.'

"Jack Manning! Have ye had yer supper yet? I hope ye weren't waitin' for me to deliver it up here to ye," Kylee scowled as she entered his chambers without as much as a knock.

"Jesus, woman! Have ye lost yer bloody mind? Ye can't just go bargin' into a man's room unannounced!" Jack hollered, "What if I were indecent?"

"Oh? And what if I'd seen yer little peter? Is that what yer afraid of? Does it possess some magical powers? If I look at it, will I burst into flames?" Kylee laughed, taunting, moving to the bed, turning down the covers. Jack's temper was on a precipice, and falling over the edge would result in this shameless, brash little sprite receiving a thrashing she'd not soon forget. He gritted his teeth, but held his tongue. After-all, he was a guest here. "Well, no matter 'bout it. I've no interest in yers! I'll be married soon, to a handsome brute, who I'm sure has some wicked, naughty things in store for me on my weddin' night," she laughed mischievously.

Jack could find no humour in her words or her behaviour. She was the crudest woman he'd ever met in his entire life. He'd spent time away from home, on crusades and missions, where the only comfort he'd had was between a woman's thighs. But no matter what he'd paid them, those women wouldn't dream of speaking to him in such a manner. She was insufferable.

'*I have to get out of Clare. She makes my loins ache and my ears ring. She needs to be taught a lesson in obedience,*' Jack thought, watching her slither all about his room, fussing over the wash basin, straightening the bed clothes, and shutting the drapery. He couldn't help but think that when she wasn't speaking, she was truly a captivating creature. Then she spoke again, reminding him of her insolence.

"Do ye want a candle set on the bedside table? Ye may need it to find yer little peter while yer lyin' awake trying yer damnedest not to think of me," she cackled. It was the cruellest laugh Jack had ever heard, especially coming from such a pretty young thing.

"Girl? Where did ye ever learn to talk like that?" Jack grabbed her arm and roared down into her face. "'Tis deplorable to hear that filth comin' from such sweet lips. Ye should be ashamed! Now get out, b'fore I send for the lady of the house to deal with ye. She'll not be happy to know how ye've been treatin' her guest." He couldn't say whether it was lust or anger, but his face burned red-hot, with every nerve in his body screaming to kiss her. *Or punish her.*

"Aye, I'll leave. But we both know I won't be gone," Kylee smirked, peering up at Jack from under her long blonde eye lashes. Before the scent of her breath could be forever imprinted on him, she sashayed toward the door.

'*What kind of game does this one play?*' he wondered, his blood fused with insurmountable irritation. He could take no more. She played her body like an instrument for his destruction.

As she reached the door, Jack stalked toward her. Catching her arm in his sturdy grip, he whipped her around to face him. He could still taste the revolting profanity that she'd been spewing just seconds before; it was intoxicating, yet infuriating all at once.

Glaring down into her shimmering turquoise pools, her focus flickering from left to right and back again, Jack uncovered the centre of her secrets. Her mask had fallen away and he could finally identify what lay beneath. Fear.

His heart sank, unable to quite understand what was happening. She'd pushed him to use brute force; she'd insulted and berated him until he could take no more. She'd been fearless. What had changed?

He caressed her cheek with his rough soldier hand, and ran a finger down to trace her bottom lip. She arched her head upward, as if she were willing to accept his kiss. As Jack leaned in close, and then closer, not taking his gaze away from her teary eyes, she quickly turned away and shot out the door.

Breathlessly, Jack ran out after her and watched as his little vixen had darted half way down the hall. He'd not catch her tonight.

Work was out of the question after the frustration she'd inflicted, so Jack lay in bed, tucked tightly under the covers, trying to shake her from memory.

He had much to do in the next few days and the last thing he needed was a distraction like Kylee.

She had been right though. She had left him alone in his room, but she wasn't gone either. Her mesmerizing lemony scent lingered, driving Jack mad with an unquenchable thirst for her plump, tender lips. *Amongst other things.*

The next morning Jack found himself standing alone in Gregory's room at the boarding house. The landlord had told him Gregory hadn't been there in over a week, and the fact that he was paid up in full until the New Year, was disturbing. *Why would he pay over six months in advance?*

When the landlord said that even he thought it was unusual, Jack's skin crawled. *Something's not right.*

The four walls were lined with shelves, filled almost to bursting with books in every size and genre.

'*Wonder how many of 'em he's read?*' Jack idly thought.

He rifled through the writing desk, finding letters from colleagues and old friends from Gregory's old alma mater. He examined sketches which were clearly drawn by Violet. They were not masterpieces, just bored illustrations of a young, uninterested girl, all signed with the same style of signature. It seemed, Violet liked to dot her "*I's*" with a flower, and for a moment, Jack was amused by her innocence and made a mental note to tease her about it later.

Jack crouched onto his haunches beside the bed, finding a steel box underneath, fastened shut with a small lock. Not thinking twice, Jack grasped his knife, using the handle to break it free.

At first glance, it seemed to house some old jewellery, a letter from a lost love, some trinkets and knick-

knacks from a long-gone childhood. Then Jack un-
earthed something worth finding. A letter from Kelly's
keep.

Sitting on the edge of the small cot, he hastily pulled
apart the creases in the parchment and began to read.

Dear Mr. Pearce,

*Thank you for your kind words regarding my fa-
ther, he truly was a great man. And I agree with you
that right now, the same cannot be said for my brother,
Brady.*

*I too have interest in rescuing Lady Violet from his
wrath, and whole-heartedly accept your offer of assistance.*

*If you can come right away, I will be waiting. But
tell no one. Brady has made it abundantly clear that no
one is to intervene. I can't bear to think of what might
become of her if he finds out we're coming.*

*I am confident that we can devise a plan to safely
retrieve your friend and student; and my one-day bride.*

Yours in camaraderie,

Liam Kelly

Jack read and re-read the words over and over.

So, Gregory is in Galway? This is almost perfect. With their help we may be able to force Brady to let her go.

Jack pondered that for a moment. But he knew he would still have to clear Robert's name – honour dictated it. Jack Manning was nothing, if not honourable.

Jack crept back into the Ryan home, looking this way and that, trying to avoid his golden-haired tormentor. He quietly entered the study to find Robert just pouring himself a cup of tea from the silver service sitting on the sideboard.

"Well, Jack? Have ye found anythin' out of the ordinary?" Robert asked, standing in front of the grand fireplace, eyes reflecting the licking flames within.

"Aye. Ye haven't seen Gregory 'cause he's gone to Galway to aid Liam in rescuin' Violet from Brady's hold. I hope they've not moved on anythin' yet, for neither of them knows what Brady's truly capable of," Jack said as he plunked down in a soft leather chair. Robert turned and faced Jack, his expression revealing the first glimmer of hope. But no sooner than it had appeared, the hope had been extinguished.

"Gregory? Gone to save 'er? Oh my," Robert worried. "Gregory may be smart, but he lacks the brawn needed to contend with the likes of Brady Kelly."

"Aye. Ye stole the words from my mouth." Jack paused for a moment, and then said, "Robert, ye say that ye'd never force 'er to marry Gregory 'cause he didn't fit the mould. Ye knew he couldn't nurture her free-spirit, as she requires? Is that right?"

"Aye, 'tis a sad truth."

"Then, why did ye consent to Liam's proposal? Gregory and Liam are the same sort…cut with the same cloth, are they not?"

"Well, yes, they are, but I thought with the merger bringin' the two families together, 'twould only make sense for a marriage of the children to solidify it. Ye see?" Robert was trying to explain, and on some level, perhaps he thought his actions were noble and excusable, but Jack knew better. What these people would do to their own children to solidify an alliance was outright ridiculous.

"Excuse me if I'm wrong, but what I'm hearin', is that ye'd rather her marry – lovelessly – to a stuffy business man, as long as the business stays within the family.

If she married Gregory, he, an outsider would be callin' all the shots, and ye couldn't retain control o'er the company. Aye?" Jack sneered at Robert for the first time since the night they met. He'd been a fool to think Robert was truly concerned about Violet's abduction. The bastard only cared about how her reputation would fare after such a scandal, and having her returned to Liam – a man who really didn't seem too concerned about her welfare either. That lad had much growing up to do.

Jack was furious at how everyone seemed to disregard Violet's feelings and wishes, and having gotten to know the lass, it was a crime to do so. Jack was on the brink of hating the whole lot of them; Robert, Gregory, Liam and Brady most of all.

Robert cleared his throat. "Aye, I guess ye can say that. Mr. Manning," *Oh, we're back to 'Mr. Manning' again.* "I've worked very hard for everythin' ye see around ye. I'll not have my daughter, who knows very little about love and serious decision makin', at the wheel. Nor will I permit her untrained husband to dictate how to run us aground."

And there it was. A match between Liam and Violet would have made sense for business, just not in love.

Jack hoped and prayed Brady and Violet were back at the cottage learning to tolerate one another. Brady might even change her mind about the beast that lurked within him.

SEVENTEEN

Violet could feel the pounding of Brady's heart through her tunic. It seemed to reach down into the depths of her entire being. Was this what it felt like to lust for someone? Or was it something entirely different?

Every moment standing on the edge of the river bank, wrapped tightly together in the blanket, increased her defencelessness until she was near to exhaustion. The torment and turmoil within, had her head swimming in a sea of confusion.

''*Tis not right for me to feel this way about such a cruel and wicked man. One to whom I am not married or even betrothed. Mother would be so ashamed of my behaviour,*' she reflected sadly, still, unable to pull herself away.

When finally she attempted to withdraw, he held her in place, his brawny arms encasing her in warmth and tranquility. Yet, the torrent of emotions his embrace triggered caused a fear that she would never again be able to recreate the moment – not with him, not with anyone. Violet relaxed within his hold and let the waves of uncertainty crash over them. He had to be feeling it too. *Doesn't he?*

She felt closer to this man than she'd ever allowed herself to feel with anyone. He buried his face in her long wavy hair, and she heard him inhale – breathing her in. His hands were wound around her in a sensual grip, leaving her panting and wanting.

"Let us stay like this for the rest of our days, sweet Vy," he whispered gently, his lips grazing her earlobe, sending goose bumps along her collarbone.

"Nay, Brady. I can't. Please, let me go," she whimpered, still refusing to fight against him. If he didn't let her go, she would certainly lose her mind, for she hadn't the strength to push him away herself.

"I can't let ye go. I'll never let ye go," he growled, the vibration in his throat shuddering against the delicate skin at her neck.

Suddenly, the weight of his words rang in her ears like the bells of every church in Ireland all at the same time – banging and clanging until she was no longer lost in the moment, but brought back to the here and now.

Panic welled inside, rising with the familiar tightness in her throat. She quickly pushed him away, finally gaining some sense of space, time and reality. When her gaze connected with his, she'd expected to find anger there – anger for her rejection and fury for her defiance. Instead, the warmth he'd only ever exposed in tiny measures, emerged in full force. His usual iron gaze had softened, the sun highlighting the tiny flecks of silver that mingled close to his black pupils.

Brady reached out and palmed her cheek. "Don't be afraid, love. I just want to hold ye and keep ye for as long as I can. I know ye don't trust me, and I don't blame ye. I've done nothin' as of yet to prove it, but I will show ye that I can be everythin' ye've ever wanted an' more. Just let me," he pleaded.

Brady fell to his knees, wrapping his muscular arms about her waist, pressing his face to her belly. Violet's heart took over, her fingers involuntarily fighting with the wet black tangles atop his head.

"Brady, there's been too much b'tween us, too much I can't forget," she whispered.

"That wasn't me, Vy. I had no right to punish ye for the crimes of your kin," he said softly, looking up, his eyes searching hers for forgiveness. "I'll be wretched 'til the day I die for what I've put ye through. Ye deserve so much better. Let me show ye that I can be better. Let me help ye forget."

The more he spoke, the tighter his grip on her became, like he was in a frenzy of self-loathing and repentance.

Softly, he pulled her down to lay into the grass. He hovered over her, gently placing tiny kisses on her forehead, her cheek, her chin, and then her neck. Her mind knocked on the doors of her heart, in a futile attempt to put an end to the madness, but it was no use. The man she'd met that first day in Galway, the man who'd made her spirit take flight and her heart skip a beat was staring down at her with such adoration it made all memory of her captivity vanish.

Flames licked her from within, from places she'd not yet discovered, threatening to burn her alive.

Brady palmed her firm breast in his hand, revelling in the way her breath caught in her throat at his touch. He wanted the clothing barrier gone, he wanted to feel and taste her bare skin. He could think of nothing else. A low moan escaped her lips, making it the most sensual sound he had ever heard.

His eager and greedy hands explored her, yearning to tear the damned garments to shreds, while he nibbled her neck and shoulders. His hand found the heated cleft between her thighs, ravenously massaging her mound until she was quivering and trembling beneath his touch.

He heard a sob, and he felt her shiver.

Panic stricken, Brady stopped.

She fears me still.

Wretched recognition clawed at him, tearing his heart apart with fierce violence

"Vy! I can't help m'self," he explained, rising from atop her unmoving form. Brady turned his back and began pacing the river side, shoulders low, head dipped in shame. "I want to feel ye, I want ye to feel me, skin on skin, heart to heart, but not like this. Not 'til I've earned it."

Brady turned to find her red-faced, yet sitting quietly, watching him prowling the bank with tear-filled eyes. He was certain that he'd scared her. He'd felt her trembling body beneath his own, for Christ's sakes! Her reaction to his advances were much the same as they had been the night when he'd nearly forced himself upon her. Today was nothing like that night, not to him at least, yet here she was, trembling with a wounded look in her beautiful eyes.

If he could only convince her that the man standing before her was hungry for the kind of love only she could give. Convince her that he was not the beast he'd shown her time after time.

With her dress sleeve, Violet wiped the tears from her eyes and attempted a small smile.

"I think 'tis best if we head back. I've had enough fishin' for one day," she whispered, even though they hadn't done much fishing at all. Brady was grateful for the suggestion, for it would be easier to be on his best behaviour – as Jack would say – when they were back at the farm keeping busy with daily chores.

"Aye, so have I," he replied abruptly. He helped her to her feet, and handed her Coco's reins. "'Tis gettin' late. I'm sorry we've not eaten our lunch. I'll fix somethin' when we get back." She gaped at him quizzically and then shook her head.

"'Tis fine, Brady. I'm not hungry after-all," she replied sharply, then effortlessly heaved herself up to sit her mare.

Oh! I've done it now! Her bloods boilin'!

With a gnawing shame inside, Brady rode in front instead of beside her all the way back to the farm. Complete silence an indestructible tether between them, yet again.

He'd already said too much in the midst of passion. There was no doubting she knew how much he'd wanted her, but her body's reaction to his onslaught of advances confirmed her distaste and now, her fury. And he couldn't ignore the fact that she still feared him.

When will I stop actin' the maggot? Again, his unrelenting remorse was enough to swallow him whole…bury him alive.

Upon their return, he'd made good on his promise, and fixed them a small supper – which she'd refused to eat, the tension thick and heavy.

Unable to withstand her silence, he leaned over his plate and took her hand in his. "Tell me yer secrets, Vy. I'll listen to all of 'em. Tell me what vexes ye so." He searched her eyes for a sign of revulsion, but only found hurt and sadness there.

Violet pulled her hand back as if he'd scalded her. "Ye stopped." Then she stood, and stomped her way to her little room without a door.

Brady scratched his head, and wiped his palms over his face.

What the fuck is that s'posed to mean?

He could choose to barge in there after her and demand an explanation, but with emotions on bust and her obvious need for separation, he respected her space and left her alone.

With each passing day, watching Violet learn and grow, tightened the strings around Brady's heart, despite her efforts to avoid him.

She'd rise early enough in the mornings to have his breakfast waiting on the table, then go about her day with the chores that he had written on 'the list'.

He'd told her on many occasions that she didn't have to do them – at least not in the sense in which they'd been written. He did however, need her help, and she didn't seem to mind the work, in fact she appeared to rather enjoy it.

Brady struggled with every waking moment that she was near him. Sleep was the furthest thing from grasp, as he pictured her alone in her room, peacefully and prettily dreaming.

On nights of the worst torment, he'd quietly creep out of bed to sit on the floor against her door frame; out of sight, just to watch her as she slept. He'd picture himself laying there beside her, her head resting in the crook of his shoulder, with her slender arm draped around his waist.

'That's what happiness must feel like,' he thought miserably. With the way things had been progressing, he doubted very much he'd experience happiness with Violet – or anyone else for that matter.

During the days, finding ways to stay away from her was becoming increasingly difficult, especially having to watch her go about those damned daily chores.

Most days her stubbornness infuriated him. Whatever compelled her to do the work of three men, he'd never understand. He wouldn't push the subject though. Instead of shaking sense into the spiteful imp, he let her be and tried his best to carry on with his own duties.

The entire ordeal was making him moody, while Violet seemed to detach even further with every waking moment.

I have to make this right b'fore Jack returns. He refused to bear witness any longer to her waning spirit, nor would he endure another night where the silence between them threatened to asphyxiate him.

Just as she'd done everyday when her chores were finished, Violet took Coco out, running the poor animal nearly to exhaustion. While they didn't venture far, Coco needed the exercise, Violet needed the wind in her hair, and God knows she craved the distraction. The illusion of freedom kept her focus on anything but *him*.

She thought of Jack often. Even though such consideration caused her great pain and heartache, she couldn't help but wonder how the investigation was coming along. His findings would become a double-edged sword, one she would surely fall upon no matter what the outcome.

'*The sooner Da is in the clear, the sooner I'll have to leave here. This beautiful place. These quiet days. Brady,*' she thought, guilt taking residence in her heart for no longer missing home. The certainty of her father's innocence had never waned, but had caused an onslaught of mixed emotions, tugging at her like greedy vines – snatching her this way and that.

On one hand, she missed her kin terribly. Especially in the first days when she was scared, or when she'd been alone in the cellar. Now, Beth and Robert had become a fond memory, their wisdom and insight only now an inner voice – one Violet rarely listened to these days. On the other hand, the thought of leaving the man who'd become more than her captor, caused a heartache so great, it nearly crippled her.

She guessed that was the way of things; mothers and fathers of young girls in love, becoming nothing more than an after-thought. The more time she spent with Brady, the less important her parents' vision for her future became. Her wants and wishes were what ruled her now, not theirs. And despite the distance that she'd wedged between herself and Brady, she wanted him, like she'd never wanted anything in her entire life.

She finally understood this enigma of a man. Understood that his cruelty had been the by-product of grief and despair. And beneath all his layers of pain, was a kind, charming and decent man who deserved her love and devotion.

When she was finally reunited with her folks, would they know she'd been kissed and touched in the ways she had? Did parents sense these kinds of things?

Violet felt a disgrace like she had never felt before. These budding feelings for Brady were inappropriate, and her behaviour, more fitting a wonton love-crazed woman. Shame slithered inside every time she thought of him, remembering the way he'd tenderly touched her that day on the river bank. She'd wanted so much more, but he'd stopped. Did he still think she was some delicate flower, whose pedals couldn't be plucked?

Ever since, she'd let him believe he'd sensed her fear, but nay, 'twas not fear which made her tremble that day, 'twas lust – and love. Two emotions she'd never experienced until then, and she hadn't the courage to reveal her secret.

His hard body had pressed her into the grass, as his hands roamed, exploring her through the nuisance of her dress. He'd pulled at the fabric, and for the first time in her life, she cared not if his strong hands had ripped it to shreds, exposing her. Remembering it now, still caused her to shiver and a full flush crept up her cheeks.

When Violet returned from her reckless ride with Coco, astonishingly, she found the cottage smelling of stewed rabbit, the aroma biting at her senses, causing her stomach to growl. The kitchen table had been set perfectly – befitting a princess really, with crystal wine glasses and fine linens.

Candles burned a soft amber glow all around the room, and a three-tiered candelabra was placed in the middle of the small table. Brady patiently waited, loafing in his mother's cushy chair.

When she entered, his expression was soft and a smile tugged at the corner of his mouth for the first time in days. His chiselled face transformed, exposing dimples on both sides of his cheeks. Her heart skipped a beat.

"Would ye sit and eat with me tonight, sweet Vy?" he asked, tenderly staring her down, his gaze transfixed, gauging her response.

'*Well, I can't say no to all this, now can I?*' she thought with a silent chuckle.

"Of course. May I change first?" Brady nodded and Violet disappeared into her room to change out of her riding habit.

Gratitude and excitement mingled passionately with apprehension. That he'd gone to so much trouble just to sit and have a meal with her, left her wondering if there were strings attached, and if there were, would she get out alive and with her heart intact.

∞

Brady held his breath, waiting for her to emerge. His heart hammered within his ribcage. How could she be so beautiful after having worked all morning, and then riding all afternoon? This woman was the reason men sang songs of love and heartache.

When Violet made her entrance, she wore a plain pale blue dress. Her hair had been plainly combed out, yet pulled off her face, tied with a ribbon, cascading down her back. He suspected she was making an attempt at being mediocre, basic and natural, but the sight of her left Brady almost gasping for air. He swallowed hard.

'*Friends first. Earn her trust,*' he reminded himself.

Brady rose and walked toward her, escorting her to the table. Pulling out her chair, he then placed his mother's fine silk napkin in her lap. She eyed him suspiciously, but politely smiled.

"Violet, ye're a sight to send me into a frenzy," he laughed. Her cheeks flushed bright pink and he yearned to rouse more of the same reactions from her.

"I hadn't known there were such beautiful table settings here. Where ever did you get them?" she asked, changing the subject.

"They were my mothers. I have a trunk of her things stored under my bed. I thought this was a good time to bring them out and put 'em to use," he replied, pouring her a glass of blueberry wine from his own homemade brew.

"What's the occasion?" she asked.

"Ye're the occasion, sweet Vy. I'm celebratin' *you*. I've seen the way ye are with the animals and how efficient ye've become 'round here. This is finally a workin' farm again and I just thought I'd do somethin' nice for ye, that's all." Brady leaned in close and whispered, "I couldn't have done all this without ye."

When she didn't respond, he held his breath, yet again. What must she be thinking? He'd been so cranky the past few days, sorting through his feelings and the misery of not being able to touch her. This little gesture of kindness was not enough, nothing he could ever do, would be enough to make things up to her.

And it's not that he hadn't witnessed a change in her, as well. She'd arrived under deplorable circumstances, a strong-willed slip of a girl who'd blossomed into a lady. She deserved to sit at a lady's table, surrounded by the finest things he could give her.

She met his gaze, pinning him with her uncertainty. He hoped she found his adoration beaming back at her, because she'd caused his heart to skip a beat.

"Thank ye, Brady. I can't deny that makin' ye proud and doin' a hard days' work, makes me happy," she replied, breaking eye contact to worry a lacy hem of the table cloth. "'Tis all so lovely." He smiled, running his fingers through her hair at the nape of her neck, but quickly pulled away again, keeping his urge to touch her in check.

Brady served her supper first and then sat across from her, his nerves in high gear. His intent when starting this today was to break their silence. Now, his male need and fantasies pounded on the doors of his mind, trying to break free. If that happened, there would be no going back. He was in the fight of his life if he was going to earn her trust before Jack returned.

They made polite conversation during their meal, discussing the weather and his plans for next year's crop, his gaze never leaving hers. She appeared completely enraptured by the topic and wholly interested in the fate of the farm. After their entirely amiable supper, Brady took his brandy out to the porch to watch the sun go down.

"Will ye come and sit with me, Vy?" he asked, lingering on the threshold with an outstretched hand. To his delight and astonishment, she placed her dainty digits in his palm, the electricity between them igniting instantly. As if it were her first instinct, she attempted to pull away, but Brady smoothed his thumb along the delicate skin at the back of her hand, calming her chaotic mind and stilling her instantly.

With the heat of her flesh branding him, she followed him outside, where they spent the rest of the evening lounging as lovers would, basking in the red glow of another day gone by.

Both of them lost in thought, neither spoke a word. It had been a truly perfect day.

EIGHTEEN

Once again, the road from Clare to Galway tested every inch of Jack's resolve. While he hadn't met many travellers along the way, the knowledge of the previous attack against Gregory ensured diligence and wariness of lurking bandits. Unlike Gregory, Jack had been ready to lunge and strike at any moment. Expectedly, his nights were almost entirely sleepless as he kept watch.

He resisted the urge to drop in on the countless shanties hidden beneath the forest's cloak where he could seek refuge from the impending dangers of travelling at night. These were homes of his retired comrades, who would surely welcome him with a warm fire and a bowl of something to reignite a fire in his belly. But the need to get the investigation cleared up was far greater than the need to avoid bug bites and knife fights.

He'd been quite content to take on the elements and the loneliness, until that is, *she* sashayed right back into his mind.

"Damn ye, Kylee. Get out o' my head," he cursed aloud, battling both the fatigue and his twisted inclinations. She was just a chamber maid, for Christ's sake! A slight, slip of a girl with an uneven disposition. But no matter what he told himself to banish his impure thoughts, there was something about the lass he just couldn't shake.

Jack's fevered desire kept him on edge, imagining how she must look under that snug, blue utilitarian uniform. He predicted perfect plump breasts, an arse he could lose himself in, and he even invented depraved scenes of debauchery they might've created together – had she not been the spawn of Satan.

Jack was a man of simple, yet barbaric needs. Kylee's haughty arrogance required a thorough spanking, coupled with methodical love making in order to tame that temper of hers. He had a sense about these things, and his intuition screamed that the little witch would love every minute of it. His keen instincts also told him she'd been hiding something.

Thankfully, Brady was the only clansman who knew of Jack's taste for the wicked – the fine, tedious art of making a lover submit. While Brady never understood Jack's predilections, he'd never judged him for it either. As long as no one got hurt, all parties involved gave consent, and Jack didn't find himself on the wrong side of iron bars again, Brady asked no questions.

Their pact of secrecy had been established a long time ago and neither of them had brought it up since. Perhaps their loyalty to one another's secrets was the root of Jack's allegiance now.

In his early twenties, Jack found himself in quite a snag over a young girl whom he'd been courting. Since then, he'd refined his skills, vowing to never repeat his past transgressions.

While she'd been a bonny lass, she'd also been base-born, and without a mother or sisters to help her learn the ways of the woman's world. Propriety hadn't been a term used much in her upbringing, and so she'd been destined to make a living as a serving wench at a local pub. She'd been a favourite amongst the adolescent soldiers who spent their days training to protect and serve the Kelly's, but by night, the pretty colleen serviced many of them – not only tasked with filling their tankards and listening to their crude tales, either.

She'd also been favoured by a dashing, young Jack Manning, who at the time had been an overzealous and eager pubescent with dark, immoral fantasies. Her winning quality – what had drawn Jack so intensely toward her – was the fact that she'd been curious, and willing to help him act on those fantasies. It seemed there were no limits, nothing she wouldn't try – as long as her purse needed filling.

Until, one treacherous night, Jack took things too far.

She'd been playing a dangerous game, one where she'd pushed all his buttons with her refusal to acquiesce. She'd teased and taunted, awarding him mere morsels of her submission, using denial and rejection as a means to raise his hackles.

In the end, her childish games had led to her own demise; at least, that's what Jack told himself at the time. The demons inside forced him to do the unthinkable.

Tying her to a support post in her father's barn, he'd brutally whipped her into submission, leaving her branded by the leather strap he'd wielded. Only when she'd finally surrendered, Jack claimed her body as well. As if possessed by Lucifer himself, he'd been unable to stop. Unable to see the senselessness, the utter chaos and pandemonium of his actions. There had been no rules, no trust, and he'd injured her so badly that her father had him locked away for rape and battery.

Back then, he'd been a foolish boy, and hadn't understood that the domination he so craved, was not about him. It had nothing to do with being callous, cold and all-powerful. It was quite the opposite, actually. He'd found that pleasing a woman – having her submit to his desires – had more to do with tenderness, selflessness and trust. If only he could go back in time, he'd teach his younger self all that he'd learned in the years that followed.

Brady had paid the debt to the girl's family, releasing Jack from prison. After-all, even a girl's virtue had a price, did it not? But it hadn't absolved him from the torment that would surely follow. Branded as a lecherous hellion, Jack had nearly lost everything. His friendships, his employment with the Kelly's, and his mind – convinced he was amongst the basest of earth's creatures. It took years for him to understand.

Those days were long behind him now, and he'd learned so much from his '*friends*' at a particular establishment in Galway. It wasn't a shady place where the women were licentious and unclean. Nay, the women at Heathen's Haven were beautiful and well tended, sharing the same interest for game-play as Jack. It had become a safe place for Jack to find himself, learn and grow. There, he need not be ashamed, nor conceal or deny his animalistic, barbaric tendencies.

He'd be paying them a visit soon.

When he finally reached Galway, instead of returning to Kelly's keep and despite being road-weary, Jack decided to tie up the loose ends on Robert's list. There were only two or three men he hadn't talked to yet, and knew respite wouldn't come easily until he had.

He opted for the tavern first, where just behind its cold, stone walls Sean Kelly had met his end. A sadness crept over Jack as he entered, sending shivers down his spine, the memory of Brady's hysteria still fresh in his mind.

Sidling up to the bar, Jack eyed the bar-keep with intense knitted brows, and ordered a tankard of ale. He suspected the man wouldn't have much to tell, as he'd been serving up the drinks that night, and had been – metaphorically speaking – tied to the bar. Jack downed a hefty gulp, then narrowed his gaze on the man wiping down the smooth wooden slab.

"The night Kelly was cut down, did ye see or hear anythin' that could help me find the lowly bastard responsible?" Jack asked, tapping the empty tankard on the bar, indicating the necessity of a refill. The barman seemed eager to oblige, noticing Jack's silver next to his cup.

"Naw, I couldn't even think straight that night with the racket ye was makin'. As for seein' anythin', a bartender sees nothin' but the shillin' and the pence," he grinned kindly, and set Jack's refill back in front of him. "Sorry I can't help ye, lad. Sean Kelly is missed 'round here," the tall, yet podgy man added, sorrow creasing his brow. "Is it true Brady's gone mad again?"

Jack rolled his eyes at that, even though the question held some innocent credence behind it.

"He's not gone mad. How'd ye feel if it'd been yer da gutted an' left fer dead in an alley? Good day to ye," Jack replied curtly, slamming down the empty tankard and striding out the door. He wondered how many people were under the same assumption.

Has Brady gone mad?

Brady's unsavory reputation left too much room for scandal and gossip, and as a result, Jack couldn't find fault in the speculation of nosey villagers.

Next, Jack approached the brothel where Robert's crew had been playing some wicked games of their own that dreadful night.

He pounded on the door with heavy fists. The lady of the house answered, eyeing him greedily, like he was a big, juicy steak – just as he knew she would.

"Mr. Manning? What brings ye to my establishment? I can't imagine I've got a girl here who'll suit yer *needs*," the willowy beauty grinned, her shimmering eyes flashing with hatred.

"That was a long time ago, Maggie. I'm not here to have an itch scratched, an'way," Jack snarled. His actions – his abuse – had been a contributing cause of how Maggie now lived. Had he not been so brutal, might she have married one of the drooling lads she'd dallied with all those years ago? Perhaps, went on to thrust out numerous babes? Who knows? But that didn't stop the pang of guilt still lingering beneath Jack's stoic surface.

A madam now. I'd caused that. There was no comin' back from what I did to 'er. Jack shook his head, culpability like a living, breathing thing, eating him from the inside out. However, with a full swing of her hips as she turned, he was reminded of one, unmistakable truth. *She was no angel then. She's no angel now.*

Maggie retreated inside, signalling Jack to follow with a graceful wave. "Well? What then?" she asked, sprawling her long, slender body across a cozy chaise in the drawing room, fanning her glistening skin with a dainty hand.

"The Ryan boys from Clare. They were here the night Brady's father was murdered. What can ye tell me 'bout 'em?"

"I do remember hearin' somethin' 'bout that," she replied, feigning ignorance. But when Jack pinned her with his impatient glare, Maggie giggled wickedly, her lips twisting into an evil sneer. "Well, the one they called Patrick, he was the worst. He nearly killed poor Sheelah! She was no good to me for days after that," she simpered.

"That's not what I'm askin', Maggie. How many of 'em were there? Did ye hear anything regardin' the Kelly's at all?"

"In case ye've forgotten, Mr. Manning, me and my girls don't do much conversin' with the clients. 'Tis not our...specialty," she replied, that glint of something sinister bubbling under her soft, feminine enamel.

Jacks patience was wearing – and fast. This woman set his nerves on edge. Coming here had been a terrible idea. The wretched whore knew exactly why he'd come, but again, she preferred to trifle with him. He fought the urge to bolt for the door and say 'fuck it'.

Bollocks, but she does test me.

"I don't have time for this. Just give me a straight answer so I can be on my way!" His voice raised now.

"Oh," Maggie puffed out, in that sweet, innocent manner of hers. "No, never heard a thing. Except for grunts and moans." Her green eyes burned with odium. "I do believe one poor man was cryin' like a babe when Rosaleen was through with 'im. Mutterin' somethin' 'bout his wife who was gonna kill 'em. Over and over again, the poor lump just wouldn't quit," she laughed, the heinous cackle twisting something inside Jack's gut. "But I can tell ye who, and how many was here. I keep records ye know." Maggie went to the desk drawer and pulled out a large leather book, opening it up and placing it in front of Jack.

All five of Ryan's men had signed their names, and Maggie had made notes in the margins about the kind of customer they'd been. Morgan had signed first, but there was nothing written beside his signature. Not surprising really, for Jack didn't quite take Morgan for a womanising whoremonger.

Beside Seamus's name read, *'refuse service in future'*. Maggie hadn't been lying when she'd said the man had left a dark, menacing impression. Next to Patrick's read, *'king of the threesome'*, raising Jack's brow in amusement.

Alongside the last two souls read, *'cried a lot'*. Jack couldn't fathom what possessed the pitiful duo to go into a brothel in the first place, but it seemed, all their stories checked out. Ryan's crew were in the clear.

Jack closed the book with a thud, the pressure behind his eyes building.

Pinching the bridge of his nose, he tersely said, "Thank ye, Maggie. Good-bye."

"Can't I tempt ye to stay and try out my new girl? She's not been broken in yet. Ye'll like that 'bout 'er," Maggie taunted, but Jack refused to bite. Going toe to toe with a cheap whore would exasperate him to no end, and he hadn't the time or the patience for it. Without a word further, Jack cast her a look of complete distain and left. The next time he was in that woman's presence, it would be because hell had completely frozen over.

'One more stop. The professor,' Jack thought, eager to fall into his cozy cot next to the dungeons below Kelly's grand keep.

According to Robert, Violet's tutor had scheduled a meeting with his former professor to discuss her progress, as she'd been Gregory's first student. According to Robert, it was important to the lad that his methods were closely monitored to correct and perfect his teaching techniques. Queen's College, the most logical place to find such a scholar is where Jack began his search.

Professor Baker's office hadn't been too hard to find. Just in asking a few students for their assistance, Jack suspected the professor had been an esteemed and well-respected lecturer on campus, and his word could be trusted.

Crossing the large quadrangle in the centre of the property, Jack found the brass, embossed name-plate fastened to an opulently carved wooden door. He knocked and waited, pacing back and forth the hallway, hands clasped behind him – he did not belong here. This place made him feel uneasy – lacking and inadequate.

A masculine voice chimed from within, "one moment please."

When the door swung open, a friendly smile greeted him. "Yes? How may I help you, sir?" asked a tall, slender man with notable, illustrious silver hair. He squared the spectacles resting on the tip of his nose, his eyes forming slits, examining the stranger at his door.

"Mr. Baker?" Jack asked.

"Doctor," he corrected. "And who might you be?"

"Jack Manning. May I come inside? I have a few questions regardin' Gregory Pearce."

The man moved aside, letting Jack sidle past. Shutting the door behind them, Dr. Baker shuffled around a cluttered desk and motioned for Jack to take a seat.

"What kind of questions? Is the boy alright? He was my best student you know," he stated earnestly.

"Is that so? Robert Ryan, his employer, speaks very highly of 'im, as well. Have ye seen him since he's been back?" Jack finally took a seat on the professor's oversized sofa, hooking an ankle over a sturdy knee.

"I hadn't realized the lad had returned. I do hope to catch up with him soon."

Jack nodded, and then got right down to it. "As ye may have heard, one of Galway's most respected families suffered a loss a while back. Sean Kelly of Kelly and Son's Shipwrights was murdered in cold blood."

"Yes, Mr. Manning. I read about that in the gazette. Such a shame about his son going insane like that, kidnapping that poor young girl." Dr. Baker shook his head and seemed to ponder the thought for a moment. "What has this to do with Gregory, besides the fact that he is the young lady's tutor?"

"Not much, sir. I'm just checkin' everyone's alibi, is all." Jack reached inside his coat, bringing forth his notebook. "According to Lord Ryan, Gregory was here in Galway the night Sean was killed. He was supposed to have a meetin' with ye, and then join the Ryan's at the merger celebration. The lad never made it. Claims he was robbed.

"He happened upon the horrendous scene, when he was searchin' for Lord Ryan. I'd really like to talk to 'im 'bout what he saw."

"Of course. But Gregory and I had no such meeting arranged. I did not know he was even in town." The professor eyed Jack carefully, and then began shuffling the mountain of papers in front of him. "He rarely checks in here. He sends his reports via messenger, once a month."

Jack stared at the man for a moment, suddenly unable to think straight. His mind racing, staring down at his notes, he double checked his line of questioning.

"Mr. Pearce did not have a meetin' regardin' Violet Ryan's progress? Am I correct? Or have I lost m'bloody mind?" Jack erupted.

"Err…I could check my appointment calendar, but I'm sure I would have remembered an appointment with him, as I'm so fond of the lad, and haven't seen him in such a long time," replied the professor, nervously pushing silver strands of hair off his forehead. He rifled through his papers, frantically looking for something, until he held up a leather-bound book in triumph. "Ah! April, wasn't it? The entire month of April there were no scheduled appointments with any of my former students. See?"

"Aye," Jack craned his neck to take a look, and then heaved a defeated sigh. "Alright. I'll have to talk to 'im myself. I thank ye for your time, doctor. I'll see myself out." Jack rose and strode toward the door, closing the distance between himself and sleep, peaceful sleep.

When Jack arrived at the stronghold, the grounds were quiet, an eerie calm encompassing even the budding blossoms on the rose bushes. The birds refused to sing, the wind declined to howl between the stockades above. A noxious tranquillity had befallen the Kelly's once bustling estate.

Entering the empty foyer, the hair on his blonde head stood on end with the absence of sound. Oddly enough, it caused his blood to rush, creating its own din inside his ears.

Jack hurried to the study where he expected to find at least Liam sitting in his new place behind his father's desk, but it too, was empty.

Mary! She'd know where everyone was.

He flew through the kitchen door to find Mary sitting at the table, feet cocked upon an adjacent chair, knitting what looked like a tiny pair of booties. Jack scanned the room, thinking it odd there were no pots on the stove, nothing baking in the oven, and Mary wasn't rushing around like she ofttimes did.

"Mary, me darlin'. Where is everyone?" Jack asked, a nervous smile tugging at his mouth.

Immediately dropping her project, Mary jumped up, hurriedly wrapping her stumpy arms around his neck, squeezing him tight.

"Oh, Jack! I'm so glad to see ye! 'Tis lonely here with everyone gone," Mary said, beaming.

"Gone? Where's Liam?" Jack asked, holding her at arm's length, studying her expression. She'd been happy to see him, yet melancholy etched her wrinkled face.

Straightening her apron, she began, "The little lord has had a visitor. He and Liam were holed up in the study for hours. And now, I fear, they've gone to the cottage." Mary hurried around the kitchen, setting the tea kettle on the stove top, and then stoked the fire. She turned, pinning Jack with an apologetic stare. "Oh, I know I wasn't s'posed to, but the stranger made me nervous, so I eavesdropped. I heard 'em talking 'bout gettin' the young lass back themselves," Mary sniffled, fear turning to unshed tears. "Lord Brady won't like it, not one bit. It'll pit brother against brother."

Jack gently patted her on the back and drew her a glass of water. She drank it quickly and continued.

"The little lord's been in a terrible state since ye last seen 'em. At first, he took the reins well enough, and business ran as usual. He even acquired a contract to build a whole fleet for a group of wealthy folks in Belfast. But, then a letter came one day, changin' everythin'."

"How do ye mean?" he asked, helping her back into her chair.

"He stopped receivin' people who called on 'im. I couldn't get 'im to eat a bite, and then when he was at 'is worst, he locked himself in that study. For days at a time, he was in there. I could hear him talkin' to himself from beyond the door.

"Folks are sayin' Lord Brady's lost 'is mind. But nay, I say 'tis Liam who's been shook loose." Mary was distraught and he couldn't blame her for it. She'd had a fair hand in raising the Kelly boys and it was as if her own children were suffering the perils of grief and loss. Jack struggled to remain calm as he listened to her tale. There was only room enough for one hysteric in that kitchen.

"And this started the day he received a letter, ye say?"

"Aye. Maybe a coincidence, but then a short time later, the strange man arrived. He and Liam spent countless hours in that study, and from what I overheard, they was hatchin' a plan to go and rescue the lady Violet from Brady. It worries me somethin' awful, Jack. 'Tis not in Liam's nature to stand up to his brother like that. And who was that man?" She asked, looking at him through old, yet innocent eyes.

"He's her tutor. 'Tis all I know. When did they leave?"

"Only this mornin'. Ye think ye can catch up to 'em? Talk 'em out of it? I can't lose another Kelly. My heart just couldn't bear it. Brady's so unpredictable. There's no tellin' what'll happen if Liam and this stranger intrudes. Jack, please do somethin'!"

Jack kissed her swiftly on the cheek, holding her shoulders with strong, yet kind hands. Even if he had to lie to do it, 'twas his responsibility to reassure her that everything would turn out just fine.

"Aye, Mary. Don't fret. I'll ride out there right away. I'll put an end to it.

Besides, 'tis time Violet Ryan is returned to her home – her family. I've given Brady long enough."

NINETEEN

As if neither of them had a care in the world, Brady was perched at the table, meticulously cleaning his revolver, while Violet was curled up like a kitten, a blanket covering her shoulders with a book in her hand, lounging in a chair next to the window.

Brady's grip tightened around the Remington when the door crashed open. But when his startled gaze met that of his younger brother's, his hold on the revolver relaxed, ever so slightly.

The last time Brady had seen Liam, had been the night of their father's demise. Standing in the doorway, clothes disheveled, out of breath, Liam hardly resembled the man he used to be. The turmoil of what the Kelly boys had been through seemed to weather Liam beyond his years. Brady's heart bled a little for the misery which had taken residence upon the once youthful face.

Then, his focus flickered to Violet's beaming smile when Liam moved aside, revealing another man who threatened to invade his domain. This man may have been a stranger to Brady, but he was certainly not a stranger in Violet's world. A familiar twinge of jealousy licked his insides. Coming face to face with an unknown part of Violet's life, reminded him that she did not belong solely to him.

'*What must she be thinkin'*?' Brady thought, as he watched her grappling with what she should do next. Her eyes flickered from the stranger's kind stare, then back to his own unnerving glower.

Brady rose from the table, and eyed the newcomer through narrow slits.

"Who the hell are you?" Brady asked with an irritated growl.

"She knows who I am. Don't you, Violet?" the man sneered, as if he and Violet had a private and intimate relationship. She made no movement and barely acknowledged his query.

Brady turned to her, scrutinizing her reaction.

"Well? Who is he?" Brady asked her with a bark. Struggling to temper the fury building inside him, he drew in a long steadying breath and asked her again through grinding teeth. "Violet?" Brady's mind conjured up all sorts of possibilities in the seconds it took for her to respond. Was the man a former lover of hers? Had Violet's affection been a ruse to pacify the beast within? His face burned as his blood began to boil.

Brady's arms barricaded her into the chair, with strong hands clasped on the arm-rests at her sides, while his arctic stare bored into hers.

"My tutor, Gregory," she squeaked. He stared into emeralds, focus flickering between irises until she sweetly smiled at him, dousing his smouldering inferno. "He's just my tutor, my love." Brady returned her smile with a sideways grin, and blew out a heavy sigh of relief.

Standing to his full height, Brady towered over Liam and the tutor, intimidation radiating off him in waves. "Why are ye here, Liam? I told ye to stay away!" he roared, and as if possessed, flipped the table on its end, sending the revolver crashing to the floor, along with the bullets and sugar dish.

"Brady, calm down, there's no need to shout," Liam protested. "Don't you think it is time to let Lady Violet return to her home, to her family? This has gone on long enough."

"'Tis not your place, Liam. Don't ye care that her father may have killed Da?" Brady tried to silence his howls, but it was damn near impossible. "And, I vowed to keep her here until I get to the truth of it, s'posin' it takes the rest of my days." Even Brady knew it sounded completely ridiculous. He'd known it was preposterous to still hold on to her, but pride prevented him from reneging. Pride, and his affection toward her.

He'd barely finished his rant, when he heard a hiccupped sob and sniffle. His attention returned to her to find a tear tracking a wet path down her cheek. "Just an instrument in yer lust for revenge? Still, Brady? After everythin' we've been through?" she whispered, disbelief shimmering behind her pained gaze. He wished he could explain it. He yearned to take back what he'd said, or at least clarify what he'd meant. What had he meant? Why couldn't he let her go? Had it anything to do with his father's death anymore?

"Nay. 'Tis not like that, Vy," he retracted, his hands outstretched, baring himself to her. But he doubted he'd find the words to heal the pain he'd caused. There was no logical explanation for refusing her release. An absurd realization weighed him down, yet he was unable to confess it.

This wasn't pride. This was pure unequivocal love, tainted by disaster and heartache. As her gaze immobilized him, he prayed she'd see through his layers, straight to his soul, where his heart could explain how he'd truly felt about her.

Then, Liam spoke once again, redirecting Brady's focus back to the trespassers. "It is not right, Brady. The entire clan thinks you've gone mad. And I must be honest, I'm questioning it myself," Liam carefully explained. Brady couldn't believe his ears. Was this his weak and spineless little brother standing before him, waging war against the head of the family? *Can't be.* The notion of it was surreal, but here he was, in his wrinkled three-piece suit, negotiating the release of his captive. *She's mine!*

"I don't' give a damn what any of them thinks, they can all go to hell. I know what I'm doin', and soon, Jack will return, revealin' who was responsible for all of this.

"God help the Ryan's if they've taken him away from us. Until then, get back on yer horse and get the hell out of my sight!" Brady snarled, grabbing Violet by the arm and leading her to her room so quickly that her feet almost didn't touch the floor. He all but pushed her down onto her bed, and snarled, "Stay here, and don't move."

"Fine. I won't," she whispered, the fear in her eyes nearly tearing apart his stony exterior. While his actions had been harsh, his motive was to protect her. If he had to show her the angry, ferocious and intensely violent Brady whom she'd come to know in her first few days arriving at the farm, he'd do just that. He had to get to the matter of Liam's intrusion.

This Gregory fellow was a stranger. He couldn't be trusted. Would he try to steal her away? How close had his and Violet's relationship really been, when he'd never heard her mention him before? Until Brady knew what he was up against, he refused to let her remain in reaching distance of them. The dread in her speechless gape told him that she'd obey.

Brady blocked the path between Violet and her would-be saviours, his massive arms folded across his heaving chest.

"What made ye think ye could come into my home and take what you want anyway?" Brady frothed at his little brother. "Get out, and take her…umm…tutor with ye."

"No, Brady! I will not leave! Not without her, I won't. Violet! Violet! You can come out here, we'll protect you, I promise," Liam shouted.

Gregory slithered toward Violet's room and the impassable fortress standing in his path. "Not one step closer!" Brady growled, his warning falling upon deaf ears, as the tutor advanced. Brady clutched an unwavering grip around the puny stick-like man's throat and pushed him backward until his back thwacked against a wall.

Gregory coughed and sputtered, pulling at Brady's hands, beating on them, losing breath, with eyes beginning to bulge. "I told ye! I warned ye not to take another step!" Brady snarled between his teeth and firmly set jaw. *I could squeeze the life outta ye!*

Liam whacked Brady across the back with a large log from the wood pile. Unfortunately, it would take more than Liam's inadequate brute force to bring Brady down. However, it had been a hard-enough wallop for Brady to release his hold on Gregory, turning his vehemence and anger toward his little brother instead. *So, its come to this, has it?* Letting Gregory slip to the floor, Brady turned to Liam. "You'd risk yer life for her? Ye'd attempt to kill me for her?" Brady asked, searching Liam's eyes for the truth. He knew Liam's affections toward her didn't run deep, for he'd barely spent time with the lass. What was his ulterior motive here? "Well? What's it gonna be, little brother?"

Liam's expression wavered, his words stuttered, "I…I just know Ryan wants his daughter returned to him. He wants the merge to go through. By keeping her against her will, you're putting our family's future in tremendous peril." The utter torment in his gaze told Brady he was ready to give up, especially when he turned toward the door.

Liam had narrowly reached the porch outside when Brady caught him by the shirt collar. He pushed his little brother into the wall next to the door and reared back a steely fist. "She's nothin' more than a pawn to ye! A way to line yer pockets! She deserves better than the likes of ye!" Just as the words left his mouth, he'd realized the lunacy of his accusation. *Jesus, almighty!*

Sensing her presence, Brady's head snapped up, his vision clearing a little from the fog of battle.

Violet was standing in the hallway between their bedrooms, her silent tears streaming down a sad, yet frightened face. "Stop," she whispered. "Just stop, Brady."

He released his hold on Liam, and rushed her back inside, a sickening shame ransacking his heart.

The threat of having her ripped away from him, without the opportunity to explain how he really felt, was all-consuming. He needed to tell her that while her captivity had started out as a disgraceful craving for retribution, it hadn't felt that way for some time now. He loved her. Perhaps, he always had. The time had come, to tell her that truth.

TWENTY

Exhaustion overwhelmed him, tearing through Jack's veins like a rising tsunami. The half days' ride to the cottage had taken a toll. He craved sleep, longed for peace. Even clutching the reins of his strong steed had become quite challenging.

When the cottage came into sight, he hadn't been prepared for what would come next. He could hear shouting and mumbled profanity. *Brady.* His skin began to crawl when he picked out Violet's dainty pleas.

"Please!" she'd cried. "Just stop all of this. Brady, he's your brother."

Jack kicked into the beast's rump to force the animal to a racing pace. As he neared, he spotted Brady's thick shoulders pinning someone to the outside wall, his arms and shoulders bulging under the strain. As he neared,

Liam gasped for air beneath his iron hold. Violet was still inside, but he could clearly hear her cries for them to stop the madness.

"Alright, alright, I think ye better give all that up now," Jack drawled, as he gently approached Brady, and placed his hands on his friend's massive bicep, pulling him away from the smaller Kelly.

Brady flashed Jack and unwelcome glare, transfixed in each other's unwavering gazes for a moment, as if they could read each other's thoughts. They were like that sometimes. One could always talk the other out of doing something they'd regret, without as much as a single word. Thankfully, today was no different.

Brady slowly lowered his fist and relaxed his stance. He shot Liam an exasperated look and walked back inside, running his fingers through his hair in frustration.

"'Twas bad enough the little bastard walloped me with a junk of wood. Then he'd leapt upon my back when I was bringin' Vy back to her room. She could 'ave been hurt!" Brady explained. Jack listened patiently, looking from brother to brother, both his fists fixed to the weaponry at his belt. If he had to take both of their foolish arses down, he'd do it in a heartbeat. *That'd put an end to this.*

Then, Jack noticed the stranger struggling to get to his feet.

"Is she hurt?" Jack asked, scanning the shattered interior, worry for the lass's well-being niggling at his insides.

"No worry. She's in 'er room. Safe. Do ye have news? Have ye finished yer investigation?" Brady asked, nostrils flaring, his breaths still labored.

"Aye, I think I have," Jack began. "Everyone, take a seat. Ye must be Gregory." Jack picked up an overturned chair, righted it and sat down. He eyed them all suspiciously. Tempers were high, pride had been demolished – there was no telling what could happen next.

"Yes, I am. And who are you, sir?" Gregory hissed from the pain of being man-handled. From where Jack stood, the man's struggle was evident as he tried to make his way back to his feet. *Jesus! What'd I miss?* Jack could only imagine what had happened before he'd arrived, and he thanked the old gods, and the new, he'd reached them when he had.

"M'name's Jack, and I've been lookin' fer you. Violet. Please come out here," Jack said, removing his cap, smacking it against his knee. He hadn't donned his armour in too long. When all this was over, he'd be eager to feel its heavy steel against his body again.

Violet poked her red head out from the safety of her room, scanned the faces both sitting and standing in the kitchen. Her eyes found Jack's and she offered a small weak smile, through tear-stained cheeks.

Jack turned to Violet then, "Violet, love, go and pack yer things. You'll be goin' home first thing in the mornin'."

Violet looked confused, gawking at Jack for a long spell, and then searched Brady's face for his consent. Brady looked at her long and hard, but as if she'd found pain and anguish behind his steely gaze, she dared not move. Perhaps, it was time for Jack to explain.

"Ye see, Brady, Gregory here, is the only one I haven't talked to in person yet. His account of what happened that night is shady at best, and I want to hear it from his own lips. I want to know why he lied about a meetin' with his old professor. I want to know why he was in Galway the night your father was murdered."

Brady looked to Gregory, whose face had turned bright red.

"What is he talking about, Gregory?" Liam asked, a suspicious scowl taking residence upon his ashen face.

Gregory quickly jumped up and grabbed Violet around her waist. He must've known it was all over. Jack recognized a desperate man when he seen one, and reminded himself to err on the side of caution. He could never live with himself if something happened to Violet; especially when he'd promised the girl's mother he'd bring her home safely.

"Oh! This has gone all wrong," Gregory whined.

"What are ye talkin' about? Ye better spill it – all of it – or I'll hold ye down m'self while Brady beats ye bloody," Jack shouted.

"Och! Gregory ye're hurtin' me. Let go!" Violet screamed pounding on the wiry man's encasing arms.

"Hurt *you*? Hurt *you*? You deserve every bit of it and more, you little bitch!" Gregory growled. "You think I didn't see you the night of the ball? Oh! I was going to surprise you, but when I arrived, I found you dancing with that animal. I saw the way you were looking at him; pressing your body to his."

"I don't understand," she cried, her gaze locking with Brady's once again. Jack watched on, his hand twitching at the handle of his dagger. The look of complete terror she wore would be too much for Brady to tolerate, and so Jack prepared himself for the chance that he may have to lunge. Be it Brady, Liam or Gregory who'd suffer his blade, Jack's devotion to saving the girl held no boundaries.

Surprisingly, Brady managed to use his head for once, instead of brute force. He listened to the sordid details, waiting for the truth to emerge.

"You expect me not to care when I see you with another man? If I hadn't seen you that night, you would have simply returned home and continued your games with me, as you've always done. All the while, your heart would've belonged to someone else. You can't fool me, Violet Ryan. You've played with my heart for long enough."

Horror filled her eyes as she and the others began to fully understand what had happened. And as if she'd read the minds of all of them, she asked the one question looming over everyone. "What have ye done?" Fresh tears emerging, shaking her head with disbelief, she shouted, causing Jack to flinch, "What have ye done, Gregory!?"

"It was never supposed to be the father to suffer my blade, it was you!" Gregory said pointing his long finger at Brady. "I hid in the shadows of that alleyway for so long, and when I saw Sean Kelly stagger outside to take a piss, I mistook him for you, you bastard! I wanted you dead! I wanted her to come home and forget you ever existed. I would've *made* her forget!" His hold on Violet forced whimpers from her as he started to move toward the door.

"I'll kill you myself! I trusted you!" Liam hollered.

"And ye framed Da for what ye did? Oh, Gregory! How could ye?" Violet cried, struggling to wiggle free of his grip. She turned to face him and thumped her fists against his chest. When he refused to relinquish his hold, she slapped his face leaving the singeing print of her hand on his flesh.

He countered, pushing her down onto the floor. She landed with a thud on her backside and looked at Brady with tears spilling down her face. Jack caught the slight shake of Brady's head, silently warning her not to move. *Stay down!* Violet obeyed, putting all her trust into the monster who had taught her *not* to trust monsters.

"The only reason Robert was framed, was because, Brady, you were a complete dim-wit!" Gregory chuckled, knowing he'd probably never leave this place alive. Were roles reversed, Jack wondered if he'd confess all his own sins, as well. "Your father wasn't warning you about Lord Ryan! He was telling you to warn Robert and Liam about *me*! The fact that my own knife – a gift from Robert – bore a scarf with the Ryan tartan, solidified the blame." Then Gregory turned, his gaze boring down upon a shattered Violet.

"And then, as if the gods themselves had arranged it, I'd been able to hurry ahead of your father's men, wait for them, warn them against returning to Kelly's. Making me the hero!"

"Why then did you appeal to me to help ye rescue Violet? Was it just a sick and twisted game?" Liam shouted. As a precaution, Jack held him back with an out-stretched arm.

Gregory's head snapped back to meet cold, narrowed gazes. "No, I do not play games. But you wanted your brother, and your would-be lady back. I knew if I helped rescue her, Robert would grant me the honours of taking her as my wife, instead of you," he smirked. Brady, Liam and Jack slowly advanced, backing the bastard into a corner. "You were never going to actually get her."

Duty dictated that Jack seize the murderous wretch, bring him back to Galway so he could be tried and sentenced. Apparently, Brady had other notions.

"And neither will you!" Brady hurled himself at Gregory, sending them both crashing to the floor, kicking and punching, while the other two men stood back to let Brady have the vengeance he'd been seeking for so long.

Violet watched through the slits between the fingers she held up to her tear-stained face; shielding herself from the deadly scene. Jack rushed to her side, and turned her away, but peered over his shoulder, in case the brawl turned in a deadly direction for Brady.

Brady had Gregory pinned to the floor, straddling his waist, beating and mashing his face with bloody and throbbing fists. Jack found no cause to intervene.

Brady's anger was boiling over. There was no turning back.

This was the man who had taken Sean's life – the man who'd been responsible for all the suffering Brady and Violet had endured – and Jack couldn't find the words to put an end to it. On some level, he condoned it.

Brady's massive hands found Gregory's throat, squeezing with such force it was a wonder his windpipe wasn't crushed beneath the weight. Then, the soldier in Jack cried out. "Brady! 'Tis enough! If ye kill 'im, he can't pay for his crimes," he shouted, momentarily distracting the beast who'd taken up residence within Brady. The distraction had been enough for Gregory to reach for the revolver that had been knocked onto the floor in the earlier scuffle.

With the weapon trained on Brady's chest, Gregory pulled back the hammer, and squeezed the trigger.

A wild fire exploded in Brady's chest. It was as if the sun had shattered inside him. Still atop Gregory's torso, Brady clutched his shoulder and then fell to the side.

'Do not close yer eyes! If ye close yer eyes, ye'll die!' he chanted, struggling for each tiny breath.

Unable to speak, Brady silently watched on as Jack rushed to kick the gun out of Gregory's hands. Pulling his knife from its sheath, he knelt and plunged it into Gregory's chest without hesitation. Brady watched the life drain from the evil bastard's body, a small sense of relief sweeping over him. The murderous fiend would harm no one ever again.

A tear trickled from the corner of his squinted eye as he tried to focus on Violet. He wanted to look at her one last time. He could die a happy man having the most beautiful woman he'd ever seen, by his side.

In an instant, he felt her warm hands cradling his head in her lap. Her salty tears dripped from her chin – he could taste them. He narrowed his gaze on her one more time, and raised his hand to her face. Then, the world blackened, swept away like ashes in the wind.

TWENTY-ONE

A fear like she had never known took hold. "Brady! Brady! No, no, ye can't die! Open yer eyes, please!" she cried. "Jack! Do something!" she yelled as she shook Brady's bloody shoulders; trying to shake him back to consciousness.

Jack turned to Liam who had been cowering in the corner since he'd heard the gun shot.

"Liam, get me some linens and bank the stove!" Jack shouted. "Shh, Violet. He'll be fine," he said in a softer tone, laying his hand on the top of her trembling head.

His words didn't comfort her; she could feel Brady's hot blood soaking through her dress and sensed the life draining from him.

Jack knelt at his friend's side and gently turned him over to see if the shot had gone straight through, and was relieved when he observed that it had.

"Liam! Where are the linens, dammit? I have to get this bleedin' to stop. The bullet never punctured his heart, but if I don't get this wound closed right now, he'll bleed to death," Jack shouted, removing Brady's Claddagh pendant and necklace and passed it to Violet.

"Oh! Brady! No! Hang on!" Violet shrieked, stroking his damp sweaty hair with one shaky hand, while the other clutched the blood-glistened treasure. "What are ye gonna do, Jack?" she asked quietly.

Instead of an answer, he rose and hardheartedly went to the wood stove and opened the heavy iron door. He wiped the evidence of Gregory's gory death from his blade and laid it in the hot coals.

Violet watched his mechanical motions in horror, sensing what he was about to do. Liam handed her the fresh, clean linen bed sheets that she had washed just the day before. Jack showed her how to press on the wound and instructed her to keep the pressure on it, no matter what.

Brady winced and his face distorted with clear agony at her touch.

"But I'm hurting him, Jack!" she cried.

"Be strong, Violet. He needs ye to be strong right now," he said reassuringly.

Liam had taken a seat on the floor against the wall, but she felt his remorse. It poured off him like breaking waves against a craggy cliff. He watched on as she cradled his brother like a babe, and he dared not utter a word.

She wondered what might be going through his mind. Couldn't he see that she hadn't needed saving? Was his anguished expression caused by the realization that he'd brought this down upon them? She warred within herself, to refrain from slapping the foolish recklessness out of him.

"Hold 'im still, Violet. Liam, come over here and help her. He's gonna thrash about; I guarantee it," Jack ordered, ripping Brady's shirt clear off his body, exposing a gruesome perforation in his sinewy shoulder. The blood oozing from the wound was the darkest shade of red Violet had ever seen, quite nearly black. Her heart raced.

Jack pulled the red-hot knife from the lava-like embers in the stove and pressed it against Brady's skin, forcing him fully conscious. And as Jack had predicted, he violently began to scream, struggle and shudder, nearly sending Violet and Liam hurling off his battered body.

Liam gagged when the smell of burning flesh reached his nostrils, but Violet held strong and done as she was instructed.

When Jack turned him over and seared the exit wound shut, Brady blacked out. No more struggle. No more blood-curdling screeches. Just stillness and quiet.

"Is he dead, Jack?" Violet cried in a small voice.

"Nay, love. He's just passed out, is all. Here, Liam, help me move him into the bedroom." Liam fought the bile back down his tight throat and picked up Brady's feet, while Jack hefted him gingerly by his shoulders.

"Violet, boil some water and get 'im cleaned up. It's going to be a long night," Jack said as he wiped his hands with his kerchief, and went outside to grab a breath of fresh cool night air. Liam joined him shortly after, looking more weary and traumatised than ever.

"We have to get rid of your *friend's* body, Liam. I don't want Violet to come out of that room and have to face it. Never mind that his plot was sinister and cruel. She was close to him; she'd trusted him once," Jack said, evenly.

They wrapped Gregory's body in the sheets from Violet's bed, and lugged the corpse out and into the barn. "I'll bring this bastard back to Clare when I leave," Jack stated with a stony expression.

Violet hovered over Brady, washing his wounds, wrapping his shoulder and beaten knuckles in bandages. With every sound he made and every time he moved in his sleep, she held on to hope that he would open his eyes and he would be all right.

"How is he? Any change?" Liam asked from the doorway.

Violet wiped her tears and sniffled. "Nay, nothin' yet. When is he going to wake up?" she sighed.

"I can't imagine why you'd want him to, Violet. The man kidnapped you, terrorized you and kept you here on this God-forsaken farm for months. I don't understand it," he said, moving around his brother's gaunt-looking body.

Without meeting his inquisitive, she sensed Liam already knew the answer. Somewhere deep within his gut, he had to. The devastation that had ripped through her should have served as indication enough. She was in love with the man struggling to stay alive before them; anyone could clearly see it. And while he hadn't always shown it, she knew Brady loved her too. Liam hadn't known her long enough to form such a bond. She may have been promised in some secret deal to marry the lad, but she suspected that Liam's first love would always be the company.

Then, the accusation in Liam's tone caused a fury to build in side her, a fury that had to escape. "Because I love him, Liam! I don't care what he's done. I don't care how I ended up here, or why. I love him, and that's all that matters. I need him to wake up," she yelled. "Hear me, Brady? I love ye, I can't live my life without ye in it…I won't!" she screamed like a mad woman, hurling herself atop his chest, resting her head next to his heart.

Violet felt a warm hand reach into her chaotic, wild hair, massaging her scalp, comforting her. When she realized that Liam hadn't moved toward her, she looked up to see Brady smiling. His eyes were still closed, but he was smiling.

"Brady! Are ye awake?" Violet whimpered. "Brady?"

"Oh, my sweet Vy, how did ye ever come to love such a rogue? I don't deserve ye," Brady coughed out. Violet jumped up and grinned for a brief moment. That he was conscious meant he would probably live, but then, a dreadful realization took hold and she wrapped her arms around him again.

"I can't help it, Brady. I love you. I've loved ye from the first time ye held me at the ball. And I think ye love me too. Am I right? Or are ye sendin' me home? I'll live in everlastin' torment without ye," she cried, sobs wracking her body, tears staining and soaking his bare chest.

"Nay, my sweet Vy. Ye'll not be returnin' home. I told ye once that I'd never let ye go. I intend on makin' good on that promise," Brady smiled, pulling her closer. Behind those cold steel-blue eyes she'd once regarded as fierce and uncaring, she found warmth, sincerity, affection and adoration.

She leaned in and touched his lips with her own.

Jack entered just in time to witness what he'd predicted all along, giving himself an inward pat on the back for having helped keep them together.

"He needs to sleep, Violet. Ye can talk everything over in the mornin'." Jack took her by the arm and tried to lead her out of the small room, but she refused to budge.

"I'll sleep here. I won't leave him, Jack," she said defiantly, as she climbed into bed next to her love and cuddled into him, interlocking her leg with his. Jack reached for the quilt which was hung across the chair in the corner and covered the lovers with it.

He signalled Liam to leave them and then closed the door behind him, "I'll never leave ye, Brady."

"I have a lot of makin' up to do, Vy. I promise ye won't ever regret stayin'," Brady whispered. "I love ye."

EPILOGUE

When harvest time had finally arrived, Brady was still not at full health. His wounds would have healed quicker, but he tried too hard to rush his progress. Violet suspected it would take more than the love of a patient woman to rid him of his stubbornness.

"What are ye doin' now?" Violet scorned, sneaking up behind him in the barn.

"Love, I have to get this done before we return to the keep. 'Tis gonna be a long winter, and I must make sure the place can withstand a cold one and a lot of snow. Just in case," he said, moving bags of heavy feed from one corner of the barn to the other. "I have to get this place straightened out to make room for the equipment. I promise I won't hurt myself."

Violet tsked, shook her head exasperatedly and hurried to help with the arduous task.

That's how things were these days. They worked side by side, getting ready for the harvest. It had been a great way to keep their minds off the seething lust they harboured for one another.

The thought of leaving their little place in the middle of nowhere distressed and pained them greatly. They had become accustomed to having a little piece of heaven all to themselves. Now they were being forced to go back to the keep to get through the winter.

Violet remembered how much she hated being there during those first days of spring, held against her will. She wished she'd come there on different terms; on her own accord. But she realized that she'd become a stronger woman because of circumstance, and in the end, it had brought her and Brady closer together.

She would have loved to know what it was like to be properly courted. On a few occasions, Brady had talked about it as well. He'd given her his soul, bared his deepest feelings of regret. He'd been responsible for robbing her of that one simple pleasure, and some days, when he was silent and brooding, she suspected he was drowning in his culpability. "Had I done it all differently," he'd said, "I could've asked yer da for yer hand in marriage - all proper like."

Instead of giving her a chance to respond, he pulled her closer, breathing his hot, hungry, breath across her face.

"When we get back to the keep, can I court ye, sweet Vy?" he sweetly asked.

Violet was shocked with such a courteous question coming from her beastly man. She didn't want to give in too quickly and thought she'd have a little fun with him.

"We shall see, Mr. Kelly," she giggled, gaping up at him from beneath thick dark lashes.

"I will court ye, I will marry ye and I can guarantee that I'll love ye. In all ways possible, Violet, I'll love and worship ye, always. If, that is, yer da will consent to it," he laughed.

Violet thought of her kin then and was filled with bit-ter-sweet emotion.

She missed them greatly and couldn't wait to see them again. But she was uncertain if they'd come to Galway to witness her marriage to the monster that'd taken her away from them in the first place.

"Do ye think Da will consent to us marryin'?"

"Love, you're not a little girl anymore and you've lived here with me for months. They have to know that ye can make your own decisions now," Brady held her tight, diminishing her fears of the future. "And I don't care, sweet Vy, I don't need their permission to spend the rest of my life with ye."

She couldn't keep the smile from creeping up her cheeks. Even though he'd softened some since learning that her Da hadn't been responsible for his father's death, he remained the same strong and tenacious man he'd always been. Not even Robert Ryan, nor his persistent remorse would prevent him from coveting his desires. Her mind flittered back to the time he'd told her, '*I always get what I want.*' In the few months she'd spent with him, she'd come to realize he hadn't been lying. She had to admire him for that.

"I don't want to leave here. Are ye sure we can't survive here for the winter? I know times would be hard, but if we work together, we could do it," Violet asked with budding hope.

Brady kissed her forehead. "Ah. Sweet lass. If 'twas only a matter of battenin' down the hatches and hibernatin' 'til spring, I'd agree with ye. But, there's just too much to be done 'round here, that I can't do 'til this heals," he softly explained, lifting his shoulder, the tiny movement still causing him to wince.

Just as if he'd sensed her sadness, his bright eyes flashed with mischief. "I do have somethin' that'll make ye feel better!"

She playfully thwacked his belly and replied, a mischievous mood suddenly surrounding them, "Aye! Of course, ye have somethin' to make me feel better." There was nothing Violet loved more than Brady's kisses. She closed her eyes, tilted onto her toes and waited.

"Aye! I almost forgot!" Brady exclaimed, fishing an envelope from his shirt pocket, shattering her anticipation, clipping the wings on the butterflies in her belly. "This came for ye today. Open it. I pray 'tis good news."

Violet rolled her eyes with a grin, snatched the letter with frisky exasperation and began to silently read.

Those lips are mine later, Brady Kelly!

My darling daughter,

I was so grateful to learn you are safe. Mr. Manning told us the whole story. We are, however, saddened and distressed that Gregory would do such a thing. We always knew he loved you more than he should've, but never imagined he would go to such lengths to have you for himself. I am so sorry we didn't see what was lurking beneath his façade. Love makes people do such mysterious things sometimes, but I bet you've come to learn that all on your own.

Mr. Manning brought him back here, and we did the only thing we could; we buried him and held a small, private service. 'Twas a beautiful send-off.

On a happier note, Mr. Manning has informed us that you and Lord Kelly have fallen head over heels in love. For the moment, you should know that your father does not like it, but I will try to get him to come around.

I know you've been searching all your life for that something to make you happy, and if you've found it in him darling, I'm ecstatic for you both.

Since you are hell bent on not coming home, your father and I have planned to come to you. He wants to see for himself that you are, without a doubt, happy and content. He loves you very much, you know.

We will see you soon.

All my love,

Mother

With watery eyes, Violet gazed up at Brady looming over her and tried a small smile. He sat down beside her and sheltered her in his arms, a foreboding tremble rattling the paper she held.

"Shh, sweet Vy. 'Twill be all right, you'll see. He's got no choice but to accept it," Brady reassured her.

"I just miss them so much," she sighed.

"Aye, I know ye do. Ye just have to cross yer fingers that they'll give us their blessin'," he chuckled, "but honestly…I don't give a good God damn who approves. I'm marryin' ye anyway," he stated, holding her face in his strong hands, searching her eyes for a sign that she believed him. She did – more than anything – and she believed *in* him.

Doing the honorable thing hadn't been one of Brady's strong points, but she loved him despite his flaws. She knew in her heart that when his mind was set upon something, he'd fight through hell to get to his heaven.

All she could think about was marrying this beast of a man sitting beside her. '*A beast no more,*' she thought, tenderly pushing a lock of his wild raven hair back from his face.

Suddenly, anticipation overwhelmed all her senses.

"Well! Let's get movin' then!" she insisted. "Can't plan a weddin' sittin' here all day, now can I?" The impish grin she gave him seemed to inspire haste in him as well, as he jumped up, with only a slight groan and resumed his duties.

She merely stood and watched him for a moment, completely in awe of her husband-to-be. Because he was the Brady she'd first come to know and adore, the rest could be forgotten. She loved him for all the layers he possessed, understood each, singular piece which made him the man he was.

Violet's journey had just begun, but the storm was finally over.

HEATHEN'S HURRICANE

Keep reading for an excerpt from the next book in the Stormy Encounters Series by Tanya Benoit:

Heathen's Hurricane

ONE

Jack Manning straddled his great steed and waved a fond good-bye to the lady of house Ryan. He knew that no matter what, this journey home would prove to test his patience, and force him to look deeper into his own inner demons.

'*I'll have too much time to think on that damned road,*' he quietly sighed, gazing over his shoulder at the beautiful Lady Beth disappearing from view.

His mind raced. So much had happened in the past few months. It had become hard to fathom just how he found himself there, once again on the road between Clare and Galway, alone, weary and mentally drained.

When he'd arrived on the banks of the River Shannon on this particular trip, he'd been accompanied by his best friend's brother, Liam Kelly. They weren't there for pleasure, but the black business of death.

Jack's efforts to clear Robert Ryan of a murder he hadn't committed had been successful. But regretfully, Jack had been forced to slaughter the man who'd been responsible, Gregory Pearce – a scholarly fellow, with his sights set upon marrying Robert's daughter, Violet. At the time, it had been an easy decision. With Gregory having already fired one bullet into Brady's shoulder, and his gun trained on his best friend's head, Jack hadn't thought twice about thrusting his dagger into the bastard's chest, ending his string of lies and sins.

Unable to control his chaotic thoughts, Jack replayed the entire scene in his mind, coming to the conclusion that there had been no other solution. It was either wield the blade, or let Gregory open fire for the second time, finishing Brady off.

It had been a split-second decision, one he'd make again if he had to. He could live with ending the man's life, but there was no way he could live with losing Brady.

The soldier in him reminded his conscience that it hadn't been his first kill, and more likely than not, it wouldn't be his last.

Delivering Gregory's gray corpse back to Clare, had left Jack with conflicting emotions. On one hand, a sense of relief that Gregory would cause no further harm to the Ryan's, spiked in his blood stream. But on the other, having to explain what had transpired, and witness the horror in Beth Ryan's eyes when she realized she'd been deceived in such a way, caused a spasm of sympathy to form in his belly. Their daughter's tutor – a man they'd employed and trusted – had been a falsifier of truths and a manipulator of situations.

Gregory's dreadful plot to rid Violet's world of Brady, had backfired. Instead of killing Brady – eliminating his competition – he'd killed Brady's father, Sean, instead. When he'd realised his mistake, one would think he'd flee. But no, not Gregory. He'd decided to become the girl's saviour.

Plotting a plan to rescue her from Brady's clutches, asserting himself as a hero, had uncovered the truth, but had consequently led to his demise. Jack couldn't find guilt or regret within himself, for having played a role in it.

How could he explain it all to the Ryan's? They'd demand more than a watered-down explanation. They'd demand to know where their daughter was, and why Jack hadn't brought her home, as he'd promised.

When first he'd set out to help them, he'd assured them the safe return of their daughter – vowed to save her from Brady's hold. Through no fault of his own, he hadn't done right by them. Violet had chosen to remain with Brady…they'd fallen in love.

He would never forget the look on Beth Ryan's face when he and Liam rode through the courtyard with Violet's carriage in tow. As she moved to fetch Violet from its confines, Jack halted her with one curt, "Stop!" Her expression would haunt him. Her soft eyes appeared utterly stricken.

"She's not in there, Beth." Jack leapt from his mount, moving to block her from seeing the gruesome sight of Gregory's body, or catching a whiff of the decaying flesh.

"Well, where is she, Jack? Ye said ye'd bring her back here, but all ye bring us is an empty carriage?" Beth's eyes were filled with rage. No doubt, she would have pummelled Jack with the bulk of her agony, but he sensed she hadn't the strength. Violet's abduction it would seem, had had a lasting deteriorating effect on everyone.

"I would've brought her back. I would've saved her from Brady, but the lass didn't need savin'." Jack walked around the horses and unhitched the carriage. "Robert, ye can take care of this, I presume?"

"What do ye mean, she didn't need savin'?" Beth asked as Robert opened the carriage door, and viewed Gregory's corpse, a disgusted scowl taking residence upon his face. Jack knew the body would have been a ghastly sight by now, and thanked his gods for not having to bear witness to it, or the stench any longer.

"Just that. She didn't want to come back with me. Violet chose to stay with Brady. She flat-out refused to leave him with a bullet in his shoulder," Jack told her, and then turned his attention to Robert, who was still holding a kerchief against his nose. "'Tis exactly as I first predicted. He loves her, and she returns his affections," Jack explained carefully. But no amount of caution could save him from Lady Ryan's fury.

Beth was enraged. "I don't understand. How could my beautiful, free-spirited and educated daughter conduct herself so foolishly? After bein' kidnapped and dragged off to some God-forsaken cottage in the middle of nowhere, Violet should be eager to come home!" Beth boomed, throwing her hands up, pleading with her own gods, to be sure. Praying for strength perhaps?

Jack could understand where Beth's betrayal stemmed from. He too, believed that Violet's actions had been impulsive. Brady deserved to be punished. He deserved to lose her. He'd done unfathomable things to earn everyone's mistrust and loathing. Instead, Violet had rewarded his misdoings by staying.

"How could she just fall in love with that monster?" Beth sobbed.

Jack drew in a deep breath. "'Tis exactly what happened. While her captivity had started out tough, I assure ye, they are happy now. She seems content to remain there, workin' the farm alongside him. He is good to her, I promise ye," Jack replied, trying his hardest to keep Beth calm. The matter of Brady and Violet's impending marriage was yet to be discussed.

For the first time, Jack locked gazes with the tight-lipped Liam. It was time to introduce him to his new in-laws, and hopefully, the Kelly's and the Ryan's could salvage what remained of their business relationship –

merge their two shipbuilding companies, once and for all.

But before Jack had had the opportunity, Beth narrowed her gaze on the young Kelly. "And who are you, lad? Haven't ye got a tongue?" she spat. Liam remained mute, shifting from foot to foot, shooting nervous glances toward Robert and Jack.

"Well?"

"My lady, I am…" he started.

'*No time like the present*,' Jack thought, and then robbed the tongue from Liam's mouth.

"Beth, may I present Liam Kelly, or should I say, your soon-to-be son in law's brother?"

"Son-in-la…?" Beth muttered, her hand flying to her lips, as she didn't quite recognise the words. Her husband hurried to her side, draping his arm about her shoulder for support, and then called the stable hands to fetch the mobile crypt.

"Let us all go into the house, for we have much to discuss. I want nothin' left out," Robert sighed, as they fell into a silent shuffle into the manor.

Once Robert, Beth, Liam and Jack were all settled in the study, Beth finally caught her breath after Jack's none too subtle announcement that Violet planned to marry Brady. Jack braced himself for an attack, when Beth's gaze pinned him to the spot.

"*Mr. Manning*!" she barked. "Please tell me what ye're talkin' about! Are ye sayin' that my dear, sweet Violet intends to marry this Brady fellow? That awful excuse for a man who stole her away from us? I want her back, Jack! And 'cause ye let this happen, and ye knew what his motives were, ye're *goin'* to go and get 'er!"

Jack winced, but no contradictory arguments would come. The lady of this house had earned her anger, and Jack let her have it.

Robert rushed to her side, engulfing her into his arms, as if his very touch could melt her icy, frantic state.

"Shh, Beth, me love. It will be alright, ye'll see. We didn't rear a lack-wit. I don't like it any more than ye do, but if our sweet Vy says she loves 'im, then we have to let her be," Robert whispered, caressing her, holding her, until her shaking and sobbing began to subside. "Ye know what she's like. If we forbid it, she'll come home and be forever miserable, and at twenty-two, she's too old to be bossin' around anyway. Don't ye think? Perhaps she sees good in 'im," he added, as if he, himself believed there could actually be good in Brady Kelly.

"Oh, Robert. I hope so," Beth sighed, choking back another sob. "I have to go lie down; my nerves can't take much more." She reached for the knob on the study door, and turned back to her audience with tear-filled, blue eyes. "'Tis nice to meet ye, Liam, despite the circumstance," she murmured exhaustedly, "And Jack, I do apologise for my outburst. Ye know where your room is. Stay as long as ye need to." Defeated, Beth disappeared through the door, out into the large expanse of the family home…an empty home.

Jack turned, facing Robert who was sitting silently with Liam at the large wooden desk. Robert had been proven innocent, so now what? Someone had to break the ice.

"So, Robert, have ye any ill judgment toward Kelly and Son's? It will be big of ye to go ahead with the merger," Jack stated, as it seemed Liam had once again forgotten how to speak.

"Nay, lad, I've no hard feelin's. At least, not with *this* Kelly. I knew ye were a savvy business man when first we met. And I know losin' yer father was a great loss for yer company and yer clan. But I hope that we can still carry on as planned," Robert said, not even looking up from his paper stacked desk, "Aye?"

Jack sensed that Robert was reaching down within the depths of his entire being to extend the courtesy. It must've been quite taxing to despise Liam's brother, and still have to conduct business with him. Jack blew out a grateful breath when Liam finally spoke.

"Yes, sir. As do I. I apologise for the hardship that Brady has caused you and yours, but I can see no reason not to carry on with the merge. I hope we can put this whole mess behind us," Liam politely replied.

Jack breathed a sigh of relief. When he felt it was safe to do so, he took his leave and went to his chamber.

'Will the she-devil *be about this evenin'?'* he wondered mischievously.

Even though he'd been anxious to return to Galway and his duties at Kelly's keep, he just couldn't leave until he looked upon this golden-haired devil, one last time. She'd haunted his dreams with a fiery tongue, and yet he'd been drawn to her like a moth to flame.

When Jack opened the door to the bedchamber, he'd expected the ill-tempered girl to meet him there, going about her duties, cursing him out for making her job difficult, as she'd done in the past. She would make him want to spank her until her arse was as red as the sun. But Kylee wasn't there. Instead, he'd found an elderly lady humming a tune, while she'd put the finishing touches on his bedclothes. Her smile was warm.

"Mr. Manning, my name is Nora. If ye need anythin', love, just let me know an' I'll try me best," she winked.

"Thank ye," Jack said, surprised. "Umm, where's Kylee? She tended me last time I was here."

"Kylee? The sweetling," Nora began, noticeably confusing Jack. '*Sweetling*' was not a word he would use to describe Kylee. "She had an emergency. 'Tis a good thing we work for Lady Beth. A chamber maid wouldn't get a week off like that, workin' anywhere else," she huffed.

Jack's gut twisted into a knot. "What kind of emergency? Is she all right?" he asked with growing concern.

"Aye, she will be. Her fiancée found her the other mornin' at the bottom of the stairs at his father's pub. What she was doin' there, I'll never know. The girl never takes part in the drink. Her betrothed does enough of that for the both of them," Nora grumbled. "Perhaps she'd been cleanin' one of the rooms upstairs or somethin'. No one knows anythin' yet, only that she was dealt a nasty blow to the head. The poor dear," Nora explained, going on and on, almost absentmindedly.

Jacks heart sank. He pictured Kylee's tiny body laying nearly lifeless at the foot of a staircase, immobilised in stale beer and whiskey. Then, curiosity got the better of him.

"Who is her betrothed. Do ye know him?" Jack asked, trying not to sound too interested. His fantasy of having Kylee would have to remain secret, for it was just that, a fantasy.

"His name's Garvan O'Shea, and everyone knows that scoundrel," she blew, and then immediately dropped the subject, continued her tune and promptly left the room, leaving Jack to ponder and worry about a woman he barely knew.

Jack scanned the chamber. It looked strange now, since he had no purpose in being there. He'd found Sean Kelly's killer, and delivered death to the Ryan's doorstep. It was time to go home.

Kylee's absence was too much to bear.

Jack ached inside, unable to go to her, and see if she was all right. He couldn't shake this girl from his mind. As much as he wanted to forget her, he couldn't. At least, not until he returned home, and put all of this behind him.

'Nothin' but a distraction! That's what she is!' Jack growled inwardly.

When Jack bid his farewell to Lady Beth and Lord Robert, he'd put the River Shannon, and the grand estate behind him. Liam would remain there for a time to finalize the merge, and talk strategy plans with Robert.

With the winds of autumn blistering his face and numbing his hands, he pushed his mighty steed onward.

With Brady and Violet's wedding taking place in a few weeks, and getting back to his regular duties at the keep, he hoped he could forget he had ever met '*Kylee the Wicked*'.

When finally, he'd stopped to make camp for the night, the loneliness and solitude forced his memories, both fond and malevolent, to taunt him.

He wondered how Emma had been doing in his absence. He hadn't seen her since before Sean Kelly's murder, and he missed her terribly. Despite being merely close friends, she'd been the one person in his life who knew his inner-most secrets. She'd been the constant tide in his raging storm. Emma had known things even Brady couldn't understand, and she'd never judged him.

In fact, she had helped him face his demons a long time ago. When he'd been only a lad, he'd been apprehended by authorities, and thrown into jail for taking his fantasy-play too far with a pubescent lover.

While Brady had paid Jack's debt, releasing him from prison, Emma had been his real saviour.

He'd had his entire life ahead of him at that time – been enlisted with the Anglo-Irish regiment like his father and grandfather before him. But when the recruitment office got wind that Jack had been prosecuted for such heinous crimes against an innocent young girl, he'd been dishonorably discharged.

Rape and battery, they'd called it. But that simply hadn't been the case, for at first, it had been consensual. It wasn't until he'd tied her to the support beam in her father's barn and whipped her until she was bloody, when she'd began to scream and cry uncontrollably. Begging him to stop.

It was like some force, deep within him had completely taken over, orchestrating every blow he'd delivered. Then, as fast as it had taken hold, he was released, and shook himself back to reality. Her pretty features had distorted from passionate and lusty, to terrified; reflecting real pain. He'd stopped dead, dropping the belt to his side, but it was too late.

With his arousal waned, he'd untied her and apologized relentlessly at her feet, with no effect. The horrified girl – Maggie – told her father, who then nearly killed Jack with the blade of a shovel. The girl's mother had saved Jack's life that day, hauling her enraged husband off. They'd tied Jack to the same blood-spattered beam, until authorities arrived to take him away.

At the time, Jack wished he had been killed. He felt utterly dejected – abnormal – and it nearly sent him over the edge. Until, that is, he found Emma, or at least, until Emma found him.

He could still see her silky black hair shimmering in the torch-lit cell when she'd first come to see him.

As she pulled the green satin hood down from her face, she revealed the iciest green eyes he had ever seen.

The glacial reflection of the torches in them were angelic, taking him by surprise.

He had no idea why this breathtaking and flawless creature had come to visit the scum of the earth, and his first instinct had been to order her away. But couldn't bring himself to do it. He had to know exactly what she wanted with the likes of him.

"Jack Manning, I presume?" she whispered in the softest old English, the tone as satiny as flower petals.

"Aye," was all he managed to choke out.

"I've heard a very interesting story about you, love. Is it true you were brought in for crimes against a lover?" When Jack didn't respond, she continued, "What exactly are the details? Why did you have the girl bound and gagged, then tied to a whipping post? Is my information correct?" Emma had asked quietly, searching his features for the tell-tale sign of remorse. Jack was oozing with it, accompanied by self-loathing.

"I'd rather not speak of it. Not now, not ever. Could ye please leave?" he growled, crawling away to the back of the cell, out of sight and that inquisitive stare of hers. Never had he ever come across someone so bold. *How dare she ask such questions?*

"Oh now, come back into the light. Do not shy away from me. I have a sense about you. Please, tell me what happened."

For some reason, Jack had been compelled to do as he was told, as if a greater force had clawed its way into his brain, completely taking over, causing him to mechanically obey. He shifted closer and met her enchanting glare as the cell bars he held anchored him there. Something about this woman commanded his obedience. Something familiar swept over him.

"What is your name, woman?" he asked, gripping the iron life-line so tightly his knuckles whitened. He stared her down curiously.

"Emma. Just, Emma."

"Well, Emma, I was involved with the girl for some time. I was not the first lover she'd taken, but I'm almost certain, she will no longer carry on with the other lads in the village like she used to." Jack stopped and thought for a moment, and then, "We'd been a little more than curious when it came to love makin', and I admit, I'd pushed her sometimes to do things that were creations of my wildest imagination. She'd always consented; always let me lead the game," Jack explained, holding nothing back. The fact that he'd been so inclined to divulge all his inner monstrosities to this strange beauty, still niggled at him.

'I've nothin' to lose at this point. I'll be dead soon. If this woman wants to know how sick I am, well, by Jesus, 'tis just as well to tell 'er,' he thought, self-pity eating him alive.

"What kind of games did you play?" she asked casually, like this was a conversation she'd had every day.

"Listen, I don't know what ye want from me! And I don't care. I'm a monster. I know it, and now ye know it, too. Who craves pain in others? I crave control, and I'm losing everything 'cause of it. Now, please if ye don't mind, I'd like to stay here and rot, so I can't hurt anyone else," Jack shouted, sinking back into the darkness.

Without a word, Emma pulled the velvety hood back up over her head, and slipped an envelope between the bars, letting it fall to the floor.

"When you've had enough of your self-contempt, come and find me. But never, and I mean never, speak of me. I don't exist," she smiled kindly, and sauntered back into the darkness from which she came.

Jack retrieved the note and held it to the tiny candle which barely still burned on the little oaken table next to his cot. With quivering cold fingers, he pulled the card from its confines.

'*Heathen's Haven*,' Jack thought, swirling the name over his tongue again and again, until it piqued an interest he could not abandon.

A safe haven for heathen's just like him. Little did he know, it would become a safe place for him to learn and harness his particular tastes for the despicable.

Like it had been yesterday, Jack remembered his first visit to the grand manor which stood regally on Merchant's Road, it's three-storey elegance putting all that stood around it to shame. He recalled having to crane his neck backward just to count the fourteen windows wrapped in smooth, grey stone. Only hours after his release from prison, Jack found himself standing on the threshold, a single wooden door begging to be knocked. He clenched a nervous fist, and made the first connection which would forever change the path of his very existence.

"Jack, I've been expecting you," Emma sweetly said, opening the door, welcoming him inside.

"I had a hard time findin' this place. Its appearance doesn't mirror its name," Jack chuckled uncomfortably. He'd expected a place called Heathen's *anything,* to resemble a gaudy site of ill-repute.

"Appearances can be deceiving. Remember that. It is only select few who know this place by its true name. Most folks just call it The Haven. A lovely name for an inn, isn't it?"

She's an inn-keeper?

Jack nodded and followed her all the way into the large sitting room, where she poured him a cup of English tea, and urged him to relax.

He could feel her distinctive, exotic gaze seeping into his psyche, like she could read his mind. What might she find beneath his layers of curiosity?

"Why do you think you are here?" she hummed after an intolerable silence.

"I'm here, 'cause ye invited me," he began, "And, 'cause I'm curious. Ye seem to think ye know what's wrong with me," he said, hanging his head in shame, refusing to meet her gaze. Would it have served as an effective distraction for the remainder of the day, he would've stared at that same splatter of color on the rug beneath his feet.

"Is that what you think, Jack? You think there is something *wrong* with you? You couldn't be more mistaken. Come with me," she said. Emma rose from the chaise and took him by the hand. She led him downstairs to a large, well-lit hallway beneath the manor. On each side, three colorful doors stood there, imploring to be breached.

Jack took notice that while none were open, he could hear faint noises coming from within.

She knocked on the yellow door, and a charming girl dressed in a costume resembling a fairy, answered pleasantly. When her gaze met Emma's, she immediately dropped to her knees in front of the raven-haired wonder and bowed her head.

"Yes, Emma. How may I be of service?" the girl asked with a strong tone of obedience.

"Will it be all right if my guest observes, but for a moment? Will it be all right with Mr. G?" Emma asked kindly.

The girl quickly rushed to the other side of the room, where a man was strapped to a large pale pink table, so entirely covered in feathers that not one trace of his flesh was left exposed. The girl whispered low in his ear, he nodded his approval, and then she motioned for them to enter. Had the man not been wearing a blindfold, would Jack's presence have embarrassed him? *Bloody fool!*

"You see, Jack, everyone has fantasies. Heathen's Haven is a safe place where the most extreme desires can come true. Safely, and without judgement," Emma explained, as they strolled the perimeter of a room decorated beautifully in bright, merry colors.

This was a themed room where pixies, cherubs and angels were painted on the walls and high ceiling, giving it an almost heavenly appearance.

"This is a brothel?" Jack asked, quite shocked. Emma didn't look like a madam from a regular whore house. She had an air about her; she reeked of high-class and exuded an unmistakable professionalism that Jack noted from the first time they'd met.

"No, love, not a brothel," Emma purred. "Both men and women come here to have their needs met – their most primal needs. Sometimes, a soul merely desires human contact.

"However, we stay in operation due to the '*donations*' from our satisfied, wealthy clientele. And of course, confidentiality is of utmost importance, as you can understand.

"We play games here, based on power shifting and control. Everyone wants power and domination. Here, you will learn how to attain it, but more importantly, how to let it go."

That first taste of the life Emma would help him discover, seemed like an eternity ago. Jack thanked the heavens that Emma had found him when she had.

With Kylee O'Roarke eating away at his mind and tearing at the fabric of his heart, he yearned to unleash his penchant for debauchery upon her. No longer the quivering and over-zealous adolescent, he longed to show her a world of pleasure, consisting of her worst nightmares and most delicious fantasies.

Cursing the possession of his mind, Jack turned over onto his side, facing the flames licking the circlet of boulders. He shut his eyes tightly against the hunger and chanted, *'Emma. She'll help release me from this purgatory.'*

Yearning to have Kylee in his bed was one thing, but now, he'd add worry to the mix.

A tumble down a staircase.

Betrothed to the town drunk.

Nothing about her situation sat well in his brain. He cursed himself for leaving.

'*I should've seen to 'er myself,*' he reflected wretchedly, shutting his eyes, praying for sleep, but sleep wouldn't find him this night. *'I should have never left without checkin' on 'er!'*

Aye, a training session at Heathen's Haven was just the necessary distraction Jack needed for a reprieve from *Kylee the Wicked.*

Thank you for reading!!

Tanya Benoit

OTHER TITLES IN THE STORMY ENCOUNTERS SERIES

ABOUT THE AUTHOR

Tanya Benoit, who currently resides in Newfound-
land and Labrador, Canada is a laboratory analyst for a
major mining company, but has been putting pen to paper her entire life. Her enthusiasm for all things historical, prompts her to create characters with many layers
and place them in the past. Her family is originally from
a small town – Lawn – on the Burin Peninsula, New-
foundland, but her ancestors hail from Ireland. The
Stormy Encounters Series has truly become a labour of
love…a means of exploration into her family's history.

You can visit Tanya's website and sign up for her
newsletter at: www.tanyabenoitbooks.com

Or follow her on Facebook and Twitter.